I0817908

ALTERED

HELIX

Altered Helix

Stephanie Hansen

ISBN 9781735042312
1 2 3 4 5 6 7 8 9 10
Printed in the U.S.A.
First printing, 2020

The text type was set in Perpetua and Times New Roman.

Cover design by inkE Cover Designs

For my kids, Ethan and Jenna.
Without the light and strength you bring me I could not have accomplished this.

PROPHASE

Some dangers come barreling at you like a freight train. Others slide right under your nose without being noticed. When I took the job at the haunted house, I never imagined I'd be kidnapped.

As I'm blacking out, it's my sense of gratitude that brings me peace in my final moments. At least I was able to experience most of my life's desires before the end.

I'd found the siblings for which I'd yearned while growing up. I'd met someone with whom to share the rest of my life. And perhaps best of all, after many years, I was finally able to see my father again.

Ironic, isn't it? To find everything I'd ever desired, just before I die. The black spots in my vision grow closer and closer together until they completely consume my sight. I imagine the cut they'll make in my body when it's gutted. My breathing becomes shallow. Then, I feel the sharp pressure from the point of the blade against my flesh as it breaks through my skin. My body won't move. I want to cry out, but my voice fails me.

PERCEPTION

As I walk through the hallway to the living room, it's disturbingly silent. I don't hear my mother's fingers brilliantly strumming piano keys. The "Silver Clouds Chasing the Moon" by Lang Lang music sheets are strewn chaotically about the room. I close my eyes and focus on my mother's energy. A vision of her on the bench in the garden under the pergola comes to mind.

I leap the stepping-stones, skipping every other. Blue hydrangeas and orange daffodils blur by me. As I approach, I notice the yellow roses are in full blossom, their smell fresh as the tide rolling in. My mother's holding a picture in her hands. Wh en she looks up, I see tear streaks on her cheeks. I sit down and put an arm around her. She's holding the last photo we took as a family. My eyes zero in on a male, mirror image of myself, my father. I was fourteen then; now I'm seventeen and graduated early. I wish he could've been there to see it. Mother should be holding a photo of my graduation day with all of us in it, smiling.

I squeeze her shoulder as my throat constricts in pain. Without looking up, I can feel my mother's eyes turn to me. I close my eyes and place my wrists on my knees. I begin playing the piece thrown from the stand in our living room by heart, moving my fingers to the rhythm and placing them where the notes should be. She squeezes my shoulder in return.

Walking to the house, she stops and points at the tire swing, offering an aching smile. I hold her hand as the visualization takes me. My father's pushing me at the age of four, and I feel like I'm on one of the roller coasters we drive by on Route 435. One of the old ones with only a handlebar for safety, no seatbelts. At the top, my stomach floats up, and the view down becomes daunting. The velocity forces me to squeal. I can still picture his smile seeing me enjoy the ride. In the excitement, I let go to raise my hands in glee. I still remember the way his face turned from elation to horror. He moved faster than I could imagine and caught me before I met my imminent doom.

Falling and your father catching you—this is every child's dream.

I awake from the vision to see my mother walking in front of me. She should have an umbrella draped over her shoulder. She belongs in a painting, that's how beautiful she is. Her clothes move with the curves on her body no matter what she wears: dress, jeans, or sweatpants. I skip the stones again so I can arrive in time to hold the door open for her. The silver, ornate door latch curves to my hand. When she walks in, I look at the neighboring houses. They're two stories high and dwarf our ranch house, but I wouldn't have it any other way. I step onto the Tuscan tile surrounded by red and tan marble walls. I almost hit my head on a hanging cooking pot when I turn on our kitchen flat screen. My mother sits at the table and picks up a pencil; I realize what's missing.

Walking to the front door, I assemble the discombobulated music sheets and place them on the stand. My finger trails on the wooden case, and a memory of my father sitting on the couch materializes. I smile, but it quickly fades. He's not really here and every time I try to use perception to find his location, which I assume is Heaven, I see a beach. Peaceful, relaxing, hot enough to bake skin to a crisp, but that can't be where he is, and I can't seem to pick up any more clues. I take a step forward, interrupting my daydream, grip the brassy steel of our doorknob, and pull the door open. I see our paper resting haphazardly against the oak tree. I grab it, remove the wrapper, and turn to the crossword I know my mother's waiting to tackle.

I enter the kitchen and hand my mother the puzzle. She blooms a smile. I sit next to her, peer at the clues, and I point to fourteen across: The Choral. As she turns to me and nods, I know she will write Number Nine before she moves the pencil. It's the perfect question for a pianist like her to answer, Beethoven.

As she finishes and walks to our mountainous recycle pile, she picks up the document on top. The neon green flier for the haunted house flaps as she brings it back to the table. My mother hands me the advertisement. I see the resignation in her face. She's feeling more than just upset with my choice of occupation. As I hone in on her emotions, a box in the attic pops into my head.

When she leaves to shower, I walk to the main hallway and grab hold of the hanging string. I pull on it, and hinges moan as the attic door swings open. The stairs fall almost too quickly to catch, but I reflexively grab the lower rung. Climbing to the attic feels like entering the mouth of a cave—obscure objects loom out of the thick gray around me. I pull another string and the area erupts in light. Boxes, a chest, and a stand-up mirror are in front of me. I know the box I'm looking for is behind the mirror. As I remove the top box the label on the next reflects the name I'd seen in the vision. BRENNAN'S THINGS.

I open the box of my father's belongings like a child opening a gift. A pair of old sneakers is on top with some team jersey below. Underneath that I find a leather-bound folder with papers inside. There are drawings worth showcasing—complex, detailed, and beautiful depictions of everyday life. When I approach a group called BOURGMONT BUILDING, I feel triumphant because this is the haunted house building, until I flip to the drawings. For some reason, the picture my mother had been holding jumps into my mind before I turn the page. Stairs bathed in shadow seem to breathe, empty hallways feel claustrophobic, and chandeliers sway in an unseen breeze. When the water from the shower downstairs stops, I drop the folder and its contents back into the box. I quickly return everything to its place, pull the light switch, and descend the stairs. Mother walks down the hallway just as I'm closing the attic door.

"Austria, what were you doing up there, darling?" she asks me as she dries her long, dark hair with a towel. I remember them telling me about the debate over my name. My mother's piano is an Austria. My father loved sports and knew the Olympics would take place in Austria during my lifetime. It was a meeting of the minds. It seemed the perfect combination to reflect their love for one another, which formed me.

"Oh, just thought I might find something I could use for the haunted house," I say as I follow her to the kitchen. I should've grabbed something up there to support this statement, but she hasn't seemed to catch on to the missing item. The mere mention of my job appears to jumble her. Still I clasp my hands together so they don't feel empty.

"Ah, that would be exciting, to provide something for the haunting. Austria, I know you like the thought of this job, but are you sure you don't want to go to college?" my mother asks me while she chews on her lower lip, a telltale sign that she's never picked up on. My mother shouldn't play poker.

I grab an orange from the fruit bowl at the center of the table and dig into the skin with my fingernail; the citrus smell overpowering the tension in the room. Lately, it seems like we're constantly at battle. She's forever handing me college brochures that I try to ignore. She's always mentioning how much college can help my career. College is also an expectation from my private schooling. I'm just not ready. I don't know what I want to be for the rest of my life yet. I take a bite of my orange, and the tang's almost too much for my empty stomach to handle.

Since I moved in with Tiff a couple months ago, my mother's chances of talking me into college have dwindled. I still come to the house every Saturday night, stay over, and spend Sunday with her. It's the only ritual we've remained loyal to since my moving out. It's what my father would've insisted upon, had he not died. The house has become awkward without him. Even though she tries to hide it from me, my mother's been heartbroken. Since I graduated early and moved in with Tiff, she's been able to become a travelling pianist, which had been her dream until she became pregnant with me at the age nineteen, and she and my father married. He would've supported her living her dream, but she couldn't fathom being away from me. She still can't; that's why I had to leave, so she could finally be set free. The door to her soundproof music room finally opens, melodic meditation floating in the air.

An announcement on the television interrupts my train of thought, "Adam Sheffield has done it again. He's reclaimed another old building, one by one turning economically depressed areas into trendy, upbeat attractions. If he keeps this up, he'll do to Kansas City what he's done before in many other cities." As the reporter talks, I think of all the history this Adam guy's removing from our city and all of the ways he finds to do it. Since the dissolution of our national government, there have been many changes. States have tried to take over, and Adam Sheffield is one of their key players. My mother's staring at me when the report stops.

"Hello, Earth to Austria, we were discussing the possibility of college. I'm just trying to look out for you."

"We've discussed this. I just don't know what I want to do in life. Do you want me to spend money on the wrong education?"

She begins nervously tearing the corner off of the poster. "I understand, but why the haunted house? I know Tiff works there, but don't other things interest you?"

"I feel like at the haunted house I'm able to step outside of my comfort zone and see what's out there. Maybe I can even write a script for one of the scenes. Why do you not like the idea of me working there so much?"

"You don't know what has taken place in that building. When your father and I lived there, he experienced more than strong perceptions, almost telepathy in its truest form, but he couldn't figure out what was speaking to him."

Just then, there's a honk outside. Tiff and Bill are picking me up today so we can move some things we need out of storage to the building. I give my mother a kiss on the cheek.

"Everything's going to be fine," I attempt to assure her.

She hugs me tightly before I leave.

PREMONITIONS

Not only is the oxygen nearly depleted from my lungs after moving and unloading numerous boxes today, but the thick heat in Bill's car is suffocating me. I wonder if maybe he could acquire an air conditioning unit that works for his car as I force my arm to roll down the window. As the fresh air hits me, relief washes over me, but I can still feel the redness in my face, sweat dampening my hairline. Bill’s hearse is an ancient car made of heavy metal instead of the light aluminum, plastic, and fiberglass used in modern vehicles. I refer to these types of old vehicles as tanks. The front seat, just like the back seat, is all one piece once the armrests are raised. What makes Bill’s hearse unique is the paintings of walking zombies and blood-dripping vampires on the side panels.

Tiff nudges me with her elbow. “Still glad you succumbed to my insistence that you sign up for this, Austria?” She raises an eyebrow as she asks, referring to our afternoon of hard labor.

Tiff has a warm smile, and her face is surrounded by curly blonde locks. Many people get along with her. Right now, I’m not sure I’m one of them.

“Tiff, you know this is better than going to college fumbling over what major to choose.”

We both smile. She knows I’ll take physical work over having to figure out what to do with my life. She’s been at my house when my mother and I have practiced Chopin, perfection expected. She gives me a sideways glance. All of a sudden, my mind sees the haunted house suffering a horrible demise. Maybe my seeing is off, and I've allowed my mother's warnings to influence me. Mother seems so against me working in this particular building because of something that occurred when she and Father were here, like there's a lurking spirit. I think that's just one more reason I'm intrigued by the job; it's a way to connect with him on some level. It's not like I can take the bus to Heaven and visit him. Maybe, she just doesn't understand how much I miss him, but that can't be it either.

Bill chimes in from the driver's seat. "Give it a chance to grow on you."

My mind picks up on his thoughts: there are many people out there without jobs at all, but the haunted house industry's currently pulsing with excitement. In the past, paranormal buzz brought people to haunted houses, but with the decline of the economy at the government's fall, more and more dollars are spent on affordable entertainment. Bill knows a lot about those without jobs. He houses half the street kids in this city when they no longer can find a couch to crash on, because he's been there himself. With the end of national government assistance, states have fumbled trying to care for those in need.

"Hey Bill, can I have a chance to mock up the scenes?" I ask as I try to focus on the job despite nagging worries about my mother and people without homes.

There's a pause, and when I look at Bill to see if he's going to answer, I'm disheartened. Images of carnage fill my mind. I don't know where they come from, but it's like flashbacks of a war scene aftermath. Bill isn't responding. Even after Tiff tugs his sleeve, he doesn't look at us or say a word.

Tiff and I turn our heads away from Bill to see what he's looking at. As he parks in front, we see what grabbed his attention. Every single prop and costume that we'd taken in is now strewn about outside. A zombie costume has landed on a bush, bent backward in an unnatural pose. Its position is almost poetic, like a Poisson ballerina move. The wig on the ground a few feet away looks as though it could be rising from the grave. What's worse is that every window of the house is shattered. It looks as if something blew up inside, forcing everything out. As I focus on the building, I see there isn't more damage inside. Could this have anything to do with what my mother warned me about? At least the bones of the structure seem to be intact—shattered windows and props scattered about appear to be the extent of the damage.

Bill steps out of the car and is pacing back and forth. He's pale, as though he's seen a ghost. He looks at the building as if it's his child. I can understand why Bill loves this building. There are gargoyles on the rooftop ledges. The craftsmanship in the statues and every laid brick is something that hasn't existed for years. At the two front corners of the roof there are lion gargoyles, poised in a pouncing stance. It feels as though any moment they could come to life and you'd become their prey—the perfect ambiance for a haunted house.

Tiff and I exit the car to join Bill and walk around picking up some of the things that blew out of the building. Luckily, most seem to be undamaged. I try to focus on the energy of these things, but there's a wall blocking my perception. I can't see what caused this. Bill, who has been on the phone the past couple minutes, returns the phone to his pocket.

"Window repairs can be made this afternoon. Let's assess the status inside before we do anything with the props out here." Bill now has his hands in his pockets and is rocking from heel to toe. He seems to be in shock and no wonder, such drastic harm to your life's work can't be easy to take. There's no reason for any of this. Why would someone target something as innocent as a haunted house?

"How in the world did this happen?" Tiff asks as she puts a comforting hand on Bill's shoulder.

I'm asking myself the same question, prodded by the cloud obscuring my vision. We were only gone fifteen or twenty minutes. How could something that took us hours to do unravel in such a short time? I wonder how Bill's going to afford window repairs and why my ability isn't picking up on what happened here. It's like when my father was taken away from me, a complete mystery.

"I have no clue how this happened. It almost looks as if it combusted internally," Bill says, rubbing the back of his neck. Then he grabs a tool case from the car and heads inside. At least I know he will find the interior mostly intact, as that was one of the insights given to me before my ability failed. I see a look of despair and anger as Bill takes in the scene in front of us. He has to believe the inside is damaged, given the evidence out here.

We walk to the building. The doors are fifteen feet tall, decorative and sturdy enough to last a century or more if not two. As we enter, the building smells like an old book when you open it and put your nose to the pages. The hallways are dark even though it's midday, but I'm able to pick up most of the details. I'm amused by the sight of genuine cobwebs that will be cleaned away so that we can set up fake ones. How did they survive the blast that threw everything outside? The air's hot and musty, but so far everything inside seems to be as it had been. There isn't any damage to the walls or the floors. It's as though whatever caused this only affected the costumes, props, and windows. Does it not want us here?

We head back to the inventory room where we'd set up all of the props and costumes. On the way, I swear I hear breathing behind me, but I'm at the rear of our group.

"Tiff, did you hear that?" I tap her on the shoulder to get her attention.

"Hear what, Austria?" she asks, giving me an odd look.

I feel a strange energy but can't make out where it comes from. My blood seems to thicken and thud through my body. I flex my fingers and relax them to keep it flowing. I turn around to see if anyone's there but see no one. I catch a familiar scent, maybe an aftershave. Bill and Tiff are talking about the walls and stairways when I see a shadow pass. I could swear the shadow looks familiar, almost like my father's when we walked to the park in the afternoons when I was a child. I'd always run forward and try to make my shadow taller than his. Eventually, he'd cave in, every time, and put me on his shoulders so I could be taller than him. It wasn't until right before he was gone that my growth spurt hit, and I was almost as tall as him.

"Well, everything seems to be as it had been inside," Bill says, exasperated. "I'm stoked the building appears fine thus far. I've seen some pretty crazy things in my lifetime, but this hits the top of the list."

We continue walking around as he tests every load-bearing beam. The electronic gizmo he holds turns green with each test. Tiff and I don't follow when he goes to the basement to assess the structure there. It's weird watching him descend the stairs, like a premonition of him going somewhere, and he won't be returning. I almost ask him to come back when Tiff backslaps my arm. She's pointing down the hall we just walked through, where a vent cover hangs down, flapping precariously. As I walk to inspect it, a numbing sensation spreads through my body. Another unexplainable happening: the vent was fine when we walked by on our way to the basement.

Bill returns with a bewildered look, "The structure appears to be sound. Let's just put the props over by the open wall in the inventory room and hang the costumes the best we can. It's going to take us at least a couple hours to manage that."

We both give him bewildered looks of our own, pointing to the hanging cover. He checks the screws and the frame. As he returns the vent cover to its rightful place, he says, "Would you two mind getting started on the costumes while I check all of the other registers?"

We have to make so many trips back outside that I lose count. I keep getting those feelings of energy, but since Bill and Tiff don't say anything, I don't mention it. I've always seemed to be able to sense more than others, so it's probably nothing. It's just a little annoying to have to flex and unflex my joints to keep my blood flowing.

##

Tiff and I go to a nearby restaurant, Novel, for dinner afterward to unwind. We often get discounts if not free meals because of Tiff's ties to the restaurant industry. She doesn't just work at the haunted house but also for one of the popular restaurants in the city, Flying Saucer. Novel is lit softly and romantically, with an almost orange glow, so a calm feeling settles over me. I order the fried duck neck with curry, smoked raisins and eggplant. Tiff gives me a look of distaste as she orders her broccoli salad; I wonder if she'll leave on the anchovy. I've always had an eclectic palate, having grown up with uncommon food. Even if we were low on money, my parents found ways to keep variety in our meals. My mother stuck to this tradition like a drill sergeant after my father passed away. I recall this morning's memory of him. My chest aches just thinking about him, so I need to think about something else.

"Do you know all the employees this year, Tiff?" I ask.

"I know most of them. Some work with me or in restaurants nearby. There are always a few bussers and hosts looking to make some extra cash. There'll also be Matt, Luke, and Ed. They're part of a fraternity that throws awesome parties."

Tiff sticks out her tongue and holds up hand horns. Then she chugs her water and slams down the glass, rubbing her mouth with the back of her forearm. She holds fisted hands up in celebration. She looks just like a fraternity guy from the movies. She's been taking an acting course this summer with the UMKC Theatre program, and her abilities continue to grow.

"And there are the street kids that Bill employs, hoping to give them enough money to survive the winter," she continues. "Not having a home during the winter in this city can be difficult. In fact, the gatherings at the haunted house are sometimes more of a holiday party than they'll see all year."

I'm happy for the diversion from my previous thoughts. Cliques seem to be growing within the states. At first, I thought it was just something I experienced as part of my high school life, but Mom has noticed the same thing. The states seem to be on the verge of war, and people are becoming polarized. Since funding from the federal government no longer exists, there've been more and more state boundary restrictions.

"So are Matt, Luke, and Ed nice? They sound like they might be ostentatious."

"Oh, they're all right. Just don't let them get to you. Last year they threw mock blood at twenty customers. While they reached their goal of scaring the tar out of them, the customers weren't thrilled about their ruined clothes."

"What did Bill do? I'm surprised they're working here again after that."

"Bill made them work without a paycheck until the cost of replacement clothes was paid. Their parents give money to the haunted house, so they think they can get away with anything."

"I wonder if they'll try a similar trick again this year?"

"Knowing them, they'll probably attempt an even bigger thrill. I'd keep my distance from them if I were you, Austria."

"What about the street kids?"

"Oh, that will probably be Joshua, Ethan, Ceresa, and Patrice. They're kind of intimidating at first, but cool once you get to know them. I tried to offer them jobs at the restaurant last year, but they shot me down. Some of their parents are alcoholics, so they don't like to be around liquor. The others seem to want to find a way on their own."

Our food arrives; my fried duck sizzles and the delicate, natural aroma of eggplant fills my nose. There are extra vegetables on top of that steam. My first bite, full of flavors, sends my taste buds into a frenzy. I'm starving after all our work today, so I have no problem putting this food away. It's also nice to be distracted from not only my heartbreaking memories, but the jitters I'm suffering from thinking about working with people I've never met before.

We're both exhausted and head to our apartment right after dinner. I close my eyes as soon as my head hits the pillow but toss and turn as doubts enter my head. I've always done well at school but have never belonged to a social clique. Tiff's my closest friend. I'm nervous to be stepping outside of my box by taking this job with the haunted house. Will I be able to act well enough to scare people? That comes naturally to Tiff, but not me. I enjoy writing but have never done well with drawing or decorations. Beyond that, I find it hard to fathom not having a home. The street kids usually find a place to stay, but their numbers seem to be increasing lately. A couple of times I've spotted kids my age sleeping under bridges. Also, I've never hung out with fraternity boys, so I'm not sure if I will fit in at all.

All this is secondary to the fear I have of the building itself. What was that energy I sensed? Why did I see shadows no one else seemed to notice? The shadow appeared almost to be following me specifically. How peculiar, and why did it remind me of something familiar? I haven't encountered that one before. Tomorrow's the first day for everyone else. I have to get some rest, so I get up to get a drink of water and read one chapter of *The Catcher in the Rye*; this always soothes me. I remember my father reading children's books to me when I was little. I would always find a way to fit on his lap.

INFLUX

At dawn's break, Tiff and I walk in through the huge doors again. The air's hot and musty even this early in the morning, but I don't sense the same energy I did yesterday. I catch a breath of relief, like surfacing from the water when a dive has lasted too long. The morning light shines on the ancient organ in the middle of the main entrance. It's taller than us and dominates the room. I picture my mother sitting on its bench entertaining people in this very building; I can hear Bach's Goldberg Variations bouncing off the walls. We begin to walk to the inventory room where the initiation meeting is to take place. We pass half-lit rooms that'll be constructed into scary scenes. According to Tiff, when fall rolls around and Halloween nears these buildings transform into the "Depths of Hell," "Ghost Riders" and other terror-inspiring names. People of all kinds will line the halls seeking a thrill and this year it's going to stay open all year long.

Three huge guys jump around the corner as we enter the next hall. All of a sudden, my mind warps into thoughts of what these guys have done. I see two of them beating someone into unconsciousness. My perceptions usually don't pick up on people until I've known them for a while. I'm not sure what to make of them as my heart jumps, and I can tell by the look on Tiff's face she's scared, too, but then she smiles. More images of carnage enter my head, but I don't want these people to think I'm a freak when they meet me, so I attempt to stifle them.

"You boys always start spooking early."

“Ah, what’s the matter, Tiff,” says the blond guy with a sinister smirk.

“Hoping Bill will forgive you for your mistake last year and just pay you with a case of beer this time?”

“Who said it was a mistake, sweetheart?” asks the guy with darker hair and a thicker build.

These must be the Frats: Matt, Ed, and Luke.

“Matt, this is Austria,” Tiff says to the blond guy.

“Ready to scare the piss out of some people?” he asks as he offers his hand to shake. He has a square jaw, long, thin nose, and piercing green eyes. I shake his hand firmly the way my father taught me when I was twelve and look straight into his eyes.

“Bet I can do better than you.”

Where’d that come from? Last night I was worried sick about my abilities, and now I’m making wagers on whom I can out-scare. He chuckles a bit and lowers his eyebrows at Tiff with a twitch in his left cheek.

“Austria, this is Ed,” she says as she turns to the next guy.

“Glad to have another hot chick on board.” He offers me his hand to shake too.

“I don’t see how looks help when we’re hidden behind costumes.”

I also shake his hand, but he tries to tug me to him. I twist my wrist so my thumb’s between his thumb and fore-finger and pull my hand free. He has puppy-dog eyes and beautiful lips that I’m sure most girls find attractive. I stare him down with pursed lips as if to say, “Don’t try that move again.” I notice the third guy give a smug grin to condone my fleeing his friend’s move.

“Ah, and Austria, this is Luke.”

"Hi." Luke, the third guy, has a warm smile and the skin around his eyes wrinkles. His handshake is firm but soft too. How does he survive hanging around the other two?

"Nice to meet you," I say. I notice Tiff's eyes linger on Luke a little too long. Perhaps she has feelings for him. Of the three, she's made a wise choice, if she does.

Tiff and I walk ahead of the group to the meeting, and when we pass the darkest hallway, a cold breeze blows our hair to the side. For a second, I fear I haven't escaped the shadows from yesterday. As my eyes adjust and I glance down the hallway, I see two boys and two girls appear out of the dark. The tattered clothes they wear make me assume they're the street kids.

"Bah, look what the cat drug in," Matt says as he rolls his eyes.

I can't help but stare. I can't even imagine what their lives must be like. I'm half afraid, and half intrigued. I notice a swagger in their walk as they approach us, like they've travelled a world none of us have.

"See you rats mustered up the courage to return," says the guy with dark hair, dark eyes, and matching dark circles under his eyes. "Name's Ethan," he says, tilting his head up to me.

I nod my chin up too, but don't say my name as I'm interrupted.

"Look, you even brought a new one." The two girls smile at each other and then look at me as if there's a hidden joke. They both have cocky smiles and daring eyes. One has tattoos everywhere—on her arms, her neck, and even her hands. The other has one eyebrow with a more angular curve than the other, giving her a look of natural dominance.

"Fresh meat," they say as their smiles fade and their eyes stare me down.

"She's with me, not fresh meat!" Tiff attempts to mediate the situation like she has numerous times among restaurant employees and students at school.

My heart rate jumps, but if I wimp out now, they'll always think I'm a coward. I stand tall.

"So is there any truth to the rumors about this place being actually haunted?" I smile at them. That wasn't really how my mother explained it, but close enough.

Even though it's hard for me to imagine being without a home, I'm very close to someone who once was. My mother was forced to live on the streets for some time with my father before I was born. One of the shelters they stayed in was here.

"How do you know about that?" The girls have lost their proud looks and almost replace them with ones of astonishment.

"Name's Austria. My mother lived here some growing up."

"Hola, I'm Patrice," says the girl with a slanted eyebrow. "And this is Ceresa," she continues as she points to the girl with the tattoos beside her. "And this is Joshua." She points to the one I haven't met. Joshua seems to just kick some dust on the floor, not exactly paying attention. His eyelashes are so long that when he looks up from the ground at me his lashes touch his eyebrows. Then he smiles and hands me a much-needed flashlight. He's blessed with a perfect smile.

From what Tiff has told me, there are Frats, Norms like us, and Streets, and an understood rule that no one dates the other side. So why am I allowing myself to focus on Joshua's lashes and smile?

He keeps looking at me. I wonder if he's noticing how scrawny I am or how long my nose is. I do have some muscle, but with my height it's spread thin. People say I have a pretty smile, and my father always told me that my eyes were full of light, but I think that was just because he was my father. Why does Josh keep staring at me? He hasn't said a word. His face is cut with sharp yet smooth edges at the same time, and his eyes penetrate into me. I breathe and try to slow my heart rate. He wears ragged clothes and a leather jacket regardless of the warmth. He seems to be hesitant or afraid of something.

Then he looks at me and speaks, "Austria, your eyes are gorgeous." He pulls on my sleeve and points me the way we're to go next.

My heart sinks to my stomach. I signed up for this job to figure out what I want to do in life and for a possible trip down my father's memory lane. I did not sign up for a romance, but if he keeps looking at me like that, I'm doomed. Romance doesn't work for me. At least the only relationship I had in high school didn't. We got along in the beginning, but once our relationship grew, he wanted to control my every move, and I felt suffocated.

Well signed up for or not, Joshua excites me. I just need to show him that I make the decisions here. So I do the only thing I can think of. I grab his face, land a peck kiss on his cheek, and walk off. I feel like an idiot, but oh well, too late now.

##

As we get closer to the inventory room, my heart rate won't slow down. There's a wall with vanity after vanity that makes me pause a moment because they're so beautiful. They all must be at least fifty years old. These must have been covered with sheets yesterday—I'd wondered what they were. Now they have occupants sitting and trying to perfect horror makeup in their mirrors. In the center is a circle of boxes, fold-up chairs, and a few old wooden chairs that must have survived with the building itself. I wonder if Bill worked all night preparing this. I hope someone helped him. Then I see the wall with hanging costumes. There are more rollaway racks than I remember. There have to be at least six now, when yesterday we only had three.

I walk over to them and start running my fingers over the costumes one by one. I walk halfway through one when his fingers touch mine. Joshua's calloused fingers brush over my hand. The touch sends a jolt of electricity that arches my spine back. It's like walking into a club where the base shakes your rib cage, uncontrollable. My fingers tingle where they touch his. Joshua looks like a nightmare I should run from, but I can't resist his pull. I put my hand on his shoulder to balance myself and keep him at a distance.

"I go by Josh, not Joshua," he says, just now correcting the introduction from the hallway. "So, which costume's your favorite?"

"I would have to say the female vampire that's crimson and black, full length with a gap at the stomach and a low neckline, but conservative enough to be tasteful. It almost has a *Phantom of the Opera* verve. I just adore the neck of the cape that's raised to the hairline. Something about it frightens you while drawing you in at the same time."

He doesn't answer at first. Probably thinks I'm an off-balance woman to go on so much about a silly costume. Then he looks at me.

"I think I know precisely what you mean."

He gives me a sideways smile, and I know I'm in trouble. Look at those eyes. They're blue as the sea, but you can see the sand at the bottom they are so clear.

ASSIGNMENTS

Bill hands everyone a piece of paper.

"I've assigned you all a team. I'm tired of you picking your own group. Our haunted rooms need variety. You know the rules. No fighting, and if you damage anything you pay for it. Now, read your papers. Team Exodus, please stand by the vanities, Team Sinister by the props, Team Decapitation by the rollaway racks, and Team Mummified here in the center."

I feel like I've been either handed a legal sentence or a winning lottery ticket. Who will be on my team? I slowly unfold the paper. Team Exodus with Ceresa, tattoo lady; Matt, scary blond; and Jack, a boy I haven't personally met, but recognize as a busser at Tiff's restaurant. Wonderful. Matt's the most intimidating to me of the three college guys, and Ceresa looks like she doesn't fear anything.

I breathe in through my nose and out my mouth to calm myself down. I head over to the vanities and watch the others to see what team they're on. Tiff heads to the props to be part of Team Sinister. So does Ed, Matt's sidekick, Ethan, the scariest of the street kids, and Lea, a girl I haven't met, who works at Tiff's restaurant as a hostess. Well, so far Bill seems to be meeting his goal of diversity. I guess Tiff being with Lea is somewhat breaking that mold, but Tiff's an actress and maybe Lea isn't.

Then I look toward the rollaway racks to see Team Decapitation and see Josh heading to them. Patrice comes up behind him and hooks her arm in his. I can't help clenching my hands into fists. Bill missed the variety there.

Obviously two street kids put together will overrule the others. If I weren't new to this, I'd file a complaint with Bill. Since me working here is kind of a favor, I don't really have much of an option but to bear the hooked arms. Maybe my mother was right about working here not being a good idea. Luke and a guy I don't recognize head there too. Four more people I don't recognize gather in the center to form Team Mummified. Bill clears his throat.

"Flip your papers over and you'll see the map of the haunted house. The room you'll be in is highlighted. Your scripts are at your current stations."

Ceresa picks up a stack of pages, takes one, and hands the rest to Matt. He takes a page and then hands me the remaining. As his hand reaches out to me, a shadow races across the room and the makeup brush on the vanity next to me falls to the floor. For some reason, the scene from *Ghost,* when Patrick Swayze is finally able to lift a penny to show Demi Moore he's there, surfaces in my brain. Jack, who is standing on my other side, jumps, startled. I wonder how long he's going to last at the haunted house. Crap. The shadows are back. I push the thought from my head, hoping the others don't notice how much the shadow has shaken me. They'll probably assume something innocent knocked over the brush. But I can't stop my blood from feeling like molasses through my veins.

"Well, that was weird," I say as I hand the last page to Jack, attempting to cover my anxiety. With big eyes, he grabs it. Jack's a sweet-looking kid. He has full cheeks like a child. He must have a growth spurt left in him.

We're Team Exodus, so it fits that our room has different groups that have moved en masse. Oppressed people pushed to suicide in Jonestown, the hundreds of movement brothers to be executed in Egypt, and slaves leaving their rulers after a plague. My mind begins reeling with ideas. I feel creativity blossoming from within. This is one of the reasons I signed up. I think my father would be proud of me. The story of his life seems like somewhat of a letdown when told by others. I know there has to be more to it. I hope I can find it here.

"We should get the props set up first. What would work for the cyanide? How do you set up a fake hanging? How do we make a scene of back in Moses' time?" I ask.

The script says that we'll have someone offering candy "cyanide" pills to customers that an employee also consumes followed by the employee dropping in what looks like the death throes of poisoning. My knowledge of toxicity is limited. I can't believe I'm getting paid for this. It's going to be a blast.

"Whoa! Don't you like taking charge?" Matt asks.

"Got any better idea where to begin?" Ceresa counters.

I smile at her, and she bumps into my arm with a smile as we walk to the props. Okay, so not as frightening as the tattoos had built up in my head. Jack kneels next to a silver platter perfect to hold the "cyanide." Now that's just creepy. Bill walks up to us.

"There's already candy set up in your room. That tray's an excellent choice for the finishing touch for Jonestown Massacre. Good eye, Jack."

Jack blushes as he smiles. Maybe he'll last longer than I thought.

I imagine someone falling over in convulsions, customers believing they're poisoned. It's simply sheer magic.

"I'm Jim Jones, right?" Matt insists.

"Of course, your personality fits that of a reverend," I answer sarcastically.

"Who's my victim?"

"According to the scripts it's me but don't think you're getting out of it." Ceresa balks as she looks up from her page.

"She's right. Reverend Jones dies of a headshot wound."

This comes from little Jack, and I have to hide my smile. He seems like someone I would've liked to have as a little brother if my father had lived longer and he and my mother could've had more children. I can see the fear in Matt's eyes. Not as tough as I thought either. Bill's shaking his head. Guess the mix of people in the group is bound to give him a headache. He starts to say something. Probably to remind us that the first rule is to not fight, but he isn't able to begin. Next to us at the costumes Ethan shoves Luke. Luke's ready to shove him back when Bill races to them and breaks it up. Now Bill will be able to remind everyone, and not just us, that no fighting is allowed.

"Quit it. If you can't find a way to get along, I'll have to ask you to leave."

"He shoved me," Luke says. "It would be only fair for me to shove him back. You always give them more leeway."

"Oh yeah, so much leeway," Ethan says. "In order to stay here last night, we had to set up the rest of the costumes. The only reason that executioner costume you were arguing with me for is here is because I worked to set it out. Rat, you should be grateful that all I did was shove you."

I guess that answers my question as to whether Bill had help setting up everything else—the street kids.

At this, Luke doesn't have a counter for Ethan, so he hands him the costume.

"Yeah, but Luke's part of Team Decapitated, so it seems fitting for him to have the costume," Tiff argues.

"Actually, Austria's going to wear that one when she hangs Jack. Look at it. It's too small for either of you," Bill answers.

Ethan brings me the costume.

"Look forward to seeing it on you," he says to me.

I just take it from him and turn away. I catch Josh sneering at him, and my heart flutters.

"Okay, everyone take turns grabbing props you need and move them to the room for setup. Then I'll go room to room and help you. Team Exodus will go first as you have already begun."

We have the tray, rope for the hanging, and some rods such as might have been used in the Moses era. We grab those and leave to head to our room. The halls are dark. I'm overwhelmed with a sense of foreboding as if I'm being spied on. It's exhaustive enough to navigate the dark halls even with Bill's map. I find myself steadying the rhythm of my breaths yet again. My foot hits something, and I trip. I would've fallen, but Ceresa catches me.

"Did your mom not tell you about those? These are the tunnels the employees use to move from room to room unseen by the customers. The builders didn't close up all of the walls, so some of the supports jut out. Better watch out for them. I'm not always going to be around to catch you."

She shakes her head, but I can see a smile tugging at the corner of her mouth. I feel the kindness in the advice she gives me even though she sees it as an unwanted responsibility. It makes me feel more like I belong here, like she's an older sibling, and I'm the brat little sister. I begin to wonder if Ceresa, one of the scariest to me when I first met her, might become a close friend. Then we enter the room nearest to the haunted house entrance. Bill's already in the room. Matt and Jack begin to place the candies on the tray. Bill checks to be sure none will fall off if the tray were to be tilted. Ceresa eats one, and after a few seconds falls to the floor, her body shaking spastically. Matt then acts out the suicidal shot to his head. He holds his index finger and thumb to mimic a gun. It appears we forgot a prop.

"Now Jack, step over here and try on this harness. We're going to have you hanging from this. The background here hides the wires that will hold you up. Austria, you'll put a noose on him for his hanging. Then you'll kick the chair out from under him. Jack must do some acting to make it appear as though he's choking."

Jack puts the harness on with an excited look. There's a belt that wraps beneath his shirt as well as shoulder straps. He'll have a specially made shirt when we go live. He steps up onto a chair. Bill adjusts the harness so that none of Jack's body weight is on the chair. I step up onto a small platform next to them. Bill shows me how to loosen and tighten the noose. It all seems pretty easy. I just have to do this placing my hands naturally around the wires holding him up. I put the loop around Jack's head, and it lies on his shoulders. Jack looks at me, and I struggle to tighten the noose. I can't bring myself to do it. I hate death. My mother has consoled me an infinite number of times over my father's death. Maybe I didn't fully think out this job.

"Are you sure the harness will hold him, Bill?"

"Yeah, it can hold a person my weight, and I weigh much more than Jack here."

"Okay."

I swallow and apprehensively move the knot. It's tight on Jack's neck now.

"His hands and legs will be tied when we're live," Bill informs us.

"Kick the chair now, Austria."

I think Ceresa's trying to coach or cheer me, but it isn't helping. I breathe in through my nose, close my eyes, breathe out, and open them. I kick the chair hard, and it slides two feet. Jack's body begins shaking, and his face turns bright red. He appears to be in agony. I grab him and raise him a couple inches. Everyone laughs at me.

"Good acting, kid. You'll have to control yourself from trying to save him when customers are around, Austria."

I should feel mortified, but I find myself proud of the kid for proving my initial impression of him wrong and being talented at this haunted house gig. Matt gives Jack a high five. I guess I shouldn't have worried about the kid surviving at all. I probably should be more worried about myself. I bet he acts with Tiff. She should've given me a heads up. I'm pretty embarrassed, but that only lasts a second. Bill's walking us to the final part of our room. It guides the customers to the hallway that leads to the next section.

"Ceresa, you'll lead the customers. You will have this staff and be dressed for the time. You'll say that Moses has split the sea, and they must hurry."

Just then Bill flips a switch and the wall surrounding the doorway fills with what looks like blue water with some kind of light causing it to glow, the doorway splitting the current. I don't know how he put this together, but it's amazing. I didn't expect to be so enamored with the creativity of the haunted house. The careful detail Bill has put into the place is moving. His technique impresses me.

"How did you do this?" I ask.

"It's just two panes of glass with water between. The hallway's the same way. Now Matt, there's a chariot and costume in the corner. You'll chase the customers to the next room. You'll wear goggles with glowing red eyes."

"Sweet."

"All right, you all go back to the inventory room. I hear Tiff's restaurant snuck in some good grub. Practice your lines. Work on finishing touches for makeup. Stay out of trouble. I need to work with Team Sinister now."

I can smell the food as we walk back. I'm so hungry that I almost feel like running. I hear people talking and laughing. I can't help but smile. Strangely enough, I'm enjoying this, the adrenaline rush of a scare, pushing myself to new experiences. As we enter, I see Josh and Luke surprisingly holding what seems to be an exciting discussion. Ceresa jumps next to them.

"So where's the food, boys? I'll torture you if there isn't anything good left."

"Oh, don't get your panties in a knot. The food's right over there on the boxes by the chairs in the center."

I'm afraid Luke doesn't realize how hungry we are. Ceresa stomps one foot right next to his and pushes her face quickly toward his. She's taunting him, but he just smiles. He softly puts his hands on her shoulders and turns her around.

"Would you like ketchup on your hamburger, babe?"

Ceresa is about to elbow him in the side when her eyes catch the food. She just smiles and runs to it. There are to-go boxes with labels. Hamburger and fries, turkey wrap, chicken tenders, and veggie burgers. The smells from the boxes make my mouth water. Each person from our team grabs a box and takes a seat. Pretty soon, everyone in the room joins our little gathering. It's nice to see such a mix of people sharing a meal and conversation together. I think this must have been what Bill was after. There's a warm feeling in my chest—a feeling of belonging that I never expected.

Josh sits next to me. He smiles and watches everyone too.

"Pretty cool, huh. Ever think you'd be hanging out with some street-kids and enjoy it?"

I smile at him and move a piece of hair that has fallen into his eyes. We freeze. Then Team Sinister enters the room with Bill.

"Okay, grab yourselves some food. We'll all take a short break. Teams Decapitation and Mummified will go over their rooms this afternoon, and then we'll be done for the day."

Team Sinister begins grabbing boxes of food.

"Oh, here, Tiff. They said this one's for you. Said it's your favorite," Ed says.

"Get out. That's awesome."

Tiff goes to Ed and grabs the box. Something bothers me about this scenario, but I'm not able to say anything before she opens the box. Tiff's scream is the highest pitched sound I have ever heard. She drops the box. It's full of wiggly worms that begin to crawl out of the box.

"Booyah!" says Ed.

"Pick up that box, Ed, and get it out of here. There better not be a worm left in this place," Bill scolds.

"If he misses a worm you should make him eat it, Bill," Patrice adds.

Nice to see Patrice sticking up for Tiff, but I wish Ed and Matt would give it a break already. Maybe someone should help them do that. A plan begins to formulate in my head.

"Tiff, Patrice, Ceresa, can you help me figure out the makeup? I've never used theatrical makeup before."

They head over to the vanities with me. Ceresa whispers first.

"You got a plan, Austria?"

I'm a little taken aback by her willingness to side with me. I'm unsure if it's a feminist move or if she's just tired of seeing the fraternity guys pick on everyone. A wave of self-confidence flows through me as I answer.

"Not exactly, but those guys can't get away with this," I can't help the crooked smile that forms on my face. It feels good to take charge.

Patrice grabs some makeup and begins applying it to my face to keep up pretenses.

"Remember last year, Tiff?" Patrice asks.

"Yeah, what about it?"

"Matt and Ed were in the inventory room and you snuck up on them with the *Scream* mask. Ed grabbed Matt's arm, and they both yelled like little girls. I've never seen those two spooked before, but something about that mask gets to them."

"You're right. Do we have any left?"

"We have four and, so far, they're not needed for any of the rooms."

"That's good. We should all have one and torment them with them until they're done picking on everyone else. Give them a dose of their own medicine."

I'm ecstatic. I can tell all four of us are filled with anticipation. I wonder if Patrice and Ceresa will be friends with me like this outside of the haunted house. What would the kids from my high school, who are pretty much all going to college, think if we went to lunch and a couple street girls approached? I would set them straight. They seem all too comfortable in their collegiate surroundings. It's like they could be happy their entire lives surrounded by only a certain type of person. The thought's utterly ridiculous. We get only one life in this world, why spend it in only one circle? If I ever marry someone like that, I would find myself bored after a year. My mother married a man with an open mind.

INCEPTION

Bill calls out to everyone, his voice reaching for us all like the fingers of a fog's mist. "That's a wrap, for tonight at least. Everyone go and get some rest, come in with fresh minds and more ideas to work in the light tomorrow. Have a good evening and stay out of trouble."

Everyone gathers to their normal groups and disperses. Tiff and I head out the door to go grab some decaffeinated coffee and discuss today's happenings before going to bed. I notice Josh running up behind us, an electric wave surpassing its perimeter. Guess we won't be discussing that one.

"Uh, hello, did I forget something back there?" I ask.

"No, not at all. Can I join you beautiful ladies? Wouldn't want you to roam the streets at this hour without a guard," Josh says.

Tiff begins to turn him down when I interrupt.

"That sounds like a good idea, Josh," I say.

I can't ignore Tiff's look of skepticism, the panic in her eyes. Broadway Café is reasonably busy at this time of night, a studious and companionable atmosphere on a caffeinated buzz. Some sit alone at a laptop or reading a book. Others are in groups talking or playing chess. We all sit and discuss our rooms and teams over coffee like we're haunting pros. The seats are comfortable, and the ones we're in are upholstered in velvet. We have also been on our feet most of the past couple days. It is exceptional. Though so comfortable and tired, I have not felt this alive in a long time. Tiff excuses herself after the first round. I can see that she is tired, maybe a little disappointed by the way she narrows her eyes at me. I'm sure we'll have a discussion about this later.

I turn back to Josh and find his gaze into my eyes to be all-consuming. He grabs my hands and asks, "Please tell me you feel the electricity between us and I'm not just imagining this all in my head."

I am so shocked that my breath hitches. He feels it too and what he describes is very similar to how I've explained it in my head, electricity. It's a tingling feeling, as if we're pulled together by something stronger than ourselves, but I'm not ready to tell him that.

"Maybe I do and maybe I don't," I say.

He gasps, "Yeah?" then half laughs, half clears his throat before continuing. "I once visited The Magic House in St. Louis and they had an exhibit with an electricity charged ball that made your hair stand on end. It's like that first second when you touch the ball, and the electricity shoots through you."

We both take a deep breath and stare at each other.

I have to focus deeply to gulp and regroup. He has to know I feel the same way. I've been unable to control my blushing when he's around.

I want to ask Josh about himself. This I am dying to know, but I can tell he's hesitant, so I start with myself. I pull my jacket sleeves over my hands nervously.

"I grew up poor but always with a roof over my head. My father died a few years ago. My mother says it was something from back on the streets that caught up with him. She hasn't told me much about living on the streets but enough to know it wasn't easy. I'm working to decide what I want to do with my life. I dream of being able to provide for her when she's older and for my own family. I love to write, but I'm torn because that doesn't always pay the bills."

There's a small silence, and then he speaks. He's spinning a butter knife between his index finger and the table.

"Life has been hard for me since I can remember. I do live on the streets and always have. Both my parents are gone. I just take it one day at a time. I love to draw."

He grabs my hands gently and pulls them toward him so that I'm facing him. "You take my breath away," he says.

I'm locked as if nothing else exists. I lean into him and peck kiss him. He grabs my chin and answers back with more passion. The electricity I'm feeling must be sending sparks shooting from me. I take a deep breath as he releases me. He's looking out the window at something and moves to shield me from whatever is outside. I wonder what he sees. Whatever it is, it seems to have interrupted us. What if it was his ex-girlfriend or something?

"I'll walk you home," he says. "I wasn't joking about it not being safe for you to be out here at this hour."

I just grab his hand and pull him close. The air has a slight chill to it, but part of that's my psychological fear of rejection. Did he feel the sparks I felt or am I totally deranged? It seems as if he's fleeing that moment, our kiss, now and I want to cling to him in hopes we can kiss again.

As we approach my place, he grabs my chin again to look at my eyes. He has tears in his. Where did this come from? He must have felt the sparks and feared rejection more than I did. I'm not used to seeing emotion like this from a guy. I wonder if it's just Josh himself or a trait he may have picked up living in the streets. I would think the streets would do the opposite and harden him. He kisses my forehead, and I hug him before letting go. It feels as if he believes this isn't possible. What he needs is someone to believe in him, and I will if he'll let me. I believe, I cannot accurately feel this quite yet... that I will love him completely one day. Perhaps my perceptions are right. I need a different artistic light to my days that he, I know, would bring to me. I need someone who will take me for how I am and not try to change me to fit in their little trophy case on their mantel. And then he releases me, and the distance in his eyes has me running up the steps to my apartment without looking back. He just stares down the street. This is extremely confusing. I don't understand his volatile demeanor.

"So...how'd it go, Austria?" Tiff asks as I close the door. I'm looking out the front window watching him run down the street in the same direction he's been staring. His strides are beautifully paced like a swimmer, but so smooth, he doesn't make a splash.

"Pretty good."

"That's it. Pretty good. You're boringly vague."

"No, I mean not just pretty good, but fabulous. We kissed, Tiff, but then it was intensely awkward. It was like he wasn't really that into it. He was just staring out the window."

"What was he staring at?"

"I don't know. Does it matter?"

"Well, maybe. Go on."

"He just seemed very hot one second and cold the next. Have you noticed anything off about him?"

"Um, no. Josh is balanced. I think I know why he might have been distracted. Did anything else happen?"

"We hugged goodnight and he got distracted at the end of that too. Maybe he decided part way through the kiss that he's just not that interested in me. After the hug, he just kept staring down the street. I don't remember seeing anything that stood out."

I try to recollect every detail of the evening to see if I overlooked anything. The first thought that comes to mind is how Josh smelled of woods and rain. He didn't reek of body odor the way some guys our age can. He smelled as if he took a nap in a forest. That memory isn't going to help me figure out what I need to identify. What was on the street? The bubbly atmosphere in the café was enticing. People seemed in their element there. Beyond them was the night outside. Then I peel back the layers of excitement I'd felt in Josh's company, and there was a moment of darkness that washed over me before he looked away. I do remember a few other faces looking outside when Josh had been. I remember seeing the rear of a vehicle peeling out, a Range Rover. At our house, I saw similar taillights. That has to be it.

"I noticed taillights belonging to a Range Rover," I say.

"Shoot. That means they've found us. They know where we live."

"What are you talking about, Tiff?"

"Matt and Ed drive a Range Rover. They seem just like jokesters, but their fun doesn't stop there. Two years ago, they beat Josh so bad he had a concussion."

I guess their opulent appearance is just a cover for their snarling and hateful true selves. My initial read upon meeting them had been right on.

"Oh no. So were they watching us tonight? What do they plan to do?"

"It sounds like they more than likely were," Tiff says. "We'll have to get an alarm system on the house and always walk in at least pairs if not groups outside. Poor Josh, they can find him in any old abandoned building he sleeps in. Hopefully, Ethan will be with him, or he can stay with Bill."

"I hope so," I say. I can't shake the images of Matt and Ed attacking. "Why did they do that to Josh?"

"Josh's the one who shone the spotlight on them when they dropped mock blood on the customers. Had he not done that, they would have probably gotten away with it. Instead the customers were able to easily identify their assailants. Don't worry, Austria. Diesel will be our guard tonight. He'll be on them in a second if they ever invade our home."

Tiff scratches behind Diesel's ear. He's a good dog, and I'm glad we have him even more so now. I sit beside them and start scratching behind his other ear. His tail begins wagging immediately.

"Sounds good, Tiff. You should've warned me about more of this before we began at the haunted house."

"I was hoping it wouldn't come up. Would it have stopped you?"

"No. I've enjoyed the experience. It's brought me out of my slump. We should probably get to bed if we want to be of any use tomorrow."

We both head to bed. I wonder if I'm going to have another restless night.

I shouldn't have wondered. I knew. I toss and turn. One nightmare that jars me awake tonight is of Matt and Ed in dark hoods surprising Josh in his sleep in a dusty, abandoned building by beating on him with objects I cannot make out. In my dream I run to interfere but am quickly knocked unconscious. It's weird to have a dream within a dream, but that is what I believe I'm having now. I see Matt and Ed doing something more cynical than in my initial dream. They're with a group of men looking at blueprints, but then something blocks my perceptive ability like when I'd been holding the costume outside the haunted house. I read another chapter and go back to sleep. I'm thankful to fall to sleep easily this time. It seems as if the next dream begins the second my head hits the pillow. I hear my father's voice.

"Ready or not, here I come."

I'm hiding inside our hexagon table. The one fully enclosed with two doors that only a preschooler or younger could fit in. I giggle when I hear his footsteps in the room. He's unsuccessful in his first few attempts to find me, so I allow myself to giggle again, louder this time. I hear his footsteps approach and then the doors open. He smells of his aftershave, a hint of ocean breeze. His eyes light up as he smiles at me. He gently holds my hand as I crawl out. Then he scoops me up and holds me in his arms. I nuzzle my nose into the nape of his neck, where the smell of his aftershave is the strongest. He pulls his head back to take a look at me.

"Good hiding, kid. You're growing too fast. Now it's my turn to hide."

He sets me down, and I begin to count.

My alarm goes off, and the sun peeks through my curtains. Guess the dream put me into a restful sleep. I wish I could've stayed in the dream with my father. I miss him so much it hurts, and I always feel like there's a void in my life without him.

ACQUIREMENT

The next day we're introduced to the three rooms that still need creating. No scene or plot has been set yet, they're blank canvases. Bill asks for volunteers and my hand shoots up before I'm even aware of it. I catch Josh's sideways smirk as he raises his hand, too. I can't seem to get a good read on him. He hasn't spoken to me all morning. I should've just steered clear of guys here altogether. Of course, Tiff's one of my creative muses so she raises her hand too, although I'm beginning to have a feeling that there may be a new muse in my life, or not. Patrice raises her hand. I hope fervently that she isn't Josh's muse, but my fear drops dramatically when I catch Ethan's face out of the corner of my eye. He raises his hand, looks at Patrice quickly, and then looks away, attempting to hide his interest. I also see Luke raising his hand while looking at Tiff. When she looks back, a blush appears on his cheeks. Apparently, crossing lines and forming new relationships must be catching. I'm even more surprised when Matt and Ed raise their hands. Of course, Matt would want to show that he can haunt better than the rest of us. If he only knew he doesn't stand a chance. Knowing what I do now about Matt and Ed, I want to get them back even more than before.

"Okay, Ethan, Patrice, Matt, and Ed are in a group together. Josh, Austria, Luke, and Tiff are in the other group. Your supplies are in the center of the room," Bill says.

There are large pieces of paper in the center of the circle with markers on top of them. Bill instructs us that there are three papers for each of the unplanned rooms. We're to work on the setting, the lines, and the overall atmosphere of the room. I take a piece of paper, Tiff takes one, and Josh takes one. We walk over to a private corner. As we go by the rollaway racks, Josh looks directly at my favorite vampire costume and then raises his eyebrows at me. Good idea. Josh and I already know what our atmosphere's going to be, but I have to come up with a way so Tiff believes she's the inspiration for this idea as my muse. So I tell her about the attraction I had to the haunted house job when she first told me about it, but about the fright too. I was running a big risk going against my mother's warning. One that may cost me a scholarship, but it could be a step toward the true career I want, to be a fiction writer, a novel writer. It could also bring me closer to my father or at least his memory. While I haven't outwardly declared this as a reason for taking the job, it's probably the most important. I have to fill the void. I don't think I can live another year splintered by the pain of his loss. I hope to find closure here.

Josh looks at me and just says, "Interesting."

The atmosphere in our room is to be one of alluring danger that draws in its prey, like a vampire. We'll have a child in one corner that appears afraid. I write out the lines here. Josh draws the scene. He's an amazing artist. The pictures are remarkably intricate—I can see a tiny tear beginning to drop from the child's eye. Tiff acts it out for us so we can see loose ends or where one train of thought might not work and needs reorganizing. It's funny watching her switch from role to role. I almost laugh when she changes from a woman to a boy. After the customers are scared by monsters while trying to check on the child, a beautiful woman will grab their hands and tell them to run this way. She will then be taken down. After that, the customers will have to fend for themselves as they see images of the child and woman being tortured by a monstrous, vampire couple. The winding path will make them nervous and, just as it clears, they will be chased to the exit only to have the risen dead woman and child be behind that door to scare them more. It is epic, and we just slapped it together in five minutes.

Bill walks around handing us maps of where our new rooms will be.

"Just like yesterday, I will walk around to each room to help set up. Everyone who didn't volunteer for one of these rooms will help move props and costumes. If extras are needed, that'll be your responsibility too. Work hard, and we may be able to call it early today."

I already know who our child will be, Jack. At least I already know he's a talented actor, but I'm unsure of how to ask him to play the role of a child without insulting him. He's seventeen but hasn't hit his last growth spurt so can pass as fourteen and after we dress him young, he'll pass for twelve.

"Hey Jack, can you help us set up?"

At least I can get him involved so he hears our script. I'm hoping he'll volunteer for the spot without me having to ask.

Luke and Josh begin gathering the equipment and props we'll need, like a television set and a camera. We can film the images of the woman and child being tortured beforehand and air it when live. We'll need plain, normal clothes for the woman and child before the change. Makeup will be crucial for when they rise from the dead. We'll also need instruments of torture for the attacker.

Tiff gives me a look and nods toward Patrice and Ceresa, who are behind one of the rollaway racks. As I walk their way, Patrice nods in the direction of the only closet in the room. It holds antique furniture that's only to be used with caution. It also currently holds Matt and Ed. Perfect, I think.

When I join the girls, I see what they have behind the rollaway, the *Scream* masks we discussed. Is it bad that I look forward to this little piece of revenge? We all put on the masks and black clothing that disguises any identifiable part—hoodies, gloves, pants and boots —as quickly and quietly as possible. Then head to the closet. Patrice holds a flashlight, Ceresa a pretend knife, and Tiff has one of those voice changers. I wonder if it works. I also wonder if we'll all fit in the closet. Patrice jumps in first, turning off the light and shining the flashlight in Matt and Ed's eyes, blinding them. Ceresa holds the knife in the light as she enters. Tiff talks with that weird anonymous caller voice as Patrice shines the light on Ceresa's mask. I step in last and growl as I close the door. Ceresa advances on Matt with the knife. Matt and Ed scream, which is fabulous. They shove us aside, open the door, and run out. We all fall on each other laughing.

"Not cool. Don't think we won't get you back. You have no idea what we can do."

Ed's trying to threaten us, but it doesn't quite work when he's as white as a sheet. Matt hasn't said a word and looks like he might be sick. All I can think of is how much fun that was. I can't wait to do it again. What's wrong with me? I like flustering these guys that have been lurking around following me. Hopefully, it will discourage them from more of the same.

"Okay, everybody calm down. You need to save the scaring for paying customers. Do you want to get out early today or what?"

"Sorry, Bill, they deserved it though," Tiff tries to explain as we walk back to our responsibilities. I notice Bill has to cover his mouth to hide a smile. He clears his throat.

"That might be true, but in order to follow the rules and not have anyone hurt, let's not do that again."

I feel bad that Patrice has to work with Matt and Ed now. At least she'll have Ethan with her. Now I see Ceresa is going to join her too. Good. Tiff's heading back to Luke and Josh. Before I turn to do the same, I take one last look at Matt and Ed. They're popping the knuckles on their hands, then they both turn and look directly at me at the same time. Why are they only looking at me? Is it because I'm the new kid? A cold sweat dampens the back of my neck as I turn to walk away.

That's when it happens. Shadows begin to swarm around me. It's like they're circling vultures, and I'm the carcass. The energy makes me as dizzy as if I were dehydrated on a desert. And everything goes black for a second. When it's light again, I'm hovering above everybody. At first, I think I've died and am having an out-of-body experience, but then I hear them. Bill's over my body on one side checking my pulse, and says that I've fainted, embarrassing. Josh and Tiff are on the other side of me and look concerned. Then I hear a voice I would recognize anywhere. When I turn to my right, my voice recognition is confirmed. My father is there. He looks hazy, as if looking at a mirage. He reaches out his hand. I reach out mine. The warmth I feel when I hold his ghostly hand is like a favorite blanket I had as a child. My father looks me in the eyes.

"Be careful, Austria."

He says that like he always did before, but this time the fear in his eyes is deeper, more serious. And then he fades away. I close my eyes, trying to memorize the moment. When I open my eyes, I'm lying on the floor, and everyone's looking at me with worried expressions.

"Austria, are you okay?" Tiff asks.

"Yeah, not sure what that was all about."

"Austria, is there someone we can call? I would like you to see a doctor," Bill says.

"I'm fine, really."

"Oh, come on. You don't want to worry an old man."

"Okay, Tiff can call my mother."

Tiff drives me to the doctor's office, with looks of concern directed at me the entire way. The smell of sanitary cleanser gags me as we enter. It's cold too. My heart palpitates when I see her; my mother's standing in the waiting room checking me in. I can only imagine how furious she is. I wonder how long it will be until she says, "I told you so."

We sit down, and I grab the closest magazine. I don't read anything, just flip through the pages browsing the photos. Tiff explains to my mother what happened.

"We had just played a practical joke on some of the employees at the haunted house and then she fainted. It was weird. It was like the life had left her and then it came back. No one touched her. I don't know what happened."

"Don't worry, sweetie. You did the right thing by calling me and bringing her here."

My mother just sits there staring off into space. I know she wants to ask me a dozen questions. The silence is worse than that. Is she upset that I took the job and might lose a scholarship? Then she looks at me, smiles, and softly presses her hand to my cheek. So maybe she's not mad and just distressed. The doctor calls me in. His name's Dr. Shipley. He's nice enough but distant. He says he wants to run some blood tests. The nurse rubs my arm with an antiseptic wipe. I don't watch when she pricks me with the needle but take a peek when she's swirling the vial of my blood. I experience another cold sweat even though the blood looks normal enough.

Back in the room my mother finally speaks to me.

"Are you feeling all right, Austria?"

"Yes, there's nothing to worry about. I think I just got overwhelmed with excitement is all."

"Well, be sure to stay hydrated and get rest from now on, darling."

"Okay, okay. I'm seventeen years old. I can handle myself."

Doctor Shipley enters just then.

"Hi, Austria. Sounds like you had a bit of a spell earlier today. Could you tell me about it?"

"There's not much to tell. Just overwhelmed."

I don't know why, but I don't feel comfortable telling anyone, even my mother, about the shadows, the out of body experience, or my father. I'm afraid they'll look at me like I'm not thinking straight.

"Well, your blood shows a high healing ability, so that's good."

"What do you mean, high healing ability?" my mother asks the question I'm thinking.

"Austria's blood has stronger DNA than usual. You know, there's been a lot of interesting new studies on DNA in the last few years. Much of what we thought was wasted space in the DNA strand, about 95%, is turning out to be a whole lot more. Instead of wasted space, it's turning out to be wasted potential. You have an Altered Helix. Human beings have always been equipped with all sorts of capabilities that very few of us ever realize, and I think that there just might be more to you than meets the eye, Austria. Of course, nothing in this world is free. Everything comes at a price, and maybe fainting is yours."

I'm not sure what to think of all this. Am I a freak of nature? It all seems subtle. No one would notice the differences in me. People have fainted since the beginning of time. Why does it have to mean that there's something different about me? Doctor Shipley must be able to tell that I'm confused by the look on my face.

"This is nothing to worry about, dear. Most of the time there will be no effects. Just keep hydrated and get some rest."

"That's precisely what I told her."

"You have a smart mother. Stay well."

We leave the room and check out. I notice Doctor Shipley on the phone as we're about to exit.

"It's as expected. Yes, I'll get it to you tonight."

Then he spots me looking at him and covers his mouth with his hand. What was expected and who is he speaking to? Is he talking about me? Did my mother hear him? My mother doesn't ask me questions during the drive as I had imagined. I figured she'd blame this whole thing on the haunted house and tell me, "I told you so." Instead, she hasn't said a word. I don't think she's intentionally giving me the silent treatment, though. I keep catching her chewing on the inside of her lip out of the corner of my eye. She's nervous, but I thought the doctor said it was nothing. Is something going on with my mother that I don't know about? When we are in front of the apartment I share with Tiff, she gives me a hug. I don't think I'm going to get her to open up tonight, but I make a mental note to check in with her later. I try to read into her emotions like I've done before but the flood of images is too much. I don't know why, but I feel nervous for her.

"I love you, Austria."

"I love you too, Mother."

CATECHISM

The next morning, I take a breather and write before going to the haunted house. I always try to draw a cartoon of the scene I'm writing about before I begin, to get the creative juices flowing. It's pretty hilarious to see, since drawing is definitely not one of my talents. Maybe I could turn them into comics to go along with the books. I attempt to draw a cartoon man trying to grab a cartoon woman's hand. I hold up the piece of paper and in actuality it looks as if he's walking her on a leash. My drawing is so awful it turns a romantic scene into S&M. Either way, it has stirred my imagination.

I boot up the laptop and begin typing. I get to a word I know but can't remember how to spell. I instantly miss living with my mother. She's like a dictionary on two legs. Anytime I wrote at our house, I could just say a word like a Spelling-Bee judge, and she'd spout out the letters like a contestant.

It had been just the two of us for the past few years. We had our routines memorized. She used to always have my shoes right by the front door every day, despite my never following her request to put them there. I always made her chamomile tea when we'd curl up on the couch to watch a show before bed. I miss how she would paint my fingernails while we watched a movie. Maybe we can watch a movie sometime after the haunted house preparations are complete.

##

At the haunted house, everyone gives me looks of concern as I enter the inventory room. Luke and Ethan ask me how I'm doing. I assure them it was nothing, and I'm fine. Tiff puts a reassuring hand on my shoulder. Ceresa claps. She and Patrice smile in unison—they're glad I'm okay. Josh doesn't meet my gaze; his face is still as a statue. I'm distraught by his reaction. I notice he's staring Matt and Ed down, but they aren't doing anything. Did they attack Josh again? I wish someone would tell Bill how serious they are. Maybe someone has, but because of the money their parents give, he's too paralyzed to react. If anything, Matt and Ed seem to be focused on only the work for once. They're organizing the rest of the props by rooms so that they can easily be moved to the correct destination. They seem to be efficient and organized. Bill gives them a nod of approval. I notice Ed make eye contact with Josh. Then he looks at me. I raise my eyebrows silently and cock my head to the side, approving of his and Matt's actions. He looks down and shakes his head. He can't even take a compliment. Guess the trick on them just made them hate us more. Are they just trying to butter up Bill with their actions? Why would they care enough? They have to be after something, why can't I figure out what? It's as if the increase of attraction and caring toward Josh is causing me to lose my sense of perception.

I busy myself to keep from feeling so lost. Patrice and Ceresa help me with makeup for real this time. There's no need to plot against the evil frats this morning. As Patrice smears white paint on my face, I'm reminded of when my mother first taught me how to wear makeup. I smile.

"Patrice, how does looking pale make me scary?"

"The white just makes the gray shadow and red blood stand out."

“Oh.”

That’s all I can manage as I look in the mirror. Ceresa has now applied some of the gray and red Patrice mentioned. It’s a dramatic change, and I do feel scary. With the lighting, props, and costumes I hope I will be terrifying. After that, Tiff and I follow Matt and Ed’s lead and begin organizing the racks by rooms. We hand-make cardboard dividers labeling each. The guys have moved all of the props, and Bill has helped them set up. It seems that everything is prepared. I wonder what we’ll do for the rest of the time before the haunted house opens. As if on cue, Bill addresses the entire group.

“Good work, everybody. I’m very impressed with your organization. Thank you. Now begins the time for rehearsals. You don’t want to be caught off guard when customers are here. You’ll need to memorize the hidden doors and hallways so you can move without being seen. First, we’ll rehearse each room one at a time. The ones who aren’t involved will walk through as if they’re the customers. Then, after each room is perfected, we’ll have a rehearsal of the entire house. You’ll have to watch your time as you move from room to room to be sure you’ll beat the customers to your location.”

The next hours we all work well together acting out each room. It’s fun. Everyone is in high spirits, playing jokes on each other here and there. Josh barely talks to me. I’m ashamed. How did I let myself believe it could be a possibility? I did enjoy writing the lines of our room, and the other two rooms’ teams see my talent and ask me to help them too. It’s utterly exhilarating. I would be thoroughly pleased if there wasn’t a slight twinge of suffering every time I look his way. Maybe no matter how great the guy, romance is hazardous for me. He appears to be watching me. Is he mocking me? I did enjoy when he drew the pictures of the rooms to complement my writing. His pictures are gifted, and they seem to capture details my words fail to. My thoughts are gravitating to him again. I have to change something.

So I go over to Matt and Ed and ask (I know this is a risk, but I'm going crazy), "Hey guys, can I help you with your room?" Perhaps I can find out more about their evil ways working with them; be prepared for their actions.

They answer immediately in unison. "Of course you can. Come on."

I follow them to their room but notice out of the corner of my eye not only Josh looking at us angrily, but also Tiff watching my moves in frustration. She even stands to head my direction a second too late. What's going on? Here I thought I was distancing myself from the drama. I should be safe from these guys in public. They wouldn't try anything crazy here, right? It's not like I'm siding with the arch nemesis. I'm just helping prepare their room of the haunted house. They're employees here too.

First, Matt and Ed begin acting their scene, costumes and all. I have to give them credit. They make such sudden movements, even I jump.

"Here, hold this skull above your head over there. We'd like to see if that placement works," Matt says.

"Yeah, just like that," Ed murmurs in my ear.

In my ear…how did he get here so quickly? I feel a spasm of panic. They're now circling me. Saying things I don't understand and then both are smiling. It feels as though I'm within a magic circle of salt, except instead of keeping evil out, I'm locked inside with demons.

Ed puts me over his shoulder and says, "See, I told you we could spook the best."

They carry me out of the room. To my relief, Ed sets me down.

Then Matt says something that has me pondering, "Better watch where you go. You tempt the demons."

I thank him and walk away. I'm not sure of what to make of that line. Are they targeting me? There seems to be more between Josh and them. Are they against me being with Josh? A sudden feeling of prehistoric self-preservation washes over me. My body wants to tense and hide, while my eyes jump about investigating my surroundings.

Tiff catches up to me and grabs my arm and asks, "Are you all right?"

"Of course I am, Tiff, they're just a couple of guys looking to scare someone yet again. We're in public so I don't think they could attack here. Guess the *Scream* masks aren't working as well as we had hoped."

Tiff drops her jaw. "So you don't know then, do you?"

"Know what, Tiff? Tell me. What else have you kept hidden from me?"

"They're closely aligned with the human trafficking in this area. How do you think their families came to so much money?" Tiff explains in a hushed whisper while she cups her mouth toward my ear. Here, my best friend has kept more from me when my perceptions of her used to be so strong. I guess her acting has hindered that ability for me. With the disruption of national law, some illegal activity has prospered. Human trafficking is hard to catch, jumping state lines by bribing guards.

I put my hands in my pockets to hide their shaking. I try sarcasm on Tiff even though I know she reads through it most of the time.

"Oh, but what does that have to do with me?" I ask. So much has gone on, I'm in a whirlwind of puzzle pieces that I can't fit together.

Tiff just puts her hand on my shoulder, shakes her head, and then walks away.

Well, I didn't see that one coming. I knew they were dangerous and giving Josh a concussion a few years back is inexcusable, but I still just believed them to be adventure-seeking. I didn't think they were intertwined with something so dangerous. Why am I struggling to engage my perceptions? Have there been too many new people introduced? Matt and Ed are characters that would fit in with our room of Exodus. Luckily, they leave. The tension that had permeated the room departs with them.

Everyone seems to be lighthearted as we rehearse the final room with Team Mummified. This is the team of people I'm not familiar with. They're full of laughter and seem to not carry the weight some of us do. Their room frightens us all. Mummies pop out from everywhere, some of them just props and some the team themselves. They all seem very acrobatic and fall from places I wouldn't be able to reach or pop out of coffins with flips. It's a good closer.

We all go back to the inventory room and begin packing to leave. Luke and Tiff are talking about the room by Team Sinister. Luke acts out the corpse that chases people. He chases Tiff a couple steps and then grabs around her arms from behind. Their laughter brings a smile to my face. It's good to see Tiff happy. She's like the sister I never had. Ceresa makes a face at them, but Patrice nudges her with an elbow. Patrice makes a face at Ceresa, sticking her tongue out. Ceresa can't suppress her laughter. Ethan approaches us.

"Guys, want to drop by my mom's tonight and hang out?" He's bouncing on the balls of his feet as he eyes us all like a basketball player ready to start a game.

"You have a place?" The words leave my mouth before I consider what the statement sounds like.

"Yeah, surprise. My mom's an artist. She's rarely home, but when she is, it's not a place you want to be."

"I'm sorry; I just thought you didn't have a place."

"Don't worry about it. I know it's not the norm. My mom's been addicted for so long I don't even think I have a memory of her being sober. She beats on me quite a bit."

"She what? Ethan, you're a full-grown man. I mean I'm pretty sure you could beat most guys in a fight. You're tough."

"I know, but it's my mom and even though she's awful to me, I can't find it in me to fight back, so I just take it."

"That's terrible." I can't imagine what it would be like to have the only rock in your life abuse you.

"Na, she's not around like ninety-nine percent of the time. She won't be around tonight. She sold a piece of her artwork last week, so she's off to Vegas or something probably blowing all the money she made, but I know she paid the utility bills, so there's electricity and everything. Come on."

"We're in." Tiff accepts the invitation. Probably what I should've done right off rather than asking all these darned questions.

"Am I included?" Luke asks.

"Yeah, I know you're just stuck with Matt and Ed because of your fraternity. You never participate in their destruction. In fact, I feel a bit sorry for you, but if you tell them anything about this evening— especially where my mom's place is—I will beat you."

He jabs Luke in the arm and smiles.

"I promise. Not a word. I'll just tell them I went out to the bar and got so drunk I don't remember a thing about tonight."

"You Frats do that often?"

Ethan teases Luke, but I can tell it's companionable. Ceresa and Patrice put their backpacks on and look up.

"Let's go."

Tiff, Luke, and I grab our stuff and follow them out. Josh and Ethan are arguing about something, but I can't tell what it is. As we go outside, I wonder if we'll all fit in the vehicle. Ceresa has her little hatchback that she lives in some of the time so we can fit four people in that. I think it's green, but it's so old and weather worn I can't be sure. I see Luke has his black Ford Escape with tinted windows so looks like we'll be fine.

"I'll ride with Luke," Tiff says.

"Okay, Tiff. I'll ride with you," I say.

"I've got room for four," Ceresa says.

"We're in," Ethan and Patrice say together.

"Great, I get to ride with you lovebirds," Josh says as he walks toward the hatchback. Maybe he feels more comfortable with his buddies, but I wish he'd ride with us.

"No, we'll need you to give them directions if we lose them," Patrice says to Josh.

"Do we need to make any stops on the way, Ethan?" I ask before we leave, ignoring Josh's look of disappointment. Before Ethan is able to answer I have to change things up. "Hey, mind if I ride with you guys?" Hopefully, Tiff doesn't care.

"Nope. Hop in," Ethan answers and then continues our previous conversation. "We don't have to stop. Mom stocked the shelves when she got her check."

"Good. Hey, is something up with Josh? He doesn't seem to be himself."

"Oh, uh, you haven't heard, have you?" Patrice asks.

I can hear the sympathy in her words. Why is it that I still seem to be on the outside of everything? Why am I the last to know?

"No…what's going on?"

"Ed likes you. He warned Josh to keep his distance from you," Ethan says.

He seems to be sticking up for Josh. I wonder how long Matt and Ed have been trying to keep these guys under their thumbs.

"I wish those guys would just go away. Why does Ed have to bully? He doesn't have a chance with me even if Josh wasn't around."

"I think they just try to find the best ways to hurt us," Patrice says.

I don't know what to think about all this, but my heart hopes this is the only reason Josh has stayed away. I don't want him hurt, so I'll stay away too, but this fills my heart with pain.

We park on the street next to Ethan's house. It is huge. Well, huge by my standards. Since the largest place I've lived in is a three-bedroom ranch house, my standards are probably lower than the norm. There's an iron gate surrounding Ethan's house. It's dark, so it is difficult to make out much detail. Some lights are on. I jump when I see a silhouette in a window.

"I thought no one was home," I say to Ethan as I point to the window.

"My mom's an artist. It's just a manikin. Seems to keep burglars out of the house though," he answers with a smile.

“This place looks enormous,” I say as we all pile out of the car.

“Well, Nelson-Atkins museum owns it. They allow my mom and me to live here as long as she continues to produce artwork that captures them.”

“Wow, that’s awesome.”

We all walk up to the door. The glass door in front of it has decorative iron bars. The roof has three peaks and above the door there’s an arch window. As we enter, there’s a staircase leading to the second floor. That was the level where I saw the manikin. The room to the left is full of artwork and supplies. Another manikin gives me a start. A huge window allows the moonlight to shine in. The thought of working in such a beautiful room has desire coursing through my veins. The room to the right should be a dining room. A beautiful chandelier hangs from the ceiling, and the wall is covered with classic square trim. Rather than a dining table though there’s a couch, some recliners, and a T.V. Connected to the T.V. is a game console with controllers. Josh and Ethan toss their backpacks down, sit on the couch, and turn on the game.

Josh looks at home. I wonder how often they stay here.

“I’ll give you the grand tour. These two seem a bit occupied,” Patrice says.

“I’ll be in the kitchen,” Ceresa says.

Luke, Tiff, and I follow Patrice and Ceresa as they walk us to the kitchen. A built-in cabinet looks like it should hold china plates. Instead of plates there are chips and granola bars and other food. I can tell this kitchen must have been built a while ago. It has metal shelves to make up for the lack of storage space. We move on to the final room on the first floor without Ceresa. It’s the official living room. Shelves full of books surround the fireplace. I step toward the shelves and remove one of the books written by George R.R. Martin. It reminds me of the vintage Facebook post I'd seen by a teacher threatening her students that she'll ruin the T.V. series "Game of Thrones" surprise by telling them because she's read all the books. A smile tugs at my mouth.

Next, we go up the stairs. They're wood as all the floors have been throughout the house except for the tiled kitchen floor. The railings are traditional. As we come to the top, I see the manikin I spotted through the window. She's sitting on a trunk holding a magazine, appearing to be reading. Pretty realistic. There's a plant next to the trunk that I cannot name but can tell it's well maintained by how green it is. There are four more rooms up here. Patrice points down the hall.

"The room down there belongs to Ethan's mom. Do not enter that room."

Then she points to the room on the left at the top of the stairs.

"This is the guest room."

I see three different mattresses on the floor. Clothes are strewn precariously about the room. It appears multiple people live in this room. I only spot girl's clothes.

"Do you and Ceresa stay here?"

"Yeah, well unless I'm in Ethan's room." She blushes as she says this. "It's over here."

She points to the first room on the right of the stairs. I peek in and can see one bed and a dresser. This room is as messy as the other. Finally, she points to the last room.

"That's where Josh stays."

My heart rate speeds up just thinking of him. I see a mattress on the floor, piles of books, and art supplies. I want to see what kind of books he reads, and I can't hold myself back. I walk in and pick up a book. It's *Foundation* by Isaac Asimov. I wasn't able to follow that one as well as I would have liked. I pick up the next. It's one of the Dark Tower books by Stephen King. I love this series. It looks like there's more Josh and I could talk about, *if* we were even talking.

Just then, as if on cue, he enters the room. I had not noticed that the others had left.

"I was just grabbing something quick," he says.

"Josh." I grip his hand.

"I, I can't, Austria," he says as his chin drops to his chest.

I touch his face and turn it up to me.

"Josh, I don't want you to get hurt, so I understand. I care about you. I wish there was something we could do."

"I'm used to my dreams being crushed. It's easier if you stay busy."

"Well, I'm not."

I peck kiss him lightly as I run my fingers through his hair. The electricity makes me lightheaded. I don't know how I've gone a second without this. I put my arms around his waist and lock my fingers so he can't run.

"Austria, this will just make it worse."

"I don't care. No one can see us, Josh. We can just keep it a secret."

"Not when you can't control the way you look at me."

"What way is that?"

"The way you're looking at me now."

He kisses me, more deeply than ever before. The heat between us burns yet feels remarkably good. He looks at me, and I can tell he cares, but then he looks away and hugs me. It feels like goodbye.

"Please," I say. I can feel my lower lip curling into a pout.

"No, Austria, I don't care what they do to me, but this will put you in danger, and I can't bear that."

He walks off. I can't slow my breathing enough to call after him. Part of me feels broken. I don't know what to do, so I just walk downstairs to see what everyone else is doing. Luke has joined Josh and Ethan playing video games. He seems to fit right in. I hear laughter from the formal living room and follow it. Ceresa, Patrice, and Tiff have set up a game of Euchre. I join as Tiff's partner. Ceresa and Patrice are pretty good. Tiff and I have to make some risky calls so we can get ahead. It's a close game, but we win in the end, even though I don't feel like a victor.

PROCURE

Ceresa jumps out of a pile of props, a jack in the box. The group of the acrobatic four, Team Mummified, that I don't really know, all pretend to be terrified. One puts the back of her hand against her forehead and pretends to faint. One guy puts his hand on his chest as though he's so panicked, he's having a heart attack. One girl runs a few steps away, swinging her arms over her head like an idiot. The last is holding his crotch looking embarrassed like he just soiled himself. I can't help but laugh. It feels good to laugh. I forget about my crazy Altered Helix. I forget about Josh and me not being able to have a relationship. I forget about the crazy shadows. I feel like one of them, having a good time. I feel like writing techniques and ideas can still be learned here.

I walk over to the group. They're possibly more people to interfere with my perceptions, but I joined the haunted house to broaden my horizons, so here we go.

"Ceresa, you crack me up. You're so energetic."

"Yeah, she's got spunk," says the girl who pretended to faint. She has kind eyes. Her face puckers when she smiles as if she just tasted a lemon.

"I'm Austria. You know Ceresa outside the haunted house?" I ask.

"Yeah. Hi, I'm Camille. Ceresa helped us get an apartment. All four of us live together. It's crowded, but we'd be on the streets I imagine by now, if it weren't for Ceresa."

I can see now that Ceresa's intimidating exterior is a cover. She found these four people a home when she doesn't have one of her own.

"And I'm Emmitt." The guy who faked the heart attack waves at me with a sly smile. He has dark skin. He has bright white teeth and when he smiles dimples show at the top of his cheeks near his eyes. I wave back at him.

"I'm Brittany," says a shy girl with curly dirty blonde hair. Her blue eyes stand out from the eyeliner that surrounds them. I can't believe this shy little thing was the one running with her arms swinging crazily over her head. I smile and nod my head.

"I'm Landon." This comes from the last one, a skinny guy with a criminal smile. He's the one who faked wetting his pants.

This group is feisty.

"You guys are lucky to have met Ceresa," I say as I nudge her and give her a nod of approval. She smiles back cautiously and then clears her throat as if to remain a person of leadership who doesn't joke around.

"I found them in the lobby of the Union Station after hours. They were lucky. Usually, just the first set of doors are left unlocked, but that night the guard forgot the final door that was closed after the last train," Ceresa says.

"That was a crazy night," Camille says. "We even camped out in the lobby of a hotel for a few hours before that. They kicked us out, so we had to move on."

"Yeah, whatever, you didn't get dehydrated because I was able to sneak into the closed bar and get you water," says Emmitt.

"I'm just glad we all had enough cash together to order a pizza that night," Landon says, rubbing his stomach.

"Yeah sure, we wouldn't have ended up in that mess if I hadn't refused to stay in the place we had. Thanks for having my back and sticking with me," Brittany says. She's running her finger up and down the outer seam of her jeans nervously. Her eyes keep darting around in fear. I wonder what happened that made her not want to stay in the place they had.

Ceresa puts her hand on Brittany's knee as if to say, "Do not feel guilty for that." It's as if she's silently reassuring Brittany that no one should ever disrespect her that way, and true friends would stick with her just like these guys did.

"I was more than happy to coax them into sharing an apartment. Since they were all okay sharing a place and I could put all their incomes together, it was no trouble at all."

Bill interrupts us. "Time for lunch. I don't have anything here today, so you'll all have to go out and scavenge for lunch on your own. Think you can handle that?"

I look over at Tiff and nod for her to join me with these kids. She and Luke head over to us. A stitch begins in my side at the sight of them. I wish so intensely that Josh and I could be together. But I need to keep my mind on the task at hand.

"Hey, Tiff. Know a good place for some grub?"

"You really have to ask, Austria?"

"Well, I was hoping to find something low-cost, high-flavor for my new friends here."

I introduce her to the four I just met. She appears to approve of Ceresa's kindness too.

"I think I have the perfect spot. Have you heard of the new joint, Zaina, near Twelfth and Main?"

"I've been looking forward to trying that place out," Luke says.

We all head out to Zaina. The prices are low, and the food is Mediterranean deliciousness. It's a "Bring Your Own Beer" joint that attracts a crowd. Luckily, it's within walking distance.

As we walk, I get to hear the stories of these new individuals I've been honored to meet.

"If you don't mind me asking, how did you guys end up living on the streets?" I ask the group.

Emmitt bursts in first. "We all have degrees, man. Graduated early from high school and had our degrees at age twenty. The recent economy caused us to be so underemployed that we didn't make enough to survive."

"We searched everywhere for jobs and found nothing," Camille adds.

"Do you know how disheartening it is to invest so much and not have the return expected?" Brittany asks. "Not only did we not receive graduate level jobs, we couldn't even find jobs that paid enough to cover living expenses. The ability to be independent was robbed from us," Brittany says. Now her shoulders aren't as slouched, and she seems more comfortable talking.

"We had all moved away from home. If we were to go back without a job and have to live with our parents, we'd all be seen as losers in our hometowns. Failures compared to the ones who had stayed and found jobs right out of high school," Landon says.

"That's awful, guys. I'm sorry," I say.

"Nah. It's a blessing in disguise. Instead of wasting years behind a desk, we've pulled together and are chasing our true dreams; anything can happen," Camille says.

"I'm really in the same spot as you guys. I have just decided to skip college to chase my dreams." I try to console them even though I can tell that's not what they want. I simply cannot resist the urge to comfort.

"You and Tiff should join us. We have enough room," Landon says, smiling. Brittany jabs him in the side.

"Well, what do you think I'm doing working at the haunted house with you?" I reply with a conspiratorial smile.

A rumble slowly stirs through the group. We look at each other and realize it's our stomachs. We walk a little faster to Zaina, laughing at each other's growling.

Zaina's packed. The line extends beyond the door. Maybe this wasn't the best choice.

"I might eat my arm if I have to wait much longer," Landon exclaims.

"Here, have some of my mints," Camille offers.

"You carry mints in your purse like my ma," Emmitt kids.

"Want to step outside and see if I fight like your ma too?"

Camille opens and shuts her hand together like a moving mouth and rolls her eyes. I notice Brittany roll her eyes at Landon as Camille does this. Then Brittany gives Emmitt a pointed look that silences whatever rebuke he was forming in his head.

The line has cleared, and we're inside. At least the service is fast, and the food's delicious. We order and find a few rare seats at the bar. We all gesture for Camille and Brittany to take the seats and, to my utter dismay, everyone insists that I take the third. I'd hoped that when I showed up to work the following day, people would realize my fainting was nothing. It appears I'll have to prove my ability. I do go ahead and take the seat as I want conversation to continue without a hitch like an argument over something so silly. So I'm sitting when conversation begins. Brittany grabs a newspaper placed on the ledge next to her that catches her attention.

"Did you hear about the disappearance?" Brittany inquires.

"What disappearance?" I ask.

"There was an athletic competition. I think most call it a triathlon, but I've never dared to compete in something like that. Everyone was biking, swimming and running, but part way through the run the competitors went through a wooded area and one of them didn't run out. When the competition was over, friends and family of the participant went looking, but came up empty handed. That was last week," Brittany explains.

"Whoa, I did not hear about that," I say as my mind reels. My father had been athletic and disappeared out of thin air. The experience of which Brittany speaks feels a little too close to home.

"Crazy," Ceresa says. "It happened in our sector too. I mean, yes, we have our 'every once in a while' runaway and disappearance, even death, on the streets, but this was different. This kid had come into the shelter looking clean-cut and well fed. He was athletic and looked like he'd outlast at least ninety percent of the folks we had in that night, but no one saw him again. He had confided in another young kid that he was on the run from people but couldn't specify who. That kid followed up with his family and friends to see if he had returned, but no one knew anything about his whereabouts."

"So any clue what it was? Could it have been drugs or a runaway?" Camille asks, full of questions.

"A couple of unidentified bodies have been located under bridges and in wooded areas of the city," Ceresa says. "They were cut open so bad. they'd bled all they could, and then someone had washed the blood away. It was as if they were gutted before they died. The forensics teams have seen nothing like this. They've recovered some blood cells but, so far, the results have been inconclusive. They say the DNA is like nothing they've seen before."

"Excuse me," Camille gets up and runs to the restroom. Brittany goes after her. Luke gives Ceresa a shake of the head as if disapproving of her going into such gory details. He puts an arm around Tiff. I look down at my hands. Sure enough, they're shaking. I'm grateful for the chair now. When Ceresa mentioned different DNA and being gutted in the same statement my breath stopped. I don't understand how they could be connected. It's not like the different DNA has much of an effect. The biggest perk seems to be the healing ability, but that didn't appear to be a bit of help to these people. Maybe their DNA wasn't the same as mine. I still feel a bit dizzy and probably as queasy as Camille did when she ran off to the restroom. Perfect timing, our food arrives.

I have to wait a few minutes for my stomach to settle, but I'm still hungry. I begin eating as soon as I think it's safe. The vegetarian platter is made of falafel with tahini and grape leaves. Even though my stomach is still upset, I chance a few bites. The food has a cleansing effect, but I'm still unable to manage more than the few bites. I wish it could erase the images that formed in my head.

Camille and Brittany have returned and are unable to even look at their gyro platters. It appears everybody was affected by the horrific conversation. No one's eating more than a small portion even though our stomachs still rumble.

We finally decide we've had enough and head back to the haunted house. I'm relieved to be moving on. Thoughts keep entering my head. The only reason something's gutted is to get to the insides. Why had the bodies been gutted unless people were removing organs? Why would they do that? I look forward to returning to work. Funny that the thought of haunting should put me at ease and release my fears.

CREATION

The next day at the haunted house the shadows are back and in force. I feel as though they move with my pulse. I wonder if yesterday's conversation is causing me to imagine the shadows. As if reading my mind, one appears next to me. Nothing could be causing this shadow. No obstacles block the light there. The shadow seems to be in the shape of a person. Could it be my father? This shadow seems more aggressive than the others. I have to squeeze the pressure point between my thumb and forefinger in order to maintain my concentration. It's rehearsals again today. We're going through rooms one at a time. As we walk to the room by Team Decapitated, a shadow flows right in front of me. I reflexively take a step back and run into Jack.

"Sorry."

"No worries. Everything okay?"

"Yeah, I…just forgot something back in the inventory room. I'm going to go grab it. Can you let the others know if they look for me?"

"Sure thing, I understand."

I walk calmly as I pass the others, but as soon as I'm out of their sight I begin to jog. A shadow lifts from the floor and rises to the ceiling. Now I sprint to the inventory room. Why is the activity so high today? Do they feed off of my fear?

When I get to the room, I go directly to my bag and retrieve my water bottle. My mouth has gone dry from fear. I take a few gulps and feel a little better. I sit down. I have an odd sensation that is impossible to even put a word to. Something between intuition and déjà vu. My arms prickle with goosebumps. I turn to the mirror of the vanity I'm sitting at. I swear I see a shadow fly up to the ceiling in the corner. Now I have a feeling of recognition. I turn back to the mirror and my father is staring back right next to me.

This time he's not hazy. He looks as clear as if he were here for real. I'm afraid to turn to see if he's definitely there. What if he turns back to the hazy appearance or disappears when I do? Instead, I smile in the mirror at him.

"Remember that camping trip we took to the lake?"

Even his voice sounds real. I cannot suppress my smile. All of the anxiety I'd been feeling is gone.

"Yeah. I loved the S'mores we made, Father. No one else puts honey on their marshmallow."

"You loved your marshmallows slightly brown, and I liked mine burnt."

"I thought you were crazy when your marshmallow caught fire."

"Those were some good times. I liked teaching you to fish too."

"Father…I didn't catch a thing."

"It was still fun."

I want to turn and hug him so bad. Tears well up, but I push them back and swallow. I don't want my vision to go blurry while I can see him. I've always wondered what our relationship would be like now if he had lived.

"Austria."

"Yes?"

"Be careful." He's hunched forward as if telling me this in secret, and the tension in his shoulders causes me to feel a sense of urgency.

"You already--" I'm interrupted.

Jack and Lea come trotting into the room sweetly holding hands. I take my eyes away from my father for one second to see them in the mirror and when I look back at where my father had been, he's gone. I miss him already. The old feeling of loss is returning. I had been to counselors after he died. The pain never truly goes away, but life goes on. The pain's rearing its ugly head now. I stand to exit.

"Did you find what you forgot?" Jack asks.

"What? Oh, um… yeah. I just needed some water."

I grab my water bottle and bring it with me down the hall to rejoin the rehearsals. They help the hours pass. If I were alone, the pain would burn a bitter hole through me. After we're done, all I want to do is head home, make some hot cocoa—Father and I had that with the S'mores—and curl up in a soft blanket.

"Can I walk you home?"

He appears out of nowhere and is causing the tingling without even touching me now. I know who said those words from behind me.

"That would be excellent, Josh, but don't feel you HAVE to."

He puts his hands on my arms just above my elbows very gently and turns me to face him.

"Austria, I'm sorry for the distance these past few days. The feelings I have for you are so strong, they scare me," he says.

"Well, they scare me too, but we have to give it a shot, don't we? This is one of those once in a lifetime if you're lucky deals, right?" I answer.

His answering smile has me quivering. How does he pack such a punch in that smile? As we walk home, we talk about everything. He finally opens up to me without barriers. I don't know what caused this change, but I don't care. It causes the shield I've put up to begin to erode. I feel like I don't have to filter anything with him. He understands everything I say. Without the shields, a warmth like a blanket fresh out of the dryer wraps around me. I invite him in when we arrive. I'm finally getting time with him. And time it is. My skin tingles everywhere and I'm afraid it will be blotchy red for days. We discuss everything, memories, dreams, and plans. His presence takes away the pain I would've been feeling missing my father. By morning, we've decided our plans are going to intermingle, screw Matt and Ed. We kiss, and it feels like what I imagine a lightning bolt would feel like, shock and heat at an unimaginable rate. As he leaves, I'm already feeling the gaping hole I know his absence will cause.

AMOROUSNESS

The smell of coffee and bacon makes it hard to not run downstairs. Tiff must be cooking. Not only is she a talented actress, she's a fabulous cook too. I'm surprised I haven't gained ten pounds since becoming her roommate. I run out and grab our paper quickly. It's cold in my pajamas and slippers, bun on top of my head. The trees seem more colorful than usual. I guess fall has fully come around then. Leaves are luscious red, little chick yellow, and sunset orange. When I come back in, I can hear Tiff singing while she cooks. A smile spreads across my face. I try to sneak into the kitchen to surprise her, but she must have eyes in the back of her head.

"Spill it, Austria."

"What? I don't know what you're talking about."

She turns around with a spatula in her hand. Instead of a bun, her hair is held up with chopsticks. She's wearing a black apron with a picture of what looks like two chef's knives in the shape of an "X." The word "cuisine" encases them with ribbon. At first, she looks upset because I'm trying to withhold information from her. Then her face lights up with a smile as she rushes to me. She grabs my shoulders.

"Austria."

"What?"

"You're all lit up. Your cheeks are all rosy and your eyes are ablaze."

"Are you saying I don't always look like this?" I should know better. She knows I'm always sarcastic when I feel uncomfortable.

"Oh my goodness. Are you and Josh? Did you?"

"No, you know I'm waiting."

"But how, why do you look this way?"

"I think…we're…in…love."

"Eeek!"

She bounces as she screams and hugs me. She is very excited for me. Tiff's like my sister reading my every move. I begin to ponder. She'd already been happy and singing before she heard the news. It's not every day that I get breakfast from Chef Tiff. Her face seems to have a new glow to it this morning too.

"Tiff? Your turn, spill it."

As the last word leaves my mouth Luke walks into the kitchen. His hair stands on end. He smiles sheepishly with his perfectly sculpted lips. His puppy dog eyes look at me.

"Morning, Austria."

"Good morning, Luke."

He walks over to Tiff and pulls her into a hug. They're adorable. As he begins helping Tiff with breakfast, I become distraught. I should've invited Josh to breakfast. I should've cooked. Super healing DNA seems to have killed my domestic genes. I take my plate to the living room. I don't want to intrude on their time, and they can't keep their hands off each other anyway. At least Luke can drive us to the haunted house so that we don't have to walk.

##

Today we're going to scout the other haunted houses and make sure our ideas haven't been stolen. First, we all walk to the Edge of Hell. This is the biggest haunted house in the area. They are known as the masters of scare. We walk down the street as a group; I wonder what we look like to others. Three preppy frat guys, multiple restaurant employees, and four street kids. Oh, and Bill of course. He is bald and tall. He has a goofy, science teacher look. He wears clothes that fit in with the street kids: stained jeans and a dark T-shirt with a flannel shirt over it. His boots are black and probably have steel toes under the leather. His appearance is intimidating until he smiles. When he smiles you see him for the teddy bear he is. Someone who takes care of everybody.

The Edge of Hell does have one thing we don't. They have a slide five stories high. It's the ride from Heaven to Hell. I think our story lines and acting abilities have them beat though. The employees spot us.

"Think you'll last against competition like this, Bill?"

This must be the owner of the Edge of Hell. He's wearing a suit, and I think I've seen him somewhere before. His hair is slicked back. It finally registers; he's Adam Sheffield. He looks like the opposite of Bill. He gives the impression of being a professional and hard-working guy to hide the Satan he really is, who would help nobody, unless it benefitted him of course. Suddenly he and Bill exchange some sort of secret handshake. They seem like old buddies. I can't imagine Bill hanging out with this evil man. Bill speaks next.

"Hello, Adam. Hear about the new code they're trying to pass in order to help your movement? When are you going to leave us alone? We're not harming anyone. In fact, we're helping get people off the streets. We're helping stabilize welfare programs."

"Oh Bill, always such a chump. You know I have interest in these buildings now. I'm no magician, but we're going to do everything we can to gain control of the ones not generating a profit, including causing you some headaches. It's time to join my team and make more money doing this."

"I'm working on it. I have a few things up my sleeve. You know I can never join your team. I've been clean over ten years and I'm never going back."

"All right, well come in any time you want. Hope you got the sneak peek you were looking for. Maybe your little group of preschoolers can pick up a thing or two."

"Thanks, but I think we have things under control. You and your little monsters should come see our place sometime. Tell them to wear their Pull-Ups."

We all walk out. We're heading in a direction that's not the way to the other haunted houses. I thought we were going to look at multiple places, but it seems Bill has other ideas. I don't realize where he's leading us until we're in front of the Nelson-Atkins Art Museum, and I see the huge shuttlecock sculpture. What are we doing here?

"It came to my attention during our last visit that we have nothing to learn from the other houses. We're a unique haunted house. We do not spend tons of money trying to get the best scare tactic. We use our minds. We use art. Now I would like all of you to spend an hour in the museum and try to create something new."

I've always felt a breath of historical resonance upon entering such a place. The art museum is in an old building with cement columns and metal doors. The hard, solid stone of the outside juxtaposes the unexplainable beauty within. I can see why Bill brought us here. Josh grabs my hand and pulls me to the Benton in Black and White exhibition. We pass by Matt and Ed on our way there. Matt looks at me and crosses his arms over his chest. Ed pops the knuckles in his hands, fisting them together while he leers at us. I swear if he were a dog, he'd be barking at us right now. Josh puts an arm around me and gives a defiant stare back as we walk by.

The first artwork we come to is called An American Treasure. It's in black and white like the rest of the pieces of this exhibit, but it sparks my interest. Clouds appear like fingers reaching to grab something. In between two of these fingers is a crescent moon that stands out even in the lack of color. I notice that it appears vitally close to the center. There's also a man facing away that, though his head's bent over so far one would fear he'll lose his cowboy hat, he appears to dominate the other people in the picture. He's also larger than the others as if closer to us. His arm hides in front of his belly. I get the feeling he could turn around any second and draw a gun on us. I shudder at the thought.

The next is of a woman at night. At least I assume that is the moon hidden behind those swirling clouds; it's hard to tell in black and white. She's at the edge of a field near the road sitting on a fence with a gas-powered lamp on the mailbox. She has in her hands a piece of paper like a letter from her love that she must read before taking one step away from the mailbox. I don't suppress my smile. She's barefoot and rests her foot on a rock. The two pieces contrast each other. One causes fear and the other joy. Emotions spurred from just lithographs. Josh smiles at me.

"You like Benton?"

"So far, yes."

"Good. Then you'll like the Reality and Fantasy: Land, Town and Sea exhibit."

His face lights up when I look at him with suspicion. How is he so sure I'll like it? Oh well, we have to cross to the other side of the museum, and he lets me loop my arm through his. The tingling this causes makes me wonder how I'm able to concentrate at all. I'm so interested to see if our tastes are the same or hear his opinion and thoughts on pieces that the tingle dulls. And then I'm lost again. As we enter the exhibit, I see what has to be at least a thousand different pieces. I'm drawn to a Giovanni Battista Piranesi black and white. There are tons of staircases and walkways that zigzag together. It makes me feel lost and found at the same time.

"This one makes me think of living in the alleys."

And now it gives me a whole new meaning. It's my turn to put my arm around Josh protectively. I gasp involuntarily. Josh looks at me and puts one of his arms around me so that we're in an embrace. His arms are strong. I can only imagine what they've endured.

"How did you sleep in a place like that? I'd be afraid to shut my eyes."

He smiles and lets out a snicker with an edge.

"I was too afraid to sleep in the beginning, but then I made friends on the streets in the area. We'd take turns keeping watch. We found enough things that could be used as weapons. If anyone unwanted approached, whoever was on watch would alert us all. Not many people want to take on an armed group. Some of the closest bonds I've made were formed in that alley."

"Wow. That's pretty cool that you had each other's backs like that."

"Yeah, definitely makes it a lot less lonely."

"I wonder if Tiff would take first watch for me if we were the ones in that alley."

I smile as I poke him in the ribs. He ducks and grabs my wrist playfully. I duck under his arm, causing him to spin. He loses his grip on my arm and I grab his.

"Looks like you'd do just fine and wouldn't need me to watch," Tiff states out of nowhere. I'd thought Josh and I were alone. I roll my eyes at her. I notice she's on Luke's arm.

"You should all just live in the basement of my parent's house. They'd never know," Luke offers.

"What would your friends think about that?" Ethan retorts.

How had I thought we were alone? My head must've been focused on the fantasy portion of the Reality and Fantasy: Land, Town and Sea exhibit.

"I'm sure your parents would love showing us all off to their clubs," Patrice adds.

"Oh, lay off, would you?" This comes from Lea. She and Jack are here too. She seemed quiet before, but now I see the rebel streak shining though.

"Want to join us one night if you're so tough?" Patrice baits Lea.

"I wouldn't have a problem with that. Jack?"

Jack has been silent. He's staring at the Giovanni Battista Piranesi black and white piece Josh and I had been looking at, chewing his fingernails.

"Too afraid?" Ethan asks the still mute Jack.

Jack clears his throat.

"How? How can you sleep in a place like that? Look at all the shadows the staircases cast."

Apparently, I'm not the only one afraid of shadows, but I'm sure it's for different reasons.

"Not much a little shadow can do to you," Patrice says.

I feel Josh's arms go around me. I'm shaking. I hadn't realized it until I felt his solid arms around mine. He looks me in the eyes, but I can't. I just can't confess to him about the shadows I see. He'll think I'm unbalanced.

“Deal. I’m in,” Jack says.

“I say we all live on the streets tonight,” Patrice says.

Tiff, Luke, and I shrug our shoulders as if this is no big deal.

Everyone looks at each other. It’s most of the couples from the employees here. Lea and Jack, Patrice and Ethan, Tiff and Luke, Josh and I, and Ceresa. Well, this will make for an interesting night on the streets. I’m curious and excited by the idea. I begin to give my approval when I’m interrupted.

“Only one way I’ll follow you all out there. We have to get something decent to eat first. Let’s all go to The Cashew,” Tiff says.

VAGABONDS

All four couples and Ceresa wait for a bus to take us from the Nelson to The Cashew. We're all discussing different things we saw at the gallery. Many pieces could inspire new rooms at our haunted house. The moon is full and lights the street with a bluish glow. There are a few figures at the bus stop with us, but not the shadows I fear. A couple of them begin a conversation with Ethan as we near. I wonder if they're street kids. The one who isn't making conversation, but sitting by himself, seems to be on edge. He keeps rocking back and forth. Now Jack begins an animated description of his favorite painting at the gallery. The moon acts as a spotlight as he releases his acting abilities.

At one point, he bends over near the man on edge. I see the man's eyes dart toward Jack and his hand reach for his pocket. Before I even have the chance to take a step forward or get a sound through my throat that now feels stuffed with wool, the man hits Jack on the head with a coffee mug. Then he runs off before anyone can react and chase him down. That's not the only reason no one runs after him. Three security-looking guys have materialized in front of us and keep us back from Jack too. These were the ones I'd assumed to be street kids that had been talking to Ethan. A woman's kneeling next to Jack. I recognize her. She's the nurse who drew my blood at Dr. Shipley's. *What in the world is she doing out here?* As if on cue one of the security-looking guys in front of us speaks.

"We're a medical team working pro bono on the streets in attempt to make it a safer place."

"What are you doing to him?" I ask.

The nurse answers without looking up. "I'm assessing his injury. He could have a concussion."

She has a small flashlight and is shining it in Jack's eyes. He's responding and seems to be okay. It feels as though she's violating my little brother. If it weren't for the barricade of security, I would go to him and shove her away.

"What happened? Why did I get hit in the head?"

"You seem to be fine. No concussion. You may return to your friends in a minute. I just need to run a test to be sure the attacker didn't infect you with anything."

"Am I bleeding? I don't see any blood. How could I be infected?"

"Sorry, protocol."

Then I see the nurse rub Jack's arm with an antiseptic wipe and poke him with a needle. By the time she's swirling the vial, I have to put my hands on my knees and take a deep breath in order to not pass out. Josh puts a reassuring hand on my back and gives me a sympathetic look. He looks up when Jack begins walking. Jack returns to the group with a Band-Aid on his arm and a bump on his head, but in good condition. I still feel violated. What's with that woman and blood? I picture her in my head with vampire fangs. If I ever return to the doctor, there's no way that woman is touching an inch of me.

"What the hell was that?" I say to everyone.

"What happened?" Jack asks, still mystified by the entire happening.

"The crazy man on the bench hit you upside the head with a coffee mug. You must have a hard head to not have any cuts," Patrice answers.

"What did I do to him?"

"Nothing. He was just out of it, kid," Josh says as he gives Jack a reassuring pat on the shoulder. But I get the feeling that this was somehow all staged. Just like with the explosion, my visions seem to be blocked.

"At least the needle that lady used didn't feel as bad as when I donated blood for extra money."

The bus pulls up.

"So are you all still game? We happened to experience a mugging even before dinner," Ethan says.

"Nah, I'm in. Can't get any worse, can it?" Jack responds, full of energy.

"I wouldn't be so sure of that." Patrice places her hands on her hips as she talks to Jack.

We all pile onto the bus. Luke gets on first and pays everyone's fare.

"Not really going to be like experiencing living on the street if you're able to pay for everything," Ethan kids Luke.

"That begins after dinner," Luke answers with a smile and a nod.

"I can't wait to get to The Cashew," Tiff adds.

"Me either. I love their Fromage-a-trois," Lea says.

"Fromage-a-what? Sounds good to me," Ethan says with a sly smile and a nod of approval as Patrice punches him in the arm.

"Oh yes, Vive-la-cheese is what The Cashew claims. And Ethan, get your head out of the gutter," Tiff says.

My favorite dish there is the Black & Bleu, but my appetite seems to be evading me yet again. The bus ride isn't too long, but everyone else is so starved that they wolf their food down in less than ten minutes. All of a sudden, I find myself nervous about the prospect of living as street kids for a night, especially putting Jack in danger. I mean, it's the time of year that nights get cold around here. A shiver runs through me before we even exit.

"Austria, you didn't eat a thing. Are you sure you're up for this?" Josh asks me aside from the group. I can't let them go alone, so I speak to the group as a whole in answer.

"So what do we do first?" I ask, hoping to borrow some of their excitement and lose my inhibitions.

"Part of the beauty of living on the street is that there isn't really a schedule you have to adhere to," Patrice says.

"Let's take the bus to Broadway and Westport. We can hang out at Broadway Café for a bit. Some of our buddies should be there at this time of night," Ethan says.

We all load onto the bus, paying our own fares this time. I notice Josh, Ceresa, Ethan, and Patrice pay in all coins. I wonder if they panhandle during the day. It's a hard picture to form in my mind. Jack and Lea are bug-eyed and holding onto each other for dear life. The night has only begun, but, then again, Jack did just encounter something none of us had planned on. We make it to our destination, and I can hear the nightlife outside before we exit.

"Broadway Café backs up to Harpo's. A lot of businesses have happy hour there, and it only gets louder and livelier as the night continues," Josh informs me.

We hold hands as we enter the café. It feels like our hands were meant for one another since the beginning of time. I don't feel self-conscious holding hands with a street kid. I feel proud. It kind of surprises me. My mother would never approve of any of this. A couple girls wave and tell Josh hello. I feel jealous, wanting to claim him as mine. He squeezes my hand. How did he know to do that? We all walk up to a big table. There are newspapers and magazines. There's also a chess table; Josh and I chose to sit by it.

"How good are you at Chess?" he asks.

"Decent."

"Oh yeah?"

"Scared to find out?"

We begin our game while listening to the others.

"Did you hear Bill and that man talking about the codes? It sounds like the government's going to make it more difficult to house us," Patrice comments.

"We should start a petition. Hey, did you hear about the gal that had an apartment improvement contest for teens without homes? That was pretty cool. Is there anything else like that going on?" Tiff asks.

"Yeah. Actually, Ceresa's trying to start a place of her own. She and Josh understand what the foster system's like. The ratio of kids that actually find permanent homes compared to kids that don't is excruciatingly small. Once they're teenagers, fosters don't even want them. They turn to the streets. These apartments were able to house a quarter of them, but they were in horrible condition. The continued improvement contests have now made half of the apartments decent living quarters. Ceresa hopes to be able to house the remaining teens without homes. Not many are runaways from abusive homes like Ethan and me." Patrice explains as she looks into Ethan's eyes and hooks her arm into his.

"Yeah, but it's difficult to get started when the government requires so many documents to be filled out and taxes to be paid," Ceresa complains.

They seem so happy, after having been through so much. I look at Josh pondering the chess board. I really should've told him that I played this game nonstop growing up with my grandmother. I wonder what it was like for him to never be claimed. I still cannot fathom being without my father in my world. What is it like never to have that parent figure?

"You really shouldn't have moved your rook there," he says to me, looking up with his crystal blue eyes.

"Oh yeah, what are you going to do about it?"

"Take it." And he does.

"Shouldn't have done that," I say as I take his queen. My cheeks warm as his eyes become huge.

He sits and deliberates for a few moments.

"How's that Adam guy able to initiate bills for the buildings?" I ask to distract myself from staring at Josh.

"Adam wants to turn the Power & Light District into a complete attraction. Having those buildings could add hotels and restaurants to the area," Ethan answers.

"But don't the haunted houses attract customers to the area too?" I ask.

"Yeah, but not quite year-round yet like the other possibilities of the buildings could. We're trying to change that."

Josh moves a piece and smiles.

"Checkmate."

"What? Oh crap."

He leans across the table and kisses me. Warmth washes all over me like when you step into a hot shower. What was I thinking about again? Oh yeah. I have to move my jaw in a circle before I speak as my lips want to pucker back up. I really want to hear about what's going on with the codes. This is something that could affect Josh's life tremendously. I want to invite him to live with me, but I don't want it to appear like a handout to him. If he really knew how much it would benefit me, maybe he'd go for it. Maybe if I take a different approach, it will work.

"So when you guys didn't have a place to stay, did you ever build communities of your own without government involvement?" I dare to ask as this would be breaking the law.

"Well, come to think of it, I visited a location in the Northeast sector of the city that had dug underground caves and tunnels. Their hidden society went undetected for a couple of years. When the authorities found it, they kicked everyone out and bulldozed it all. I guess some of the inhabitants had been burglarizing local businesses. Had they not done that, the society probably would still be there today," Josh answers.

"Did you ever live there?" I ask.

"Yeah, but it wasn't for me. They were sort of hippies but enjoyed being separated from society. I thrive on society and couldn't stand more than a couple nights with them."

"All right, it's time to go." Ethan stands. I wasn't able to ask the question, but we have the entire night so there should be time.

We all stand and follow him into the night. He walks south on Broadway. Patrice is by his side. Tiff and Luke follow them first. Jack, Lea, and Ceresa are following next. Josh and I bring up the rear. When we reach 43rd Street, we turn left. There's a park that we all sit in. Like many parks in this city, there's a fountain in the center. This one isn't as big as some of the others. The angel in the center is a young child. It's sweet in the middle of this ghastly park; the bubbling water creates a peaceful meditation spot. The place makes me feel alone yet watched at the same time. A shiver runs up to my skull. My chin lurches forward in response.

"Who wants to check out The Levee?" Josh asks.

All of us but Ethan and Patrice raise our hands.

"You know we don't like to go to establishments that sell alcohol. Look at how abusive it turned our parents," Ethan says to Josh when he thinks no one else in the group can hear.

"I get it," Tiff says.

"I'll stay with them too," Luke volunteers.

I see Tiff's look of disappointment, but I don't want to leave Josh and since Jack appears to be interested, I feel committed to stay with them.

"There are ground apartments around the corner that are open to respectable looking street kids for restrooms, water, and a safe house if we need," Ethan says.

"Great." Tiff rolls her eyes.

"They're not that bad," Ceresa adds.

Jack, Lea, Josh, and I head up the hill to The Levee. I could hear the music from the park. As we walk closer, I recognize the band. It's Arctic Monkeys.

"What are they doing at The Levee?" I grab Josh's arm as I say this.

He smiles at the shock and excitement in my face.

"Sounds like they're starting "Do I Wanna Know?""

I can't help myself. I begin jogging, my worries abandoning me in the thrill. The others join me. I can barely contain myself as we're carded at the door—luckily they allow ages seventeen and older. Once inside we head to the stage. I find myself falling into the rhythm of the crowd. The song seems fitting for our evening. Josh, Lea, and Jack surround me dancing. I look at them all with one of the biggest smiles I've had recently. I completely let go and let the music rule my body. I feel the beat pound through my chest. We're all shiny with sweat when we find a table upstairs after the song. Jack gets waters at the bar for us all. Now I find Josh putting a protective arm around my shoulders. I follow his eyes to see what he's looking at and find a group of guys that seem to be checking me and Lea out. I guess he's getting the jealous feeling that I had at the coffee shop.

Once our waters are guzzled down, an employee from The Levee approaches us and asks if we'll be making any purchases this evening. I notice Josh turn a shade red as the guys who had been looking at me now laugh behind their fists at us. We shake our heads no and head back out to meet up with the others. Another girl is with our friends. They're all talking about the stars and moon phases.

"Hey Tiff," I say.

"Hey yourself. How was it?"

"Guess who is performing…Arctic Monkeys."

"Get out. You suck even more now."

"Whatever."

"Oh, hey you all. This is Jenny," Tiff says to everybody, ignoring our bicker.

"She says she has an apartment and that we should stay with her tonight instead of under a bridge. I'm sure not going to stay under a bridge if she has an apartment," Luke says.

"What, you don't want the real feeling of being on the streets?" Ethan replies.

"There's a full moon out tonight, Ethan. You know how Gunner gets on full moons," Jenny points out.

"How'd you find an apartment?" Ethan asks.

"I got a job at the pizza joint connected to Kelly's Irish Pub."

"Sweet deal. So where's your place? I guess these yuppies can't handle the streets for real."

"We're going to have to walk halfway to the KCPT tower."

"We can handle a walk," Lea says eagerly.

We all begin walking north on Main Street. I'm again struck with wonder. What will people think seeing us all walking down the street together? Most of the people we pass by seem to be three sheets to the wind, so they're probably not in a judging mood. As we pass a liquor store, a man recognizes Josh.

"Hi, kid. How are you? Who's the sweet thang on your arm?" the man says.

"Hello, Tom. You didn't just buy a bottle, did you?"

"What's it to you?"

"Tom, it isn't quite 10 p.m. You can still make it to a meeting. It's on our way. We can walk you."

Tom doesn't say anything. He falls into step with us but stays a couple feet behind. This doesn't bother me as his odor is quite rancid. How many times has Josh saved this man from himself?

"It will be okay, Tom. Tom?"

We both turn around. He's gone. He disappeared without a sound. Well, I guess we won't be saving him tonight.

We get to the apartment. The building's another old, brick building. As we enter, I notice other people plan to stay here too.

"How many are you housing, Jenny?" Josh asks.

"I don't know. Ten to twenty depending on the night."

"Watch yourself. You're such a hard worker, and I would hate to see you taken advantage of."

"I can take care of myself. Thank you."

Whoa, I wonder if Josh and Jenny have a past. I find myself jealous without substantial evidence.

"Your group can stay in the living room. I have sleeping bags in the hallway closet. Due to the number of visitors, I'll need you to pair up and share the sleeping bags. I haven't paid all the utilities. It gets a little cold without heat, but you'll stay warm paired up. The water bill has been paid, so restrooms are available. Food is limited, but there's a convenience store down the block."

"Thanks, Jenny," Josh says.

"Not a problem."

My shoulders tense at their exchange, but I'm quickly relieved when I find Josh and myself sharing a sleeping bag.

It does get pretty cold in the night, but I'm warm being curled up next to Josh. I regret when I have to leave the comfort of the sleeping bag to use the restroom. I take care of business and wash my hands. As I'm about to turn the doorknob to leave, it twists, and the door opens. There's a young man I don't recognize in the doorway. He gives me a look that makes me feel ill; it doesn't take a strong perceptionist to know what want lies behind his eyes. He steps forward, and I feel his breath on me. It reeks of booze. I step to the side to go around him, but he blocks me with his arm. He grabs my left arm fiercely and holds my chin up with his other hand. I use my right hand to remove the hand under my chin.

"Such a pretty little thing. Don't you want to hang out with me?"

I try to scream but nothing comes out. I just shake my head from side to side. I bring my right elbow down on his forearm, hoping to release the grip. He yelps and I'm released. I take a step to the door, and he grabs me from behind. His arms are around mine. They squeeze so hard. Then he readjusts and now he holds both my arms with just his left arm. He starts reaching down my shirt with his right hand. I scream, but he claps his hand around my mouth. At least it's out of my shirt. I don't know if anyone heard the scream. I'm shaking with fear. He's bigger than I am. I stomp on his foot and bite his hand at the same time. He groans as he limps a little forward. He must be drunk. I try to take a step to get out, but he stumbles, and we both fall down. He's lost his grip on me. I pull myself forward away from him. He tries to grab my ankle. I kick at his hand with my other foot, but he gets my ankle. He begins pulling me toward him. Oh no, this is the worst possible position. Lying down as he pulls me underneath him.

Then there's someone else. They punch the guy in the face. My attacker's head falls to the floor. It was a good punch. I think he's out. The person who punched him turns around and offers me a hand. It's Josh. Josh shoves the guy off me with his foot.

I can't talk. I grab Josh's hand, and he helps me up. He hugs me protectively. I'm still shaking. I can't make it stop. Tears well up in my eyes, but I don't want to cry. Josh seems to understand. He walks me to the closet and grabs a couple coats. We put them on, and he walks me outside.

"Austria, are you okay?"

"Yes," I say through chattering lips.

"I have to walk. Is that okay?"

We walk. My shaking subsides, but now I'm able to notice how much he's shaking.

"Are you okay?" I ask.

"Yeah, I just had to get out of there. The rage I felt was uncontrollable. What a jerk. I wanted to punch him again. Punch him over and over until no one would recognize his face."

"Josh, it's okay. We're out here. Try to calm down."

"Do you know what he would have done to you if I didn't get there in time?"

"Um, yeah, but do we really have to talk about it?"

The dark black sky is turning to a navy blue.

"Want to see one of the beauties of being a street kid?"

"I don't know how much more I can take, Josh. I guess I'm not built for living this way."

"This will be safe."

He holds my hand as we walk to the park on 31st Street. He takes me to a tree at the top of a hill. We climb it. He folds his hands and gives me a step up. We sit on a sturdy branch. He points to the east. The sky's now becoming lighter. There's a harmonious mixture of blue, orange, and red. The sun peeks out above the horizon. It's breathtaking. I curl into Josh's lap. He strokes my hair.

"What do you think?"

"I think it's gorgeous."

"Not as gorgeous as you."

I look up at him. He kisses me with a deep passion. I twist to face him more. Heat courses through my body as we kiss, erasing the hurt and fear. I feel like we're the only two people in this world, and this sunrise is meant for just us. When we come up for air, his eyes are dilated almost completely. They quickly change in the light, and I can see the blue again. He smiles and gives me a peck kiss.

"Happiest morning ever," he says.

I smile and embrace him. I'm amazed by how his emotion has changed. Maybe that's something you pick up when looking for a home on a daily basis.

How am I experiencing such polar opposites of emotion in such a short time?

"We should probably get back, so the others don't worry."

"Oh, they'll be fine." I hold onto him tighter.

"Austria."

"Josh?"

He exhales and smiles.

"Okay."

He helps me get down, and we walk back to the apartment. I hear a ruckus before entering. People are all yelling at one another as we walk in.

"You can't just tie people up in my apartment," Jenny's yelling at Patrice.

"He deserved it," Patrice answers.

Then I see what they're talking about. Patrice has my attacker duct-taped to a support beam. I can't hold back my smile. People have used markers to write on the duct tape that holds him up. All vile words and pictures. He's still unconscious. Probably passed out drunk. Patrice notices me and Josh. She looks at me.

"I saw what he did to you, but you and Josh disappeared before I could talk to you. I taped him up so he couldn't try anything like that on anyone else."

"Yes, but I don't want him stuck in my apartment." Jenny pouts.

Ethan takes out a pocketknife and begins cutting the tape. Josh holds the guy up so he won't fall and wake up. Just then, Jack strolls in with a shopping cart. They get the guy free and put him in the cart. Jack, Josh, and Ethan take him outside. I watch from the doorway.

"We should just push him down the hill on Main Street and let him roll," Jack kids.

"If I could be certain it wouldn't hurt an innocent bystander, I'd be all for that," Josh answers. I can see he's struggling to keep his smile hidden.

Instead, they push him to the convenience store parking lot. They return, and we all take a bus to the haunted house. On our way, we pass by a blood donation center. In our epiphany of what a life on the streets is like, we all decide to donate blood. When the needle enters my skin, I have to suppress the angst that rises within. I automatically look for the vampire nurse who had taken Jack's and my blood before. Afterward, Tiff and I walk home. Luke and Josh escort us. It's comforting having them there. We all take showers. I attempt to cook everyone breakfast. Everyone's polite as they slather jelly on my burnt toast and mix their scary looking eggs with sausage to make them taste better. They must not mind too much though, because all of the food is gone in five minutes. I smile. Maybe I can figure out this whole domestic thing.

SOLITARY

The days seem to breeze by with Josh. I'm walking on the clouds. We struggle to keep our hands to ourselves. Our spirits are only dampened when Bill receives a notice that Josh, Ceresa, and Patrice can no longer use the haunted house as a mailing address. Often street kids use shelters as an address on job applications. I think about Ethan's house, but he informs me that his mom would be kicked out by the Nelson Art Gallery if they house others officially. Bill has a meeting with the city and is able to work out a temporary deal. They won't have to worry for another six months about the address usage.

I don't even realize the time has passed when suddenly it's the night of the opening. We're all in full costume, including the hideous makeup. We're excited to finally put our practice into action on real customers. The first group that comes to the house is a bunch of high schoolers. They scream, and the girls cling to their guys. In fact, the first four groups appear to be teenagers, while this is entertaining, I'm growing bored and want a new genre of victims. Wow, this haunted house gig is positively getting to my thought processes. Ah, wonderful, the next group's a bunch of men who look pretty tough. Their muscles stretch their shirts. They have facial hair and tattoos. One even has a snake tattoo that slithers behind his ear and around his bald head. It almost appears to be a halo in the dark, but the head of the snake stretches over his forehead and the mouth is open above his eye as if to eat it. Spooking them will be quite a thrill. In the room, I helped to develop I stand still as a statue in my favorite vampire costume. I stay that way until they're inches away from me and then jump. They'd all been so transfixed on me that I truly frighten each and every one of them. This was pleasing. As I try to sneak to the hidden passageway that connects the rooms for us employees to move through without being seen by customers, I realize the men still have their gaze on me. I'm afraid to let the secret out, so I freeze. That's when I see Josh on the other side of the room, and I can't help but smile.

One second, I'm smiling at Josh full of love; the next scrounging for air as the cloth covering my mouth and nose will allow none. Someone has grabbed me and is holding something over my mouth. I feel myself being pulled back into the hidden passageway and then upward, but how could that be? There's no known exit above the passageway that I was pulled into. I was unable to make out any features of the man who took me, and I only assume it to be a man because of the sheer size of the hands, but now I'm blacking out. My last glimpse is of the roof, and I definitely feel the chill of the outside air before things go completely black. Great, I have no clue where I'm headed and then I awake just to more blackness. I try to feel around the room they seem to have put me in to make sense of anything at all. I'm alone in the dark but seem to be surrounded by walls. My eyes are slowly adjusting as there's a sliver of light coming from under what I assume to be a door. A door. Oh sweet escape. I crawl quietly to it as I press an ear to see if I can hear anything.

"Doc called in the information and sent a photograph."

"I don't know. Are you sure? Is it really her?"

"Yes, go see."

I don't react fast enough and "whack" the door smacks my head, lights out again.

The next hours pass slowly for me, and I'm unsure how long I was out or where I am or whose voices I hear on the other side of the door. I search the room for an escape and find only the door with the voices behind it. I heard them say "it is her"—they apparently believe I'm someone of value. They mentioned someone called Doc phoning information in. I remember Dr. Shipley's phone call after my appointment and him covering his mouth when I spotted him. They've more information about me than I realize. Someone's been clueing them in on my day-to-day tasks; feelings of betrayal twist inside. I wonder who it could be until they say names. Apparently, Matt and Ed have been filling them in. Of course they knew where I work, but what did Matt and Ed have to gain by the knowledge of who I am? I quickly remember something Tiff told me about Matt and Ed and human trafficking and fear rises within me. The voices outside the door mention that I'm his daughter. Could they actually be speaking of my father? How could they know or care who he was? He lived on the streets until he and my mother found an escape. They found a way to live a normal life, but how can this information be of such value to these men? Then they say things about my father I've never heard. By the physical description they give, I know it's him. No one else has a scar on the neck like he did or the star tattoo on his shoulder. Then they give me knowledge I've never known about him. They say he'd been an Olympic gold medalist before succumbing to the streets. How could this be? How have I never heard about this? I remember the sneakers and jersey I found in the box. Why had my mother never told me? Then I remember her being so worried after my doctor appointment. I never did find out what was bothering her. Why did I not ask her right then?

At that moment, the voices fade, and it becomes silent. This may be the only opportunity I have to escape. I quietly open the door and make a mental assessment of the room. I'm in a basement I believe by the cement walls, and I find the staircase that, hopefully, will lead to my freedom. I scan around to find the owners of the voices I'd heard. There are two men asleep on sofas with the television on low. One's the creepy snake tattoo guy. The sight of the gurney behind them and in front of the stairs puts my nerves on edge. What's that for? I don't even want to know. I tiptoe successfully by the two sleeping men and make it to the stairs. I have the first feeling of hope since this unfortunate adventure began while I'm climbing the stairs. This hope quickly fades as I open the door at the top of the steps to find another man, and this one's not asleep.

"Well, hello, Austria," he says with a sadistic smile.

I look around desperately for an out. I take the old-style phone on the counter next to me. This is one of the rotary dial phones you never see anymore, but I know it weighs a decent amount. As I lift it to hit the man on the side of the head, a hand grabs my wrist from behind. I know the face as I turn. It's Matt's face. How dare he do this? Then there's the sharp pain of a needle poking me in the arm. I don't know what they've just put in my system, but I instantly go limp. He catches me as I fall. The man I was going to smash with the phone grabs my legs. He and Matt carry me down the stairs to the gurney. They strap my arms and legs down at the wrists and ankles. I can't help thinking of the disappearances, special DNA, and gutted bodies. Now I see the other two men are awake and staring at me with smiles on their faces. I don't know if I black out this time from the drug or the inexplicable storm of psychotic images that flood my brain.

This is it. This is the end.

##

It's amazing how easy it is to let go when you realize you have no other choice. Something changes in my body. The blood flows so fiercely I must be bleeding out. I'm dizzy. There's a strong metallic scent. My eyes roll back. I must be spinning. Could every particle be floating away from me one by one? I feel weightless, as if I'm floating in the air. As if I don't have a body, but just my soul is rising. I feel emotions I've never felt. I don't have fear, anger, or regret. Facts and figures that I never knew before run through my head. I know planets that I've never seen in a textbook or on the internet. I know the rate at which a black hole rotates. I feel emotion from the clouds, empathetic with the wind. I feel love from the sun. Not just light and heat, but actual love like a dear friend's. What is all this?

I want to take a deep breath or smile, but neither of those physical things belong to me now. This means I have no physical pain either. I have no idea how long I've been gone. I get the feeling time here could pass very quickly. Although I'm not a parent, I get the strong sensation that this is what a parent feels like when their baby laughs for the first time. The thought reminds me of someone who enjoyed my first laugh. My mother. She'll be devastated. First, she loses my father and now me. It can't be. I have to get back. Then I feel the love of a sparkling star. It's like first love when you count down the seconds until you see the person again. Josh. This will break Josh's heart. He has no family. How do I get back? The desperate feeling I have is indescribable. How did I let myself go this far? It still is tempting, though. What am I talking about? I'm losing my mind. If I still have one left.

##

All of a sudden there's a forceful rush against me from all directions. Now my particles swirl at the same rate as a black hole. They're closing in on themselves. Forcing the small items to meld into a solid form. I hear sounds whirring past me. The light behind my closed lids is as bright as the sun but without the love. It's cold. I shiver. I shiver—that means my body's back. The metallic scent fades. My lungs expand with air. I exhale and try to open my eyes. I blink a few times. There are specks. Maybe I am still with the stars. Beyond the specks is a rectangular sun. No. That's a man-made light. I look down a bit. I see a board with names written on it, a T.V. and a generic picture of a flower in a nice frame. I'm lying down. Oh no. No. No. It's a gurney. Wait, I'm not strapped in. I look to my left. Josh sits asleep in a chair. Oh, Josh. I want to go to him, but I have tubes poking in my arm, and I'm not fully confident in this body being real yet. I watch him as he sleeps peacefully. I don't know if this is real or not. I try to soak in every detail. How long his eyelashes are and how he makes faces with his dreams. Then his breathing alters. He twitches. He's waking up.

EXTRICATED

When Josh wakes up this is what he tells me, reliving the memory:

I was lost in a misery I didn't know could exist within me, and if there's one thing I'm well acquainted with, it's misery. This misery was not like the freezing of my body in the streets in the dead of winter. This misery was the freezing of my soul. One second I saw you there by the hidden door the employees use to exit one haunting scene to the next unobserved. Your beauty had stunned me even covered with that decrepit vampire costume. The next second I saw a masked man with a cloth over your mouth. I didn't get to you before he took you through the door to the hallway. Some idiot, big men had been blocking my way. When I opened the door and walked into the hallway myself, I couldn't find you. I couldn't find you in any room of the haunted house, in any hidden passageway or even in the meeting room. Where could you be? You were missing. Now the misery I felt was much stronger than my soul being taken. This misery was worse than the lonely feeling of nothingness. The pain was unbearable. It made it difficult to think, but I needed to think clearly. I had to find you. I let the adrenaline take over as my search into the night began.

The worry I saw in Tiff's eyes was blinding. I noticed that Matt and Ed were nowhere to be seen either, and that was when I pulled Tiff aside. I had noticed her eyeing them skeptically before and assumed she knew something about them she did not trust either.

I said, "Tiff, have you seen Matt and/or Ed tonight?"

Tiff turned her face to me slowly and then, as if I'd unveiled something vital, her jaw dropped. I could see she was upset she hadn't noticed this before, but I didn't want guilt, just knowledge that could possibly help.

"I didn't notice that. I think that means they're involved in this. I know they're involved in an evil out there that I would never want Austria near. I'm sorry I ever brought her into this," Tiff had exclaimed.

"Don't blame yourself, Tiff. Let's just work together to bring her back," I answered. "What exactly is this evil they're involved in?" I asked her.

"Human trafficking."

"What? Damn it. Do you have any more information than that?"

We worked together to figure out how to get you back. She knew Matt and Ed were involved in a human trafficking ring nearby. She had even tailed them to see where they met. We decided to go to the nearest house immediately. We recruited the few we knew could help: Ethan, Ceresa, Patrice, and, believe it or not, Luke.

Apparently, living on the streets gave us some benefits as we knew our way around, could survive on little to nothing, and knew many kind and giving civilians in all areas. When we came closer to where the house Tiff had tailed them to was, we recognized the place. Then we put two and two together and realized what was happening there. The citizens who had come to this place had been citizens who regularly break the laws and reap power. They had also been seen leaving in hospital garments appearing to be recovering from something. An organ transplant, that's it.

"You're right, Tiff." I regretfully accepted your possible fate.

I wanted to storm in, beat the living shit out of everyone inside, and get you out. I had heard through the black market that this had been happening. Not human trafficking for slavery and/or prostitution. Those were scary enough, but they wanted you for healthy organs. This unnerved me. I revealed this knowledge to the others, and we began our advance into this house. It was like when we were planning out the haunted house. We thought about the entrances to the house we were aware of. We knew our cues and placement. Ceresa and Ethan, our best fighters, would distract the kidnappers while the rest of us got to you. We knew what roles we were to take. What we did not know was the setting of this scene. We did not know how many "customers" would be in attendance.

Patrice had a brilliant idea. She mentioned Gunner from the market. Gunner's a veteran who hasn't come into full grasp of reality since his return to civilian society. He is a good soul and doesn't intend harm, but every once in a while he thinks we're all enemies. I have never been to war, and I feel bad for him, but I sincerely hoped his wits were about him now. We were going to see if we could acquire sleeping gas and masks from him. When we reached him, he seemed together, and that was good. What he had for us was something he called ether. Given the urgency of the situation, we wasted no time with explanations and rushed back to the scene. We began searching out entryways for the ether. Luckily, although the air was frigid, almost every window was cracked. This had me second guessing. Wouldn't you be screaming if they were already in action with their plan? If not, did they already have you unconscious and if so, how much ether could your body handle? There wasn't enough time to play this fully out. We would just have to get you out as fast as we could.

The gas streamed into the house without a hitch. We'd covered our mouths and noses with masks to keep from passing out ourselves. As the thuds of bodies hitting the floor reached our ears, we made our entrance. This is when having Luke around was really helpful. While he didn't speak up in the beginning, he had now mustered the courage to tell us everything about this place. He told us you'd be in the basement and pointed to the door I assumed would be our entryway. I could see two of the men unconscious on the floor as I reached the top of the stairs. We made our way down. Now the true showstopper hit me. You lay there on the gurney, breathing tube in place and a fresh incision on your belly. What were we going to do? Did they make more headway than what I could see? There didn't seem to be any removed organs. The sight of the cooler in the corner of the room made me lose my balance, and I fell. I pulled myself up to the cooler to lift the lid. Nothing was inside. One positive after so many negatives! Now I thought aloud as I went to you and held your hand.

"How are we going to get her out of here? We need to keep oxygen on while she's out and, if we lift her, she may bleed to death."

Luke seemed to be more on our side than I would've ever imagined.

He said, "You know I'm in medical school, right?"

He began grabbing things and putting them to work. He assessed your wound and pronounced it to be only external damage. He started to stitch you up. Then he injected your body with two solutions. I hoped one was to wake you so you could breathe on your own, and then I prayed the second was something for the pain. He also removed the breathing tube, and I removed the restraints they had on you. Just then, one of the unconscious men began to stir. Ethan unleashed a violence I knew he worked his best to keep in check and knocked the man out in one swift move. We began our exit up the stairs. I heard another man mumbling something and Ceresa revealed the defensive tactics she picked up on the street. After one powerful kick to the man's jaw, he was sailing down the stairs. This ruckus woke the others so we began to run as fast as we could outside. I had no idea what we would do once we were out there, but the feeling of freedom was too strong to slow down.

The lights of cop cars as we exited assured me everything would be all right even though usually those cherries have me running, like when I was living in an old abandoned warehouse the state decided they did not want street kids inhabiting. I saw Bill at the front of the group holding his hands out to help all of us.

"How did you get here? How did you know? Oh, thank you, Bill," I breathed out.

"I went to check the market when you, Ethan, Ceresa, and Patrice all ran off. Gunner led me right to you and, lucky for you, was aware enough to be able to tell me what was going on. He didn't have the look in his eyes like when he sees everyone as enemies, so I knew it was true. What were you thinking, attempting this on your own?" Bill asked.

"We had to get to her in time, Bill. If we had been a minute later...." I could not bear to put the thought into words.

You were safe then and waking. You looked at me with desperate eyes and then looked around.

"You saved me," you said with a scratchy voice before you passed back out.

I stayed by your side as the ambulance took you to the nearest hospital. I felt a rush of relief as I saw the men being handcuffed and put in the back of police cruisers. You still weren't responding, but the paramedics said your vitals were stable. I was worried that you must be in shock and wanted to bring you out of it. I settled for just holding your hand. As they rolled you into the hospital, the doctors applauded Luke's work. Your incision appeared to be stitched as well as if one of them had held wielded the needle. Your vitals showed that he had effectively brought you out of the sleep those monsters had put you in. So why were you not waking? They told me you were in a state of shock, and we should allow you to rest. I stayed in your room and slept the rest of the night. When this morning came, I saw you had risen before me.

"You should have woken me up, Austria."

I just smile at him. I can't believe he did all of that for me. I'm so glad they came for me. I'm so glad I still have my organs. I touch my stomach and feel the stitches. There's a little pain, but not much. I wonder if the time I had been in shock was when I was having the weird "out of body" experience. Then my mother walks in. She wears a look of pain and regret, but not one of surprise as I expected.

"Mother, I'm fine," I say.

She half-runs to my side and embraces me. I notice Josh looking at us with a longing in his eyes. This must have been the way he dreamed of his mother embracing him.

"I'm safe. Josh saved me."

My mother looks at Josh and says thank you with her eyes. She doesn't have to say the words, and before Josh can even form any in return, she has a bear hug on him. I can tell what he's thinking—so this is what kindness and warmth from a mother feels like. It has been too many years since he has felt this and I can tell he doesn't want to let go, but she releases him to turn her attention to me. I begin telling them what I remember, and I can tell Josh is calmed by the detail my mind is capable of recalling. I can tell he's also afraid, as he is unsure of how these memories are going to affect me. He has too many memories he wishes his mind would omit. Maybe it would have been better for me if I didn't remember any of it, is what they both seem to be thinking. The next statement from me has Josh wondering just as it had me.

"They said Father was an Olympian. Why had you never told me about that? Why did they know when I did not, and what does it mean?"

My mother is silent for only a heartbeat. The same fateful look of worry she had after the doctor visit has returned to her eyes.

"Oh darling, we had hoped you never would have to know this turmoil and felt it best for your safety for you not to know. Your father was a marvelous Olympian, and so was I, but that has all been stricken from the records. In the last events we participated in, they called us in for testing. Many of the Olympians had turned to steroids that year. But what bewildered your father and I is that while I was put in line with the rest, your father was pulled to another room with more official-looking doctors. What he told me, and this cannot go beyond this room…"

She hesitates to look at Josh and Bill, who had somehow appeared in the room without my notice. They both nod their willingness to comply with her request.

She continues, "They'd known something about your father before that day. Your father didn't take steroids, for he didn't require them. There was something in his DNA that made him stronger than the average human being. That day began our plight into the world of the streets and the unknown. We tried our best to make a living so that we could raise you out of harm's way, but the people who wanted your father's DNA wouldn't allow it. He ran off so that you and I could be free, and I've been able to hold my end of the bargain with him to keep your DNA a secret until this fall. I'm sorry I didn't tell you about this. He wanted you to have as normal a life as possible."

When she finishes, we're all struck silent. And then I regain my strength to speak.

"Thank you for telling me. It's not your fault. I wish I could've had more time with Father, but I understand his desire to keep me safe. He gave more to me than I'll ever be able to give in return. I'm glad you were able to keep us safe the past few years and, thanks to Josh, we're now safe again."

I rise from my bed. Maybe the DNA is stronger than I'd imagined. I give each of them a hug. We all look at each other and vow to keep the secret. If my DNA is different, like my father's DNA, are the people who captured me the same ones that were after my father?

INCOMPLETE

The doctors make me stay in the hospital for another day. I feel fine, but they want to monitor me. I'm afraid they will find more of what Dr. Shipley found. After a few tests turn out normal, I realize they must not be performing the same test he had. I guess he was specifically looking for the stronger DNA. He'd been right about the healing ability. The hospital staff is amazed by my fast recovery. It upsets me to be kept from the haunted house. Apparently, Bill has cashed in some debt from friends, and they're doing us all a favor working as security. It'll be safe for me to go back. I can't wait. After such a short time, I miss my new family. I wish I could make my sentence here speed up, but there's nothing to do. I read and write for a bit. After this, the exhaustion hits. Even if I do have special healing powers, I'm still tired by the trauma. I quickly doze off.

I fall into the dream easily. It's not a dream, but a nightmare. I'm back on the gurney strapped down. The same guys are around me, including Ed and Matt. They're talking.

"The shot you gave her will only keep her out for a few minutes. We need the anesthesia." This voice sounds like the man at the top of the stairs. The one I was going to hit with the phone. He's not just talking but giving orders. I think about Matt and Ed's involvement. Is it purely voluntary?

I hear movement and feel another poke but this time in my stomach. Then I feel a mask being placed over my mouth and nose.

"All right, this is your first time. You have to put a breathing tube like this in. Otherwise, she'll pass too soon for us to get the organs out in good enough condition for her type of DNA to survive."

Wait a minute. These guys do this for a living. Why are they training someone on me? Then I'm unable to form a thought. I feel searing pain. Something sharp is entering the skin in my abdomen. The pain sends tears into my closed eyes. I try to scream out, but my vocal cords are clogged with the breathing tube, and I'm unable to move any part of my body. The tube would probably muffle what little sound I could muster. Then the pulling begins. I'm in agony. This is a whole new pain mixed with the sensation between a burn and a broken bone. They're breaking open my skin. Why? Oh. I have special DNA with healing capabilities. Who knows how they could use my body? Since they're slicing my abdomen, I believe they must be after vital organs. I cannot breathe. I black out.

"It's okay. You are in the hospital now, Austria."

I open my eyes in my dream, but my dream has changed. I see my father now. He's clear and in front of me with his hand on my cheek. The warmth almost makes me forget every fear, but not completely. I try to imagine what he went through. What pain he may have endured.

"Father, it was awful."

"I know, honey. But not now. You're stitched and safe. You are safe."

"You keep saying 'you' very emphatically."

"I know, honey."

"So who is not safe?"

“It’s still not safe for all, Austria. You’re right. You’ll also have to continue to keep yourself safe, too.”

“What do you mean? They’ve arrested the perpetrators.”

“You really think they’re the only ones?” He’s leaning nonchalantly on something outside of my vision’s periphery.

“Well, uh, really, there’s more?”

“Yes.” Now it’s as though he’s taking an aggressive step forward to reach me.

“Wouldn’t it be a little suicidal for them to come after me again? I mean, the police and community know it was me that was targeted.”

“Oh, Austria, there’s so much to explain.”

“Well, you’re here now. It’s been so long. Why now? Do I have to be in danger for you to be able to converse with me?”

“Austria, there’s too much going on to get into it now.”

“Wait. Mother said you ran…Father, are you dead?”

“That’s something for the scientists to debate.”

“What?”

“I’m running out of time, honey. Listen. They’re coming back. Just as I’m not the only one with my capabilities, you’re not the only one with strong DNA.”

“I’m so confused.”

“Think. Did anyone else at the haunted house notice the shadows?”

“Not that I can think of.”

“Did anyone else jump? Did anyone seem sensitive or keep extra quiet?”

I wake to a nurse taking my pulse. That was so odd. I hope I don’t have recurring nightmares of being cut open. At least I saw Father. I haven’t seen my father in so long, and now I see him all the time. It's never in the flesh though; only when I fainted, in the mirror, and my dreams. I notice he didn't answer my question. Is my father somehow still alive? I have to find him. He was so worried. He tried to warn me before. I should have listened. He didn't really give me anything concrete to go on. I try to recall in my memories if someone else saw the shadows besides me. Nothing. How can I help?

The nurse removes my I.V. and applies gauze to my arm. Someone enters with food. I hadn't realized how hungry I'd become. I wonder if the healing process depletes me, causing drowsiness and malnourishment. I don't even attempt to smell or look at the food. I just gobble it down like I haven't eaten in ages. My mother enters the room.

"Hey."

She has a sparkle in her brown eyes. Her lips aren't full, yet they're more than thin strips. The upper lip has a perfect heart shape, and the bottom lip is round. Her dimples show on her cheeks when she smiles. Her nose is a little long, but thin. She always says to be glad I have my father's nose. The light in her eyes shows how much she has held on her shoulders throughout these years and how relieved she must be to be finally opening up about it. I'm seventeen. It's time for me to take the burden. Can you ever really get a parent to stop worrying, though?

"How are you, darling?"

"Ready to get out of here."

"Take things slow. There's no reason to hurry."

But there is. Father warned me something else was coming.

"Don't fret."

"It is such a relief to no longer be hiding things from you. I knew it was for your own protection, but I still felt guilty."

"What else is there?"

"Shortly before your father left, he claimed to have met others like him."

"Did he tell you who they were?"

"Unfortunately, no. He felt the knowledge would only put us in more danger."

"Mother."

"Yeah?"

"Is Father really dead?"

"I've had to tell myself that so I wouldn't go crazy missing him, looking for him and hoping for his return. I didn't want you to go through that pain either, but I don't know for sure if he is dead or alive."

"Oh."

I still hold back the conversations I've been having with him. Here she's finally sharing information with me and, in return, I'm withholding from her. It's just that I can see the pain in her eyes that has been building all these years. What if Father has never talked to her like he has me? Wouldn't that depress her a little? He's been the only love she's had. My heart aches just thinking about her having to let him go. I clear my throat to keep back the tears.

"Oh darling. I'm so sorry. This has to be so much. Please try to relax. We'll get it all worked out."

"Thanks. I am feeling much better."

I let her stroke my hair while I rest. I close my eyes and bring my breathing to shallow breaths so she will believe I'm asleep. I am actually thinking back on the days at the haunted house, trying to relive the moments when shadows had been around. Attempting to recollect any differences from the other employees.

The nurse enters again.

"The doctor's signing your release now."

"Thank you," my mother tells her as she begins packing some things she'd brought for me.

I get up and hug my mother.

"Do you want to stay with me?"

"That would be nice, but I think it will be good to get back to my place."

"I'm sure Tiff has been worried. You two are like sisters."

"Yeah, and it will be nice to hear about what's been going on in my absence."

"Okay, I'll give you a ride there."

I give my mother another hug and tell her I love her. As I exit her car and walk to the apartment, I find myself looking all around to be sure there isn't someone waiting to attack. I open the door and can immediately smell the food Tiff has cooked: steak, potatoes, and pie. My mouth begins watering. I set down the bag. I hear footsteps; not just one set. Tiff, Luke, and Josh run down the hall to me. I'm so happy to see them tears threaten to spill down my cheeks. They give me a group hug.

"So glad to see you're okay, Austria." Luke speaks first.

"Welcome home, Austria," Tiff adds.

"Missed you every second," Josh says.

I remember the sparkling star that made me feel love when I was unconscious. Josh is my sparkling star. I hug him, and he helps me to the table.

"Thank you guys so much. The food smells amazing, Tiff. Is that pecan pie I smell?"

"Your favorite. Consider it a homecoming gift."

We all sit and eat. The food's wonderful. The steak is cooked to perfection, and I don't know if it's the chives or cream, but the potatoes are scrumptious. It seems surreal to feel so normal after being through everything we've been through in the past few days. Then I remember my father warning me that it's not entirely safe. Josh grabs my hand under the table. I hadn't noticed, but my leg's bouncing in a nervous tic.

We all say goodnight and head to bed. Exhaustion hits, but I'm so happy to not be alone. I feel protected in this home and with him. Josh carries my bag to my room. He keeps watching me as we're getting ready for bed. I don't know if he's expecting me to break down, but I can see he's ready if I do. I probably would, but I'm too tired. He wraps his arms around me as we fall asleep.

The dream comes suddenly as they always do. I've been having so many recently, they feel eerily similar to reality. I'm going to have to focus to keep everything straight. I dream of Jack jumping when the makeup brush fell, but now I notice in the dream that his jump occurs a millisecond before the brush makes a sound. HE saw the shadow too. Then I remember us bumping each other when I saw the shadows in the hallway. I had stopped out of fear. Why had he not seen me, but run straight into me? Because HE was looking at the shadows too. Even his fear as he looked at the Giovanni Battista Piranesi black and white piece. My father had also seen shadows while in the haunted house building. The image of Dr. Shipley's nurse swirling the vial of his blood, after he was hit with the coffee mug, quickly flashes to her swirling my own. HE has different DNA too and now they're going after him. Little Jack, so young, he's such a great actor. He is so helpful and full of joy. He's always ready for adventure. I know he's only a few months younger than me, but I feel protective of him. I always have. Like the little brother I never had. They're going to try to cut him open and take his organs.

"NO, not Jack too," I scream as I sit up in bed.

STRANDED COIL

METAPHASE

When someone you love plans to sacrifice themselves to save innocent people, do you really have a choice? I think so. I think there's always a better answer. Unfortunately, the only answer I can come up with in the time allowed will sacrifice me.

You know those funny old cartoons when the character's floating on a rug or some object in the air, and it's pulled from beneath them? I feel like the character running in place in the air for a couple seconds before the fall.

How do you choose between two people you care about? As time runs out, I have to go ahead and take the leap and hope I've chosen wisely.

DISCOVERY

The bed shakes as Josh jumps from his sleep at my scream. He leaps up to fight an attacker if necessary, but then he sees it's only us in the room. I can hear my heartbeat, it's pounding so hard. He relaxes and puts his arm around me. My room is a mess. The bonus of having a boyfriend from the streets is that he doesn't seem to notice things like that. His forest smell almost causes me to forget my previous thoughts, and I have to hide my smile. How does he make even an undershirt and flannel pajama pants look so attractive? I can see a sheen of sweat on his forehead. I wonder if he'd been having a nightmare in his sleep too.

"Did you have a nightmare?" Josh asks as he gently squeezes me.

My previous thoughts rush back to me. "They're going to go after Jack next if they haven't already done so," I say as I look at him pleadingly. "When did we last see Jack? He wasn't part of the rescue team. I wonder if Lea's with him right now?"

"Why do you think they're after Jack? He was at the haunted house today as we met with security. He even left a little early so he could get Lea a surprise."

I know I should confide in him about everything that has been going on with my father and the warnings, but I'm not ready to yet and, anyway, there's no time. Little Jack, who I couldn't bear to mock hang in the haunted house, is in danger. I think about how he blushes every time he smiles. How he hasn't grown into his extremities, like a puppy with too big paws. Then my mind warps, and

I imagine him cut open, even gutted, with blood spilling everywhere. I have to put my head between my legs as I sit to keep the dizzy spell away. I look up and continue talking to Josh because, if there's any way we can save him, we must.

"He has different DNA like mine too. That's why he was hit with the coffee mug that night and a pro-bono medical team magically appeared," I say.

"Are you sure?"

"Dead sure."

##

Tiff and Luke wake easily. I think my scream had already stirred them from their sleep. They make a cute couple in pajamas with matching disheveled hair. We all sit in the kitchen now drinking caffeinated coffee. The smell reminds me of the first day at the haunted house when Josh joined Tiff and me at the coffee shop. Could that really have been just a month ago? It feels like I've known Josh for years now.

"So you think they're after Jack next?" Luke asks as he rubs his eyes.

"I don't have time to explain right now, but yes, they're after him," I confirm.

"Tiff, do you know how to locate him from the restaurant?" Josh asks.

"Um, let me see." She scrolls through the contacts on her phone. "Yeah, here it is. I have his number."

"Call him, Tiff," I beg.

"It's three in the morning. Are you sure?" she asks.

I'm so tired of everyone not believing me. It cuts deep into my pride. Here we've been working together, and this is my best friend, my roommate. They've seen my capabilities, yet now they don't take my word. I guess they think that after being through what I have, my head isn't clear. The stitches in my abdomen still ache. I imagine the men that were going to take my organs and tremble. Josh puts his arm around me and hands me a blanket. I don't feel as tired as I should. I'm alive with fear. The only thing making me tired is the fact that we're wasting time.

"I'm sure," I state, hoping this ends the questioning.

Tiff hits the green button on her phone. She's like the sister I've never had. She sees that I'm serious now. She puts it on speaker so we can all hear. It rings and rings. After four rings, we're forwarded to his voicemail. Shit. He could be anywhere. He could be safe at home asleep or strapped to a gurney as I'd been. What are we going to do?

"Do you have Lea's number?" I ask frantically.

"She just started working, and I haven't gotten it yet," Tiff answers, giving me a consoling look.

"Should we call the cops?" I plead.

"They should be better able to locate Jack," Tiff says.

"I don't trust them. Why would they help you if I'm involved? They despise the street kids," Josh says. He's looking at the floor as he talks. I put my arm around his shoulders. He has to see that this might be our only hope for some help. I have faith that he can set his distaste aside. They were there when he rescued me, so I'd wished a bridge might have been formed. It looks like it might not be that easy. Past grievances may not be put to rest; ghosts haunting outside of our haunted house.

"I'm with Josh. I've seen cops take payoffs from both Matt and Ed. Who's to say that isn't happening with other parts of the human trafficking ring? I think, if we contact them, we could possibly increase the odds of a bad result for Jack."

Luke's siding with Josh and not with Tiff. This I didn't expect, but what he says makes sense. If he's witnessed it with Matt and Ed, I don't think we have a choice but to find Jack ourselves. I don't know where to begin. The look Josh and Luke give each other reminds me of when kids silently converse behind their parents' backs. They nod their heads as if they understand each other completely without saying a word at all. I wonder what they have up their sleeves.

I wish my father could visit me from the dead as he has recently in my dreams and visions. He had warned me before I was captured. Maybe he could tell me where Jack is. I don't know how to summon him. How does one call the dead, or undead for that matter? I bet Tiff doesn't have that number on her contacts list.

"Tiff, you tailed Matt and Ed to the house and, Luke, you knew about that place before our rescue mission. Do either of you know of other locations?" Josh asks. His forehead creases in concentration. Luke nods at him like he knew this was the direction Josh would take.

"There are two more houses that I know of, but with the arrests that took place, they might have disbanded them," Luke responds.

"Where are they?" I ask.

"Do you have paper and pen?" Luke replies.

Tiff gets up and rifles through the desk in our kitchen. This is where our mail piles up, an abyss of the unknown. It's nice to have a place for that so our table can remain clean and available for meals. The desk is tucked into the wall so as to not make the entire kitchen appear messy. It's so cluttered it's like the black hole of our documents. She's successful in finding paper and pen, though, and returns. Luke draws a map. I recognize some of the downtown streets. He draws a house near Olive and 39th. This is a bit southeast of where we are. The next house is near S. Minnie Street and Lake Avenue. This is southwest of here. Luke's drawing is nowhere close to the intricate artwork Josh could produce, but it's readable, and that's all we need for it to be functional.

"I followed them to the one on Lake Avenue too," Tiff puts in.

"Do we know where Jack's staying? Let's stop by there first, then we can go by the house at Lake Avenue as that's the one we're most familiar with. After that, we can take 39th over to the Olive house," I say.

I'm ready to be doing something. Every second that passes worries me. I find myself massaging my hands to release tension.

"We should get some help. Can we stop by Ethan's first?" Josh asks. There's a hint of resignation in his words, but Luke's nodding his head in approval. This must have been what they had up their sleeves. They want more people on this mission. I can't really complain, but what time could it cost us and how much does Jack have left if he's taken?

"That's out of the way," I reply, exasperated.

"We can go to Jack's place first and then to the house on Olive," Josh says.

"But Luke and Tiff both have witnessed the Lake Avenue house. I think we run the risk of losing Jack if we don't go to the Lake Avenue house first. If we go to the Olive house, they'll tip off the Lake Avenue house and relocate Jack to an unknown place," I say.

"Or they *could* be at the Olive house to keep a low profile after the arrests of their colleagues," Tiff says. "If they've been watching us as closely as I fear, I may have tipped them off when I followed them to the Lake Avenue house. I'm sorry."

I hate when Tiff apologizes to me. It's not like she's part of this human trafficking ring. What does she have to be sorry for? She followed her intuition and tailed them to see what was going on. She's been more aware than I apparently have been.

She's right. It's a huge possibility. We really have no clue where they are. We have to split up.

"Okay. Let's recruit more people and split up. We can simultaneously approach both houses," I suggest.

Luke and Josh nod their heads again as if this was expected. Maybe Josh even led me down this trail on purpose. Then Luke looks at me.

"Um, Austria, are you up for this? You just got out of the hospital. They were already after you. Won't we run the risk of them recapturing you?" Luke states.

I see the muscles around Josh's jaw flex. His hands clench into fists too. I grab one of his hands and massage it open, out of the fist, hoping to release the tension as I had in my own.

"I'll be okay. I'll stay out of their reach. Now, can we go already?"

DEBATE

We pile into Luke's Escape. It oddly feels like we're a couple of husbands and wives setting out on a Sunday drive. If only we were enjoying something that relaxing. His car even has a new car smell. Instead, we're driving to Jack's apartment, hoping to find him asleep and not kidnapped by people who want his organs. Just the thought of it makes my breath catch. Jack lives in an apartment within a tall building across 31st from Penn Valley Community College. The gray cement feels like a prison. It towers over us and curves around us. It gets cold as thunderclouds blot out the sun. We buzz his number. Luckily, Tiff had the apartment number saved in her phone too, in hopes that he'll answer, and all of the worrying tonight will be for nothing.

"Hello." It's a girl's voice.

"Lea," I say.

"Yeah? What are you doing out and about? Shouldn't you be resting?" she asks.

"Can you let us up? It's me, Josh, Tiff, and Luke."

There's a click, then we open the building door, and head up to Jack's place. The stairs are laminate with black rubber footholds. The stairway's depressing and dark. It smells dusty. The metal railings are cold to the touch. I'm glad we only have to climb three stories. My abdomen aches with each step, but if I say anything, they'll put me back in the last place I want to be, bed. I'm glad I'm at the rear of the group so I can wobble up the stairs attempting to scale them without using abdominal muscles. I feel like a pregnant woman. Lea lets us in when we're at the door to Jack's apartment.

"What's up? Have you seen Jack? I've been looking all over for him. He isn't at any of our secret hangouts." She blushes with the last statement. She's adorable. Jack and her both are. She looks flustered. Her hands are shaking. Her hair is in disarray.

"No, that's actually why we came here," Tiff says.

"Shoot. But your group doesn't always hang with him. Why would you come all the way here?" There's a wall of silence. We all glance at each other awkwardly. She looks at us one by one. She gasps for breath. Luke rushes over to her and has her sit down.

"What is it? What aren't you telling me?" Lea says shakily.

Everyone looks uneasy. Lea's eyes get so wide, I'm afraid they might pop out of her head.

"Lea, do you remember Jack being hit over the head with the coffee mug and the pro-bono medical team?" I ask.

"Uh, yeah. What does that have to do with anything?"

"Jack has different DNA." I pause. I'm completely breaking our promise to my mother. I wish I didn't have to tell so many people about my DNA being different, but I don't see how I can explain this and its urgency to Lea without doing so. "I know because I do too. The same people who had me are after Jack."

"Oh. Wait, so do they have him now? This is out of control. We have to find him." Lea's putting on a jacket and her shoes. Her jacket is leather, and her shoes of choice are sturdy boots. These outside appearances contrast with her trembling hands. Now I feel like Luke. He'd thought it might be best for me to stay back and not join in the search.

That had really upset me, but here I am thinking the same thing of Lea. She really isn't in the best emotional state for a rescue mission.

I walk over to her and put my hands on her shoulders so she has to look me straight in the eyes. She appears as impatient as I had felt earlier tonight. I take a deep breath. "Lea, you need to be able to keep your head if you go with us. Can you do that?"

She follows my lead and takes a deep breath and exhales. Her eyes focus on mine. "I'm fine," she says. I can see why Lea was able to work at the haunted house. The look she gives me tells me that if I try to stop her, I may lose a limb. Not as sweet and innocent as my first impression of her had implied.

We're back in Luke's Escape headed to Ethan's place. His mom is still out of town. I wonder what he, Patrice, and probably Ceresa are doing right now. I rest my head against the window next to me and look up at the stars. I find the Big Dipper and the North Star. The North Star falls behind us as we head south, like the hand of a clock. It's four in the morning. If we take much longer, we're not going to be able to sneak up on the houses in the dark.

When we pull up to Ethan's house, I see more lights on than I'd been expecting. He must have people over. This could throw a wrench in our plans. The three peaks of the roof appear to be reaching toward the sky more than the last time we were here. We all exit the Escape and head to the door. It opens before any of us knock.

Ethan greets us, "Did you hear what happened? Is that why you're here?"

"No, man. What happened?" Josh asks as we all enter.

Then I see Camille on the couch in the Game/Dining Room. She has a small towel up to her face. The towel is drenched in blood. Emmitt's by her side massaging her shoulders and neck. Brittany and Landon are on the floor playing a video game. Patrice and Ceresa walk out of the kitchen toward us. Patrice has another towel, and Ceresa has a baggie of ice.

"Hola, see the bloody nose our coworkers dragged in here," Patrice says.

"What are all of you doing here? We've had enough action tonight," Ceresa complains as she removes the bloody towel from Camille's face to inspect her nose. Luke walks over to examine her. Without his medical school experience, I may not have survived my kidnapping. I have him to thank for my very professional sutures.

"Jack's missing. We're sure he's been taken by the same group that took me. There are two possible locations that we need to seek out." I eye them and hope my words are sinking in. I don't have time to explain this more than once. What if they think I'm hiding something? Would they really think I would do that right after they saved me? Just as in the beginning, I'm questioning my read on people, but I am hiding something from them. I've been seeing shadows and my dead/undead dad.

"Why would they take Jack? Are we all doomed to this fate? Why are they targeting us?" Patrice asks viciously. Her shoulders have tensed.

"They're not after all of us. Only the ones with different DNA," I say. And here we go, more explaining.

"What are you talking about?" Ceresa asks. She has grabbed Patrice's hand.

I know we promised my mother that we would keep the secret, but I've already told so many. I might as well tell my entire haunted house family. I feel goosebumps rise on my forearms.

"Jack and I have different DNA. We have Altered Helixes. It isn't really that big of a deal. We heal faster, so that's why we've been targeted. I guess the investors in the stolen organs want ones that heal quickly."

"Whoa. Are you like the Wolverine or something? I had wondered how you were able to be here so quickly after being cut open," Ethan chimes in. He punches Josh in the arm with brotherly love.

"Like I said, it's really not that big of a deal. Plus it makes me dizzy sometimes. Remember when I fainted," I say.

"Wait a minute," Camille says. "Did you just say dizzy? I carry mints in my purse all the time because I have fainting spells. The reason why I have a bloody nose is because I was attacked earlier tonight. We'd all been walking home to our place, and I fell behind. This stupid man grabbed me from behind. He tried to cover my mouth and nose with a cloth, but I got a good elbow in his ribs first. I've studied karate and other self-defense techniques, but he was still able to hit me in the nose. As soon as I had him down, Emmitt, Brittany and Landon were with me, and we ran." She seems to be awestruck.

Josh and I exchange a glance when she mentions that a man tried to cover her mouth and nose with a cloth. That's how I had been taken, and he had witnessed it. Too bad I didn't have reflexes like Camille. Maybe we wouldn't even be in this mess if I would've been able to fight back. I feel a pang of guilt in my stomach. We have to get Jack.

"So I have different DNA like you?" she asks.

"I think these occurrences lean toward that fact," I say as I try to calm myself down.

"Did you recognize anything about your attacker?" I continue.

Camille twisting a strand of hair in her fingers as she concentrates. "Come to think of it, I think I saw the man at the blood donation center."

I'm in shock now. Camille must have an Altered Helix too. I cannot believe three of us have different DNA. I'd thought I was a freak, but it seems to be more prevalent than I had realized.

"All right, you three are like blood siblings. Great. Can we please go get Jack? I'm so afraid for him," Lea pleads, pacing back and forth.

"You're right, Lea. We can discuss our DNA later. It just startled me for a second. Let's get Jack," Camille responds reassuringly.

"Okay, Luke, you've been inside these places. Can you give me the general layout of the floor plan?" Josh asks. As usual, he's keeping us on target. He knows just how to make a comment that will get the ball rolling in the direction we need. His forehead creases yet again.

Luke draws out the floor plans to complement the previous drawings of locations. Ceresa makes sure he marks where the windows are. We may need to visit Gunner and get more ether and gas masks so we can knock out the bad guys again and save Jack the way they saved me. Lea wants to see doorways and other points of entry and exit. I try to split us into two equal groups since going to the cops is out of the question. Our biggest guys are Ethan and Emmitt. They both have experience fighting, so one will be in each group. Luke and Landon are next. I put Luke with Ethan and Landon with Emmitt as they already know each other. I see the flaw here. Who's going to treat Jack if he's cut and Luke isn't in their group?

"Does anyone besides Luke have medical experience?" I ask everyone.

“I went to nursing school,” Brittany says.

I put Tiff and Brittany with Emmitt and Landon. That leaves Camille, Lea, Josh, and I. Tiff can’t be in Luke’s group as they are the two who know the locations. When I say this out loud, I see the pain in Luke’s and Tiff’s eyes as they look at each other. To even things out, I put Lea and myself with Ethan. Josh speaks up and states that he should be with me and Lea. I can tell he’s being protective, and I want to protest, but Camille will feel more comfortable with her group. I think Ceresa will be good with that group too as she has medical experience on the streets. I see the look of relief on Ethan’s and Patrice’s faces as they see they’ll be grouped together.

I try to tell them as much about my experience as I can so they’re prepared, but my memory is fuzzy. I remember the chloroform, but Camille’s own story about chloroform is newer than mine. Plus, we unfortunately are more than likely past that point. I tell the group that I think the gurney will be in a place like a basement away from windows and where possible screams may not be heard easily outside of the house. Luke fills Brittany in on the two shots that he had used on me. They’d been available for him when he rescued me. Do we hope the same will hold true for Jack, or do we try to get them from Gunner with the ether? If he doesn’t have these things right on him, I’m afraid we don’t have time to collect them elsewhere.

We assign someone to man a phone for each group. There’ll be a call between the groups, so we unleash the ether on each house at the same time. There will also be a phone call when Jack’s found. The person manning the phone for the group that doesn’t find Jack will call Bill and ask him to notify the authorities because, by that point, even if they’ve been paid off, it will be too late for them to be a danger to Jack. We all study the layout drawings Luke put together. I feel like I am part of a S.W.A.T. team strategizing to secure a hostage situation. It's kind of exciting, but a blanket of anguish smothers us. We're experienced in haunting, not in rescue missions. I wish we could call an adult, like Bill, but I know if we do, they won't pay heed to our misgivings about the police. They would call them at the first chance.

"Okay, I think we've planned this out the best we can. Let's go get Jack," Lea almost yells.

CAPTURE

We have to backtrack to get to Gunner at the market, but in order to keep us all safe and give Jack the best chance of recovery, it's a must. It is like our own version of the SWAT team's armored tank. The market's quite busy, even at this hour, and I'm afraid of all of the people that surround us. We can't chance anyone overhearing our game plan. What if they're somehow connected to the human trafficking ring? My fear subsides when I see Gunner. He has a crew cut and wears army fatigues that are tattered from years of use. I don't know why I had envisioned him with messy long hair and looking deranged. His eyes are bright and, the second his gaze meets Josh's, he ushers us over to a more secluded spot. Two for two, Gunner has his wits about him again. Thank goodness. We had not made a backup plan if we couldn't get the ether from him. I hope our plans don't have any more holes than that.

We separate from there. I find it difficult to watch Tiff go in the group that's not my own. My group is in Luke's Escape. Ethan and Luke are in the front while Lea, Patrice, Josh, and I are crammed in the back. Lucky for Lea and Patrice, I'm in Josh's lap shrunk down so we aren't pulled over. Emmitt has a full-size van for the other team. No one has to sit on anyone's lap in that vehicle. Not that I honestly mind sitting on Josh's lap. It's reassuring to be so close to him before we encounter danger. My own version of the SWAT helmet and bulletproof vest. What are we thinking, attempting this on our own? It worked before and I hope, despite all odds, it works again. The ride seems to make everyone thoughtful, for it is silent. Lea keeps biting her fingernails. Ethan is pounding a tune on the dashboard like he's playing the drums. Patrice is looking at him with an appraising smile. Josh and I hold hands, as if praying for the success of our next actions.

We make it to the Olive house; the other team went to the Lake Avenue house because that's the one Tiff is familiar with. We pile out of the car and stretch our legs. We are a little ways down the street so as to not be detected. We walk to the house in an even larger silence than the one we had travelled in. A shadow flies across the street. My breath catches. I'd only been seeing shadows in the haunted house. No one else seems to have noticed it. I'm not sure if these shadows are just straight up following me or if they appear when danger's near, but it sends a shiver through me either way. I'm grateful for Josh's hand in mine. I squeeze, and he holds tighter.

When we're next door, we crouch behind a bush away from the streetlight.

"The windows are open again. What is it with this group?" Luke asks as he peers around to view the house.

Lea, Patrice, and I take turns running hoses to the windows. We're the smallest and can move the easiest undetected. The house sits on top of a small grassy hill. It has brick with white side panels from the top of the first floor to the roof. The windows are within reach. They have metal frames and must be at least twenty years old. I'm grateful they're open. I know these old windows creak when opened, and I don't think we could've opened them without being noticed. We should acquire some glass cutters. Once the hoses are in place, Patrice calls Ceresa while the rest of us put gas masks on.

"We're ready," Patrice whispers.

She gives a thumbs up, and Josh turns the switch that forces the ether into the house.

"Talk to you soon." Patrice hangs up the phone and puts on her own gas mask.

When Josh had made his testimony of how they saved me, I had not been able to understand fully what he meant by hearing bodies hit the floor. Now I do. How intense is that? I know some of these guys are large, but to be able to hear their bodies hit the floor out here is astonishing. I guess dead weight can do that. We all jog to the closest window of the house. Ethan pries it all the way open. Lucky for us, this window isn't behind bars as many in this neighborhood are. Maybe we should also acquire some metal cutters. That's another thing we had not planned for. I hope the Lake Avenue house doesn't have bars on all the windows.

Once we're inside, and the perimeter has been checked, Ethan gives us a thumbs up.

"The way to the basement is over here," Luke says.

We all head that way as quietly as we can. Josh opens the door and peeks his head in to be sure the coast is clear. He turns back to us and nods. Then we descend the stairs. I can hear my heart beating in my ears when I spot the gurney. That brings back memories I would be glad to forget. Everyone seems to sense my uneasiness, and they spot the gurney too. They walk to it. It's empty. I still haven't managed to move my feet. It's as if they have dried in cement.

Another shadow flies by me, right in front of my face. If I were faster, I would've reached out to touch it. It flies up to the ceiling and then through the crack under a door. I remember the room they kept me in before hauling me to the gurney when I attempted to escape. I'd spent a long time conscious and unconscious in that room. That's where Jack is. It has to be. I have to get to him. I remember how alone I felt in that room. My feet are free now, having somehow rid themselves of the cemented feeling. I run to the door. As I open it, I hear Josh say "No." I take a step in ,and someone grabs my arm. They pull me into the room, shut the door and lock it. It's so dark I can't see a thing. Then I feel the all-too-familiar prick of a needle penetrating my arm. My body goes limp, but I'm awake. I still cannot see anything.

My assailant throws me over their right shoulder. On the back of the assailant's head are straps from a breathing mask. My eyes have adjusted to the dark. It seems they did somewhat prepare for a possible rescue mission. I'm surprised they still left the windows open. Had it all been a trick to lure us in? Then I feel a hand hit mine. I look to my left with my eyes only as my head won't move and see Jack in the same position as myself but on the opposite shoulder. Here I am another victim when I was supposed to be helping Jack. At least the paralyzing sensation numbs the pain I would feel with my attacker's shoulder gouging into my abdomen. I'm so sorry, Jack. Maybe they'd only wanted to lure those with different DNA. They had to know I'd be the one to recognize the room first. I feel something clutch my heart. It's the grief of my errors. Here my friends had come to save Jack, and I just led myself straight into the lion's den. Maybe they'd been right after all about my ability to help in their mission.

No, I will not let this happen. Then my assailant climbs a few steps and pushes something with their head. Two doors swing open, and we're crawling out of the earth next to the house. This is not a good sign. They could take Jack and me to an unidentified place and have twice the organs. What can I do? Father, help.

I see a flash as Ethan tackles the assailant. He's faster than I thought. Jack and I tumble to the ground, still unable to move. The assailant rises and grabs something out of his jacket while heading in Ethan's direction, but Patrice hits the attacker in the back of the head with a pipe. I can see Ethan smile at Patrice. He runs up, and she jumps into his arms. The others come shortly after that and help carry Jack and me to the car. We pile in, and Luke starts the engine and peels out.

Luke's driving, and Patrice is in the front passenger seat. Lea's in the middle of the back. Ethan is to her left with Jack in his lap. Ethan sees Lea's need and lays Jack's head in her lap so she can brush his hair with her fingers. I'm in Josh's lap. He holds me like a child. I see the terror in his eyes when my head flops from one side to the other. I have no control. I wish I could make it stop so he could be at ease. He takes his hand and holds my head on his shoulder. We're speeding down the street. Patrice calls Ceresa so her group will know we have Jack and can call Bill. She never speaks. She hangs up the phone.

"No answer?" Luke asks, concerned.

I bet they're still looking for Jack, but it's odd that they aren't answering. I hope they haven't run into issues like us. Oh shoot, did they get Camille? I recognize how flawed our plans had been, but we do have Jack.

"We have to go to the hospital," Luke says. "St. Luke's on Broadway is closest. There'll be authorities there. I know you Streets don't like the cops, but the hospital's such a public place, they'll have to help us; bribes, Streets, or not. I haven't been able to ascertain if Jack's injured. Both Jack and Austria need shots to take the paralysis out of them."

Just then, the phone rings. Ceresa is so loud that even I can hear her, and she's not on speakerphone.

"We didn't see Jack. They woke up, Patrice. Some wore gas masks. It was like they knew we were coming. Tiff got cut. We had to get out of there. They're tailing us. What do we do?"

"Go to St. Luke's on Broadway. That's where we're headed too. We have Jack," Patrice says, but she doesn't hang up. I think Ceresa and her need to hear each other to know they're safe. Patrice stares at the phone.

"We're being tailed too," Luke says as he floors it.

We screech into the hospital emergency parking lot at the same time as the others. Our tails speed off into the night. Looks like the crowded hospital scene was a good choice on Luke's part. I see both groups exit their vehicles as my head rests on Josh's shoulder looking out. Everyone's hugging each other. Tiff almost knocks Luke down when she runs and jumps into his arms. He smells her hair and smiles. Guess the cut wasn't too bad, but I still watch to be sure she isn't vitally injured. Luke says something to her I cannot hear, and she shows him a gaping hole in her shirt. He lifts it, and I can tell she's going to need stitches. Josh is holding me and walking to the entrance.

"Ethan, thank you for carrying Jack," Lea says.

Hospital staff surrounds us now, putting Jack and me on gurneys and attending to Tiff. I know this is a safe gurney, but the feeling still makes me sick to my stomach. We're rolled into the hospital. I think I hear a nurse say Tiff just needs ten stitches and with Luke's look of agreement, I'm relieved. At least Tiff wasn't harmed too badly, but I detest putting the ones so close to me in such a situation. I have to find an end to this so they can live the lives they're meant to live. I hear Luke telling them what he believes we were injected with and what he used last time to wake me. I can feel them work on me, and I can see Josh's look of concern, but I feel disconnected. I can't be going into shock again. It wasn't like last time. It wasn't quite as scary because I knew I wasn't alone this time. I can't help myself. I have to close my eyes and try to get a grip.

"You're safe. This has to change. You're putting too much at risk." My father's back. I don't know if I fell asleep and am dreaming or if it is like the out-of-body experience when I fainted. I do not see my body from above so I must be in shock and dreaming, or whatever you call this.

"Father, I don't understand what's going on. Why, now, are they after us all? Why are you able to talk to me so much lately?"

"I didn't have time to explain earlier, but I do now. At least I can explain part of it. They are after you because you have different DNA. The results of that don't fully set in until you're between the ages of seventeen and twenty-two. These differences caused by your DNA don't manifest themselves until you have the ability to recognize future consequences, which is after the frontal lobe fully develops in the human brain. I was unable to communicate with you until you reached this point. Plus, we're better able to converse when you are at dangerous moments because of the way adrenaline kicks the special abilities you have pushing your DNA to another level."

"Okay. So why did you disappear? What are you?"

"Oh, you're waking up now. I love you. Talk to you later."

"I love you too, Father."

That was weird. He just said "talk to you later" like he knows we'll be conversing soon. He also said that it's easier to speak to me in times of danger. Does that mean I'll be in danger again soon? When will it end?

My closed eyelids look bright red from the hospital lights. I hear the sound of a monitor beeping next to me. I feel Josh's hand on mine. I slowly open my eyes. He's asleep in a chair next to my bed with his head resting on the bed. I take my hand from under his and begin patting his head. He wakes up disoriented.

"You're okay. I knew you shouldn't go with us. What would I have done if that man had gotten away with you and Jack?"

"What would you have done if they'd come after me while I was alone, and you guys were off to rescue Jack?" I ask while raising my other hand up to the sky with a bend at my elbow and shrug.

He smiles. I put my hand on his cheek and smile back at him. "I'm fine, Josh. How's Jack?"

"He's in a state of shock. What is with you DNA people and shock?"

"I don't know. I'm trying to find out." I've gone too far. The only way I've been trying to find out is through my father and I haven't told anyone about that.

"Oh yeah, how are you doing that?"

I'm silent. I don't know how to backtrack and cover my misstep.

"Austria?"

"It's a long story."

"Doesn't look like we're going anywhere soon."

I tell him about how my father has been contacting me lately. Much of his contact has been warnings. I tell him about how I'm unsure if my father is really dead, but that I only see him when I'm not in completely conscious states. My father's appeared in dreams, out-of-body experiences, and as a hazy figure in a mirror reflection. I worry that Josh will look at me like I'm crazy, but he never does.

I tell him that I fear there's more to come given my father's confidence in seeing me again. Then I have to explain that the adrenaline rush caused by fear allows us to communicate easier. While he has the look of understanding and reassurance I'd been hoping for, I catch another look pulling him from within. He's jealous. He lost his parents and never had a relationship with them. Not only do I have a living and supportive mother, but my father's trying to help me from the dead or whatever he is.

"At least they're not after you for your organs," I say as I brush his cheek with my fingers.

He puts his hand on mine and holds it against his cheek. He looks me in the eyes. My monitor beeps faster. He looks at it and then at me. I do believe my heart rate is about to the maximum it's allowed before the nurses outside my room are notified. He smiles, but then his face turns serious.

"If you think for a second, I wouldn't rather them be after my organs than your organs, you don't understand how much I care for you."

"Josh, don't say that."

"What would society lose if my organs were stolen? It's not like I'm an upstanding citizen with collegiate aspirations. Hell, society would probably benefit more from my donated organs than from me living."

"Stop. Don't say things like that. If anything were to happen to you, it would be the end of me. I would be crushed. I wouldn't be able to give anything. You give more to this world than you give yourself credit for. I've seen the way you support people and inspire them to have the courage to fight for their dream."

“Oh, Austria, you’re like the family I never had. I don’t know what I’d do without your belief in me,” he whispers as if telling a secret.

“What about Ceresa, Ethan, and Patrice? They’re like family, and they believe in you.”

“It’s not the same.”

“Okay, let’s just agree to keep each other safe the best we can.”

“I will try to help you figure out what’s going on with your father. You can talk to me about anything.” He leans over the hospital bed and hugs me.

STATUS QUO

Once Jack and I fully recover, we return to the haunted house. The organ at the entrance isn't as terrorizing as it once was. Though the pipes still tower above me, they don't seem as foreboding. Instead, they seem like a wall of comfort, like my mother really should be sitting there playing *Beautiful Torment*. Even the dark rooms and props of evil seem to have lost their eerie luster. Everyone looks as if we're returning home. Everyone applauds as we walk in. Jack runs and picks up Lea. This different DNA really does give us better healing capabilities.

The others have been able to somewhat cover our spots while we've been gone. Bill now wants us to run through a rehearsal with everyone in their original places. There's also a new element to the house that Jack and I aren't used to. We now have guards at appointed positions within the house. We need to rehearse getting from one place to another while checking in with the guards. In order to remain concealed, they get to wear costumes too. It's comical to see Ceresa putting makeup on these tough guys. The smallest one has to be at least two hundred and fifteen pounds and six feet tall. It feels as though we've recruited a football team to join the haunted house staff.

Everything comes back slowly. I remember my parts and placements but find it difficult to act. I've been so petrified lately, I find it hard to ignore my inner emotions. Jack seems to pick up everything faster. His acting ability helps. Ceresa coaches me if I falter. After mock-hanging Jack, I remember that we lost Matt and Ed. We had skipped over the part of Ceresa taking cyanide. I don't know if Matt and Ed are in jail or out. The thought of them being out freezes me. Jack seems to notice and puts his hand on my shoulder.

"Everything okay?" he asks me just like a brother would.

I have to clear my throat to talk. "Yeah. Matt used to ride a chariot at this point. Do you know where Matt and Ed are?"

Ceresa answers for him. "Don't worry. Tiff made sure to file restraining orders against them for this location, your place, and Ethan's. I found a couple street kids to fill their spots. We have guards. Everything will be okay."

I take a deep breath. "So, they are out. That's intense. I wonder what their parents had to pay for that. Thank you guys for putting up protections and finding replacements."

Ceresa did find a stocky guy to replace Matt. He stops by us before mounting the chariot.

"Hi, um, I'm Brian." He offers his hand awkwardly for me to shake. I like him already. His personality is about the complete opposite of cocky Matt's.

I shake his hand. His shake is firm but not overbearing. I smile at him. "It's nice to meet you, Brian. Thank you for filling in last minute."

"Not a problem. Ceresa has helped me out more than a couple times. Plus, it'll be nice to fill my pockets before winter."

I'd almost forgotten the street kids' troubles while concentrating on my own. Here they've gone out of their way to help me and what have I done for them? I don't care what my past perceptions of the street kids had been. I've found them to be some of the most selfless people I've ever known. Once again, I find myself grateful for this opportunity. Then Brian's on the chariot, and we all prepare to run. Jack flips the switch to the water for the "splitting of the sea" scene. The lit water rushes through the glass panes. It makes me think of being cleansed. I feel like, with these people, my haunted house people, I could be cleansed of the fear and pain that's filled the past few days.

I smile as Jack runs screaming through the doorway and into the hall. I join with everyone running. My heart races but not in fear. I look forward to seeing the rest of the rooms, but Bill has an announcement. He tells our group to head to the inventory room. We're having a meeting.

As I walk into the room, Josh catches up to me and grabs my hand. I take my arm and hook it into his so we're closer. He smiles at me as he brushes a bit of dust from my shoulder. The sight of vanity after vanity is not as impressive as before, but it now is filled with memories. Memories bonding with the street girls in our pursuit to put Matt and Ed in place. Memories of seeing my father. The haunted house feels like returning home after a vacation. It's familiar and warm. We sit on a box in the center. Others sit on the chairs and boxes or stand. Bill's in the center. I see he now has a Carhartt coat over his flannel. It enriches his rough exterior that I know covers his true and kind interior.

"You've done an excellent job today. To see you jump back from such dire circumstances gives an old man hope. Thank you for being you. I don't want to push those who have been through so much too soon, so we're breaking for lunch. I don't have food so you're free to do as you choose. You have two hours today."

We all look at each other amazed. Bill's never given us two hours for lunch. Our group has grown, and I'm not sure we'll find a place to fit us all. Ethan, Patrice, Ceresa, Josh, myself, Tiff, Jack, Lea, Camille, Emmitt, Brittany, and Landon head out the door trying to come up with a solution. A party of twelve is going to find it difficult to be seated at a table last minute. Oh, and we have a guard assigned to us for lunch too. That makes thirteen. We decide to go to Zaina and get food to go to eat at Tiff's and my place.

Zaina is packed as usual, but their service is also quick. People are bustling through. Many come from the street. Some come from the walking bridge over Walnut. On one wall, there's a mural of a Mediterranean city on luscious green hills with mountains in the background. I'd been too busy to notice that before. We're waiting for our food when Camille and Brittany break from the group to use the restroom. Our guard asks them to be quick. Conversation resumes about parties that had been scared in the previous nights.

"This kid jumped back three feet when I scared him. I thought he was going to take out half of his friends," Landon says through a laughing fit.

"That was nothing. I swear the one with the pink Mohawk peed his pants," Emmitt adds with wide eyes of disbelief.

I can't help but laugh with them. It's fun to scare when it's not in harmful ways. I notice it has been awhile and look toward the bathroom to see if Camille and Brittany are headed back. What I see takes the oxygen right from me. Brittany is by herself walking back to our group. She has a confused look on her face.

"What kind of trick is this, Camille?" Brittany asks, looking between us like she's trying to find Camille. "You've got to be kidding me!"

"What are you talking about? Isn't Camille with you?" I ask her.

"Great, you're going to play along with Camille's trick. Like we haven't had enough to fret about recently. That is SO funny."

"No, really, she's not out here. Are you sure she's not still in the restroom?"

"Crap. I looked everywhere and didn't see her."

The guard now starts his way to the restroom. He knocks and, when no one replies, enters the restroom. I follow him. He looks in one stall while I look in the other. We turn circles to see if there's another place someone could be. There aren't any windows. There isn't a closet. I look up, but the ceiling doesn't have a possible exit either. It's a complete ceiling, not a false one made of rectangles that can be moved to access a crawlspace.

"This doesn't make sense. There's no way she could have left," he says after checking the stall I'd checked.

As we return to the group, I hear everyone debating.

"This isn't a funny trick if that's what you two are doing, Brittany," Emmitt says.

"This isn't a trick. I don't know where she is. I swear," Brittany answers as Landon puts his arms around her.

"I think she's done it again," Jack says.

"Done what?" Lea asks.

"She told me that she thought there was something else the ones with special DNA could do. We can heal fast, we faint, and we can see and become shadows," Jack answers.

"What?" I ask. "What do you mean by see and become shadows?"

"I know you've seen the shadows too. Like when you were startled and told me you had forgotten something back in the inventory room. I saw it too."

"I kind of figured that out, Jack. That's one of the reasons I knew they were after you too. What I don't get is the part about 'becoming' shadows."

"When Camille visited me at the hospital, she mentioned out-of-body experiences and a close to death encounter. She said she was able to be invisible to others apart from people like us being able to see her shadow. She could converse with people that weren't really there. She said it felt different. It was almost like she was a spirit."

I remember the out-of-body experience I had when I fainted at the haunted house and talked with my "dead" father. This all has something to do with my DNA. Guess that makes sense to me. Then I remember when I'd almost died on the gurney and went into shock, or at least that's what it seemed to be. I remember feeling like a different being and sympathizing things such as the wind that has no control over where it blows.

This really is the time to choose. I've already shared so much with everyone here. Now I'm not the only person going through it. They can't treat me like a freak the way I fear they will. Even though they are my friends, people can only understand so much outside the norm. It's time to confide in them all. I'm glad Josh knows about my father talking to me. I wish I'd told him everything.

"Um, yeah, but I didn't realize I was becoming a shadow during those times," I say.

"So you've had the experience. I haven't. What's it like?" Jack asks.

"Camille was right when she said it's like becoming a spirit. I felt things I've never felt before. I've been able to communicate with my father, who *died* when I was fourteen."

"Wow. That sounds exciting. Can I try?" Jack asks.

"What I don't understand is that during my experiences my body has been where people could see it. When I fainted, you guys could see me, but I was looking above and over my body and the group. When I was in shock, people still saw me in the hospital. We can't find Camille anywhere."

"So can Camille get back now that her body is gone too?" a very worried Emmitt asks.

"I…don't know," I state flatly. I wish there were more I could offer, but I truly do not know.

DISAPPEAR

"What do we do? Do we leave without her? Our two hours is almost up," Jack says.

We all had pretty much lost our appetites with Camille's disappearance. We only make an attempt to eat outside of Zaina, instead of going to my place, to keep our strength so we can search for her.

"You all head back. I'll wait here to see if she returns. If she doesn't after an hour, I'm going to check all of our usual places. What if when she comes back she doesn't get to choose where?" Emmitt asks. He looks as lost as Camille is.

"I'll stay with you for protection. The rest of you stay in your group until you're back to the haunted house with the other guards," the guard says.

"The shadows seem to be able to place themselves near others like them or near danger. I think she'll either return here, at your regular places, or at the haunted house, Emmitt," I say, trying to reassure him.

The rest of us head back to the haunted house. We're unsure what to tell Bill, but I feel since the rest of the haunted house family knows, Bill should too. Bill's at a loss when we try to explain what happened.

"Well, I guess we'll finish the rehearsals with Ceresa and Patrice taking Camille's roles where they can. Are you sure she wasn't taken, and we shouldn't be going after her?" Bill asks.

"There was no way she could have exited without us seeing her," I say.

"Wasn't it busy and there were thirteen of you," he answers.

"I don't see that as possible. The way Zaina is laid is somewhat like a galley. There's just no way she could've left. Plus Brittany didn't hear her exit the restroom that we all saw them go in." Josh backs up my claim.

"All right, let's finish up rehearsals. I'm worn out already," Bill says.

We finish the day's work without the enthusiasm we had begun with. The roles seem tedious when we all are tormented by where Camille could be. Patrice and Ceresa do a pretty good job of covering for her, but there's no way they can do this and make it to their roles and check-ins in time when we're live. Camille has to return by tomorrow, or we're doomed.

We finish and Bill calls a wrap. We head home with our heads held low.

"I'm calling Emmitt to see if he's found anything," Brittany says.

We all freeze and wait in silence for the answer.

"Have you come across anything? No, she didn't show up here. Okay. See you at the apartment." Brittany hangs up her phone.

Landon gives her a hug. We all head home.

"Can I call you in the morning to see if she's appeared?" Tiff asks Brittany.

"Sure. I just don't understand. What can we do?" Brittany says.

"Just keep yourselves safe. I'm going to see if I can contact her through the night," I say.

"Thank you," Brittany exclaims. The look of despair that I see on her face makes me revert to primitive behavior. I clutch my arms around myself as if I can shield away the evil haunting us. My adrenaline picks up a little, and I want to investigate every sound and sight.

##

At home Tiff, Luke, Josh, and I get ready for bed. No news turned up during dinner or the hour after. Josh walks with me to my room. We sit up and talk for a while. I sit on my bed with my knees cradled to my chest. He rubs my back.

"I just get a weird sense that my father understands what's going on. Maybe this is the explanation for how he could disappear and not die, but he's never returned in the flesh that I know of. What if Camille can't return either?" I say while my eyes dart around beyond my control.

"We'll figure something out. We won't be any help to them if we don't get the rest we need, though. Do you need some chamomile tea to help you sleep?" Josh asks. He's so caring. How many guys would think to ask a girl if she needs tea to relax?

"That would be great, Josh. Thanks," I say as I lie down.

I don't know if he brings back the tea. I'm asleep before he has the chance. All of the commotion of the day petered me out. My father's talking to me before I even realize I'm asleep.

"Your friend is with us. We're the shadows you see. We're trying to warn you of precarious situations," my father says.

"Camille's with you? Is she okay? Can she come back?"

"Yes, and yes she's okay. She can come back, but it's a little difficult right now. She didn't come here alone. See the people after you in your world have members like us that can travel between worlds too. One of them came after

Camille in the bathroom, and that's why she disappeared. We have her safe from the one who went after her, but it's rather trying to teach her how to travel back, since she travelled here against her free will."

"What world, where are you? How long do you think it will take for her to learn?"

"Telling you about my world is a little difficult. Camille's working real hard. I think she should be back by tomorrow."

"Oh, that's good. So how many of our enemies have the ability to travel too?"

"Quite a few, but don't worry. We have it under control."

"Are they after you guys there, too? Can you come back to your body and be with us again, Father?"

"Please don't concern yourself, Austria. Get some rest."

"Wait, I don't understand, and I want to know."

"I'm sorry. We're running out of time. I only get a small window with you each visit."

"Fine. Good night, I love you."

"I love you too, honey."

I wake to Josh snoring beside me. I smile at him. All uncertainty has seemed to leave me. I know beyond a shadow of doubt that Camille will return today as my father said. I'm still confused about all of the details, but it's relieving to know Camille should be back soon.

I walk downstairs to find Tiff sitting with an untouched bowl of cereal in front of her. She has her phone in her hands. She keeps touching the screen to refresh it to see if she has a message or missed call from Emmitt. She looks up at me when I enter. She looks like she didn't get a minute of sleep.

"Is it too early to call him?" Tiff asks me.

"No, he'll be awake. Go ahead," I say.

She dials Emmitt. A few seconds pass.

"Emmitt. Is she back?" There's a small pause. "Yes. Oh, that is great news. What? She's disoriented?"

Another small pause, "Okay, we'll see you all at the haunted house."

Tiff hangs up the phone, relieved. She hops up and gives me a hug. "She's back."

"My father said she would be."

"You talked to your father last night?"

"Yes, but only in a dream. I don't know how to travel back and forth, and it sounds like Camille just learned to travel back. She was taken by force. Apparently, we not only have enemies here, but also in my father's world."

"How in the heck are we going to protect you three from that, another world?" Tiff asks.

"My father says he has it under control."

"Not complete control if they were able to take Camille." Tiff gives me a look of desperation.

I am distraught. I'm angry that she's questioning my father's words, but she has a point. I'm going to have to find another window of time to speak with my father.

RETURN

Everyone surrounds Camille when we get to the haunted house. They're asking all sorts of questions and I can tell by the bewildered look she's wearing she doesn't have answers.

"Calm down, everybody. Give the girl a chance to breathe," I say.

Camille gives me a look of appreciation. Emmitt has his big arms around her. In fact, throughout today's final rehearsals he doesn't leave her side unless absolutely necessary. He seems to have to keep touching her by holding hands, putting his arms around her shoulders, or even sitting her in his lap. I think he's afraid she'll disappear again, and he believes that if he's touching her she can't or, if she does, he'll go with her.

"Emmitt, she can't disappear on her own," I say.

"How do you know? Do you know about how I was taken? It was the worst," Camille says.

"I spoke with my father last night. He *died* when I was fourteen. He has different DNA like us. I don't believe he truly died, but now lives in that Other World that you were in."

"What does he look like?"

"He has brown hair and bushy eyebrows. His whole face lights up when he smiles. He has a star tattoo on his shoulder."

"Yes, I saw him. He helped me get back."

"Do you remember the process? Do you think you could repeat it on your own?"

"I do know the process, but I don't intend to ever go back to that world." I can see the look of fear in her eyes. Emmitt's grip on her tightens.

"I would never ask you to do that against your will. I would just like to know for myself. It would be good for Jack to know just in case too. Hopefully, we'll never be forced to use it again, but I feel better being armed and equipped." Josh squeezes my hand as I finish.

"Okay, I can see your point. It's really difficult to explain." Jack leans forward, trying to get as close to Camille as he can so he can learn the process.

"Maybe if you compare it with anything you've experienced before it would help," I offer.

"It's similar to meditation. I focused on where I wanted to go, home. My understanding is that to get to the Other World, one has to be in a state of emergency with high adrenaline. It's the opposite to get back. You have to control your breathing and be as calm as you can be. Meditation helps."

"That doesn't sound too bad," Jack says.

"It sounds easier than it is. When you're in that world everything is different. It's so disorienting that concentrating and keeping calm is almost impossible. If it hadn't been for your father, Austria, I don't think I could have done it."

"He was really good at focusing. I remember him teaching me as a child. Now that I know he was an Olympian, I believe he picked it up in the competitions. Think about being in another country with the world as an audience. You have to be able to focus through it all. Maybe that's why he is so good at it in the Other World."

"How did the person take you from the bathroom to that world?" Brittany asks. I can tell she's disturbed that her friend had been taken from right under her nose. She's popping her neck and her shoulders appear tense.

"He appeared out of nowhere. He was there in the stall with me. Thankfully I had finished and was fully dressed. He popped in with a hand covering my mouth and, before I could react, adrenaline coursed through my body. I had closed my eyes to try to think of an escape. I did escape but didn't recognize anything around me. It was so weird. In the Other World, you feel emotions from everything. Not just people, but plants, streets, anything. It's almost like everything has a visible bubble around it. People have the brightest. When your father first approached me, it was blinding."

"Wow, really? I remember feeling great emotion when I went into a state of shock," I say.

"Can we change the subject? I'm still reassuring myself that I'm really here. It is a somewhat of a downer thinking back to then. Until your father showed up, I had thought I was lost and would never return."

"Yeah, how about everyone grab some dinner before we open for tonight. Camille, are you sure you're up to working? No one would blame you if you wanted to take the night off," Bill says.

"I'm sure. If I don't work, I'll just get lost in thoughts and worries. I'd rather be busy and with everyone around me."

"Well, we have the guards, and you know the check-in schedule. Please adhere to it, everyone."

"No problem," Camille says.

##

Everyone disperses. Each couple goes a different route. Ceresa's by herself and looks a little mystified as to where she should go when Bill side hugs her and asks if she'll join him for dinner. He says he'd like to discuss some of the projects he's working on to help the street kids.

Josh and I walk off with clasped hands. He moves the hair away from my eyes and looks at me. "Where would you like to eat?"

"Have you ever tried Novel? Tiff and I went there once when I first started working for the haunted house, and I've been craving it ever since."

"Sounds perfect to me."

We walk to Novel still holding hands. I still can't seem to drive the thoughts of Camille's kidnapping from my head. If someone took her, why were they not in the Other World with her? Walking in calms me the way it did last time. There are so many questions, but I'm able to set them aside in the comforting surroundings of Novel with my hand in Josh's. Soothing, soft lights and a Tuscan décor cause my muscles to relax instantaneously. Josh puts his arm around me and smiles. I grab a menu as we're waiting to be seated. I explain to him the variety and deliciousness of it. I wonder what his meals have been like growing up.

"What sort of meals did you have growing up?" I dare to ask.

"Pretty dull. I mean I usually had whatever was the cheapest. Fosters had variety. Once I stayed with an Indian family, and their food had such a kick, my stomach was upset the first couple of days. Once I grew accustomed to it, I enjoyed the flavor."

"What about when you were on the streets?"

"Canned goods, non-perishables, and every once in a while a car driving by would see one of our signs and offer leftovers from whatever restaurant they'd just had lunch or dinner in. Those were a nice treat."

"Were you ever starving? Is there anything we could do to help? I know there are soup kitchens. I have volunteered at one, but they can't cover all the meals."

"We should've gone with Ceresa and Bill. They're probably having a very similar conversation."

I wrap my arms around him. "Yeah, but I don't mind being alone with you either."

"Okay, a table has opened up. Follow me, you two," the hostess announces.

We walk to a table toward the back. As we're walking we go by a table of some of my old classmates. This is it. The moment where I stand up for the street kids and do not let this proper yet judging group uproot my feelings.

"How are you? I haven't seen you around lately. What have you been up to?"

"Hey, Monica. I'm good. How are you? Oh yeah, I started a new job and have been really busy."

"Right this way," the hostess says. She must not want us to block the walkway. Novel isn't the biggest restaurant.

I feel like I've lost my chance, but Josh and I are holding hands, so that has to count. Josh and I turn to follow her.

"Can we join you for a bit and catch up? The rest of the group's heading home," Dave says as he pulls Monica by her sleeve and steps to follow us.

"Sure," I return.

We all sit down at the table. Josh and I look at the menus. I realize the flaw I've made. I haven't introduced Josh.

"Monica and Dave, this is Josh. We work together at the haunted house. That's my new job."

"A haunted house—that has got to be exciting."

"It is."

I glance at the menu but already know that I want the crab salad with puffed rice, nor, and ginger. There's a lull in conversation. It feels like pulling teeth trying to think of something to say about the haunted house. I could go on and on for hours about it with certain people, but I do not think my old classmates will understand. I look over to Josh to discuss food choices. He appears to be somewhat hiding behind his menu. Does he feel the tension too?

"What's it like to scare people?" Dave asks.

"It's a blast. The employees are artful and talented, and I've been able to put my writing skills to use on scenes. Josh is extremely gifted when it comes to drawing the scenes."

"I bet it's a thrill. So, Josh, are you in costume? That garb you have on would put me on edge in a haunted house," Dave prods.

Josh isn't in costume. He's in the clothes of a street kid. The clothes he always wears.

"No, these are my street clothes. The costumes in the haunted house are epic and would probably make you run if I were in them now," Josh responds.

"Oh, I see," Dave says.

The silence returns. I notice Dave and Monica sizing Josh up. They're just now seeing him for the street kid he is. Then they're looking at me and whispering. Why do they have to be so judgmental? They're going to be talking to all of our classmates, and I'm going to have to explain myself. Why can't they just go?

"Well, we need to be heading off. Everyone's meeting at Tom Fooleries later. You should join us," Dave says.

I notice they don't include Josh in the invite. How rude, but I'm just relieved to have them leaving.

"I'll be working after dinner, but I'll see you guys around," I say.

They get up and walk out. I turn to Josh to help him decide what he'd like from the menu.

"I've heard the Pig Head Pie is to die for, Josh. It comes with asparagus, summer truffle, and comfit lemon."

"I can read the menu, Austria. How come you introduced me to Dave and Monica as your coworker and not your boyfriend? I thought we were beyond the point where you would be ashamed to be with a man from the streets. You were so awkward with them. It was like you were embarrassed to be with me."

"Josh, no. We'd been holding hands. I guess I thought they'd assume the boyfriend part. It was difficult trying to explain the haunted house to them. I just don't think they'd understand this part of my life. Our private school was so rigid and controlled."

"You don't think they'd understand the haunted house part of your life, or dating someone who's from the streets part of your life?"

Josh's face looks broken like he could cry at any second. I guess I really did foul things up. How can I make them better? I'd have us go to Tom Fooleries if we didn't have to work. I'm tongue-tied and don't know what to say.

"Don't worry about it. I'll go back to where my kind belongs. I just thought you were different. My bad."

He gets up before I can reply and storms off. My heart drops to my stomach, and I'm dizzy.

"Josh, wait."

He walks too quickly for me to catch up with him before he exits. The hostess stops me.

"We've scheduled a server for your table. Can you please sit back down and eat?"

Shoot. Well, maybe Josh needs some time to vent. I'm not completely sure how to prove to him that things aren't as he believes. Plus, I need to sit until the dizzy spell ceases. Maybe I need some time to convince myself too. Had I been too embarrassed to introduce him as my boyfriend? What does that say about me?

Dinner's boring by myself, but I'm able to think. Unfortunately, I haven't come up with answers when it's time for me to get back to the haunted house. I don't understand. Josh and I have been through things most people don't face in a lifetime together. How can he believe that I'm embarrassed by him? Or is there something going on with him that's more than that? Have his feelings of inferiority resurfaced with my different DNA? Great, now things are going to be weird between me and Josh again. We're different, with people chasing us and another world. We don't have time for this kind of argument. There's a pain in my side like the stitch you get when you're running.

ALONE

Walking to the haunted house in a gloomy state, my first destination is the inventory room. Everyone's getting dressed when I head to the costume racks and find the outfit I need. I spot Josh by the vanities. He sees me but looks away without saying a word or waving, or anything. It feels like back when Ed had threatened Josh not to talk to me. Only now, I know this silent treatment is Josh's own decision. That's worse than before. I walk over to Ceresa and Jack to head to our room together. Ceresa gives me a look of disapproval. Josh must have spoken to her about the scene at the restaurant, or at least his version of events. I don't want to misinterpret her. Maybe she's upset about something else.

"Is everything all right, Ceresa?" I ask.

"Don't worry about it. We can keep our distance from you outside of the job if you're embarrassed by us. I'd just allowed myself to believe that, after all we've been through, you would at least respect us."

"It wasn't like that, Ceresa. This whole thing is a misunderstanding. Please don't be upset with me. I do respect you."

"Yeah, whatever."

She walks to the room ahead of us. Jack gives me a confused look.

"Sorry, it looks like Josh talked to the whole group, and a lot of people are upset. I hope you can get this misunderstanding remedied. It feels weird working without people getting along. It feels more like a job when before it just felt like fun," Jack says with a miserable look on his face.

"I know, Jack. I'll do my best. Sorry. Now let's go scare some people."

I'm so furious with how everything has turned into a mess that I look forward to scaring complete strangers. Jack and I sit in the dark corner that will light up when it's time for his "hanging." Ceresa drops to the floor shaking, and Brian shoots himself in the head. I hear gasps from the customers when they believe they're doomed. Jack and I are next. I fit the noose around his neck. I can feel the customers' eyes on us. I kick the chair from beneath him, and he begins to convulse. A customer actually steps to him to help, but Ceresa intervenes. She instructs them to run just as Brian starts after them in his chariot and the lit water illuminates their exit. I'm about to leave so I can check in with the guard and make it to the next room in time when I spot Jack still struggling. He's not acting this time. He really is being hanged, and the convulsions are real. I am lightheaded as I run to him and lift him.

As I'm lifting Jack with one hand and moving the noose off him with the other, shapes appear. They look hazy, like my father did when he conversed with me after I fainted. As Jack is freed I recognize the shapes. It's Matt and Ed. Guess they're still with us when we had thought the haunted house was free of them. Jack slumps down, but now Ceresa has joined him and is caring for his wounds. Matt's shape looks at me and begins talking.

"Looks like your pops isn't the only one who can make physical occurrences happen in this world while being in the other."

So Matt and Ed are like us, the ones with the different DNA. Otherwise, how could they be in the Other World? What do they mean by occurrences?

"What are you talking about?" I ask.

"Oh, you don't remember when your pops busted out all of the haunted house windows trying to warn you there was danger here? Come on, your memory is sharper than that."

"Okay, but what did you do?" I know the answer before they respond. Jack shouldn't have actually hung. The hidden wires should have held him up. The convulsions should've just been merely an act, but they weren't.

Ed gestures toward Jack. Ceresa looks at me like I'm out of my mind. Since she can't see Matt and Ed, she probably believes I am. She doesn't think much of me now anyway. Jack's looking at Matt and Ed fearfully. He's probably coming to the same conclusion I am. We really aren't safe in this world if there are bad guys in the Other World. Apparently, not only can they kidnap us, but they can harm us physically as well. Great, just what we need.

"We just played with the strings that were supposed to hold the kid up. Looks like they're not as effective if loosened a bit," Ed says with a smirk on his face that I wish I could wipe off.

"You wouldn't want to actually harm him though, would you? Your bosses might not be too thrilled to have his organs go to waste now, would they?" I'm mocking Matt and Ed for making a stupid error. Jack's one of the ones with special DNA. It was foolish of them to put him in danger.

"We knew he'd be saved. Plus that wasn't really what we were after," Matt says.

I'm furious. I wish I could hurt them. Maybe if they're able to make physical occurrences, I can make one happen to them too. The adrenaline almost makes me dizzy as I go in for the attack. I hear Ceresa say, "What in the world?"

I land on a grassy patch near a beach. It's so bright I'm blinded. As my eyes adjust, I look around. A bird trots up a stone stairway. I can feel its excitement. I can feel the grains of sands' love for one another as they cling to each other. A wave hits the beach, and the grains are separated; I feel their longing. I must be in the Other World. One second I had been barreling toward Matt and Ed. The next, I'm in a place I don't recognize even from any dream. I remember Camille mentioning adrenaline having to do with how she moved to this world. So did Matt and Ed take me or did I come of my own free will? I don't see them around, so I hope it was of my own accord. Maybe I'll get back faster because of that. I stand and brush off my costume.

As I begin to walk to the stairs, a bright light makes me shield my eyes. Then I hear his voice. As my eyes adjust again, I recognize the face that goes with the voice. It's my father. He is real. I run up and give him a hug. He hugs me back. I can't stop the tears from flowing down my cheeks. He's really here. I can feel him. He's hugging me back. Again, he smells of the aftershave he used in life.

"Father. So this is where you've been all these years."

"Yes. I've been here watching over you. You won't want to be climbing those stairs just yet."

I step back onto the grass. "Why? What's up there, Father?"

"That's Heaven. We're stuck in a middle world here."

"What? I don't understand any of this."

"Do you feel different than you did at home?"

"Well, everything is different here. I felt the sand grains' emotions." I also feel something different that I hadn't noticed before. I feel dizzy, like I'm about to have a fainting spell, but it isn't bad. It feels like that's the norm in this world. At home, this would feel strange. Here, I feel dizzy, but not bad."

"That's because we are on the Stranded Coil of a Nebula. You see our society is evolving. Some of us ahead of others. One day all of society will live in this world, and we'll all be a step closer to Heaven."

"What about the bad guys? They're here too. Do they get to go to Heaven?"

"I really don't have all of the answers as I'm still here and have not moved on. Since our DNA pulls more energy through the double helix, we have evolved ahead of others. We're within a part of space that will still exist when the Earth no longer does. Because of our DNA, we're able to travel from here to Earth and other places. That's also why you were able to sense shadows and perceptions unlike anyone else, just as I had."

"What? This is intense. There are other places?"

"Yes, but first I need to get you to a safe location. As you know, there are people here who would like to harm us."

"I thought you said you had it under control?"

"I'm sorry, Austria. Their numbers have grown, and I lost control, but we still have something on our side. Let's go to the safe place, and we can discuss it further."

"Okay, Father. What do we do? Do we travel here like on Earth or can we orb somewhere or something?"

He smiles as I say this and takes my hand. "Just walk like you would as if you were on Earth."

"Okay."

I take a step forward, and I swear the sun smiles at me. I take another step forward, and the flowers near the stairway begin to sing. I feel like I'm in a cartoon I saw as a child. I'm walking with my hand in my father's. I've dreamt of holding his hand for years. Is this real? Could it all just be a dream? I think. The wind blows my hair from my face, and I swear I can feel the elation it feels.

"I get to the safe place by thinking about your favorite hiding spot when you were a kid," my father tells me.

"Oh, the hexagon table we had, right?" I can see it perfectly in my head. I close my eyes and remember how I used to open the doors under the table and climb in to hide. When I open my eyes, I see our house in front of me. The blue shutter on the far-right window's still loose as it had been years ago. The daisies are still behind the birdbath to the left of the door. The sweet potato vine drapes over the flower bed to the right of the porch. The door's wide open, and the smell of home-baked cookies wafts out at us.

"Right," my father says with a smile.

HEAVEN

This can't be true. To have things like they used to be. It's what I've dreamt of for many years. Yet, something plagues my heart. My mother isn't here. My haunted house family isn't here. If it weren't for my father beside me, I'd feel as alone as I'd been in that room in the basement where my capturers planned to take my organs. I will enjoy this time with my father, but there are a few things I need to get straight.

"Father, are there others like you or are you all alone?"

"There are others. Come on inside."

We walk inside, and I see a dozen people in our old living room. I don't recognize anyone, but they all offer me warm smiles. An aura makes me feel at home. I follow the scent of cookies and, when I find their tray, I see a face I do recognize.

"Grandmother?"

"Yes, sugar bear, it's me. You didn't think your father got his special DNA from nowhere, did you?" She sets down the tray and gives me a bear hug. "Now eat one of these cookies before they get cold."

I hug her back and then take a cookie. I take a bite. They're delicious as the ones grandmother made me when she was living.

"So we can taste here too?"

"Of course, sugar bear. It's just more in your head now than actual senses. More like waking up memories and triggering your brain the same way they had," my grandmother informs me.

I don't know what to think of all of this, but it feels good, so I take a seat. Sitting on our couch with a pull-out bed as I have dozens of times before gives me comfort.

"We know this must be dreadfully frightening for you," a man I don't recognize states.

"I'm listening with open ears," I reply as I try to prove that I'm here for a purpose, although I'm not sure what that is. I would really like to just spend time with my father and grandmother, but something has to change. We can't continue to be attacked.

"Your grandmother is right. What you experience here is different. A flaw to our foes. You will be able to tell if we're lying or telling the truth as if it were written upon our foreheads," the man states.

"Well, that makes things easier than Earth. It always seems to be a game of poker in my world. You don't get to know others' emotions completely."

"True. I'll begin with history, as that's what I'm most knowledgeable about. I've been here for a long time. Our DNA began evolving as long as a hundred years ago. I'm sure you've guessed that, seeing your grandmother here."

I'm only able to nod; Grandma's definitely not a hundred, but if it began before her, who knows? I don't really want to interrupt this man. The information he is sharing's too valuable.

Fortunately, he continues. "Those with the different DNA also have psychological, physiological, and intellectual aptitudes."

"Well, given my father's Olympic experience and the healing capabilities, I presumed physiological aptitude was involved, but what's this about psychological and intellectual aptitudes?"

"You pick up quick. The psychological is part of the reason you're able to travel here and why your father can communicate with you between worlds. My theory is that with these mental exercises, one's brain grows, increasing intellectual aptitude. So it may not surprise you that, included in our different DNA species, were John Fitzgerald Kennedy, Martin Luther King Jr., and Ronald Reagan."

"Whoa, for real? I have something in common with those guys?"

"Yes you do, as do I. What I'm wondering is if you have put together that they were all either assassinated or experienced attempted assassination."

"Oh, well yeah, I guess so."

"The fight against us has gone on for a long time too."

My grandmother sits beside me and pats my leg. My father is on the arm of the couch and massages my shoulder as if to lighten the load I'm hearing. I hold my grandmother's hand with my right and place my left hand on my father's. "Go on," I say.

"The evil in your world believes that if they can make up the majority of this world, they can gain control. This world's population is much smaller than yours so it would be easier to control this one. When organs are transplanted from someone with our DNA into a normal human in your world, the DNA changes. So by transplanting organs they can move more of their own into this world."

"So that's the true purpose of the human trafficking ring. That's why they're targeting Camille, Jack, and me."

"What you say is true, and we do need to get you, Jack, and Camille prepared. But please let me finish."

"Of course."

"There's a weakness in those with the transplanted special DNA. The ones implanted with the organs aren't able to completely feel emotions here. They can't tell if we lie to them. And they also only get three visits here—"

My father squeezes my shoulder involuntarily. He coughs and interrupts the man, "I don't think we need to dive into that. Let's focus on what has to be done to stop these evil ones."

The man clears his throat and looks my father in his eyes. I feel a sense of apprehension. I know there's something they're withholding but don't know enough to know what it could be.

"Yes, we believe the best way to stop this from happening is to disband their medical research and discontinue the human trafficking," the man continues.

"How are we going to do that? My group has struggled just to keep from being captured and rescuing those of us who have been captured. We can't go to the authorities. Well, except for our restraining orders against Matt and Ed and the arrests made at my rescue. Don't we run the risk of bringing more unwanted attention if we ask for help? There have been bribes passed from our enemies to the authorities," I say.

"All very level-headed questions. We have to do something. They're getting too close. It also appears the ones we don't want to know about us already do, so I don't think we run the risk of bringing more attention to ourselves. That being said, it's still wise to keep this as quiet as we can," the man adds.

I push my fingers across my forehead and then squeeze them over the bridge of my nose. This is all so much to take in at once. My grandmother seems to sense my tension.

"Don't worry, sugar bear. We're going to be with you the entire time you're trying to work things out in your world. I'll even talk to you and give you advice the way your father has been. I was just afraid I'd scare you to death if I did before."

I smile at her. Grandmother always understood. When I was in trouble one day as a child for drawing on the walls, she came into my room when I was in timeout. She explained to me that most children do this when they're young. She said she believed it was just their creativity and understanding of the world blossoming. She also let me know that, unfortunately, doing this caused my parents extra work either by cleaning or having to buy paint. So as adults, we forget what it is to first learn such things and instead focus on the responsibilities at hand. She said as a grandparent looking back she can understand both sides. Finally, she said it would be best if I just tried to focus my creativity in areas that didn't damage my parents' property.

"Thank you, but I don't even know where to begin," I answer and squeeze my grandmother's hand.

"With the medical research. We need to locate anything that points to our DNA. We've already seen which facilities have the information from this world, so we can give you that. We need their research to be corrupted. The human trafficking ring needs legal intervention. We have the locations of the precincts that would be best. They're closest to the houses of internal organ theft. You just need to deliver evidence to their desk and have charges pressed to get the heat on the ones after us. That'll only last so long, though. We were hoping you could work with Bill. He seems to be involved in promoting street-friendly legislation. We would be ever grateful if he could help in this cause too," the man says.

My mind reels back to the street kids. They don't have a home, just as everyone here except me seems to not have an earthly body. This Other World reminds me somewhat of the street kids. Look at how they've all bonded together. I wonder if it's certain shared experiences that cause us to draw together, or if it's things inside of us that cause that. Thinking of the street kids also makes me recall how upset they are with me right now. I find myself massaging my hands out of old habit. It's what helped me when my blood thickened on Earth and what I did to Josh's hands when they tensed in anger. I remember how warm his hand had felt in mine, but that was before. Will I ever feel that warmth again? I wonder if Bill will be interested in helping me. Maybe I should ask Camille or Jack to approach him instead. I can handle the medical research with the assistance of Luke and Brittany. Even though I'm not wholly confident in this course of action, I'm glad to have a strategy.

"Thank you. It does feel good to have a game plan. This has been an excellent visit. Can I travel back and forth as need be?" I know I'm pushing the envelope here. My father had seemed quite frustrated when the man mentioned this topic with regard to the non-legit DNA individuals, but we don't have time to be withholding information. I mean, I've gone basically my whole teenage life thinking my father was lost to me forever. And here I sit next to him. I feel his hand on my shoulder, which has tightened once more. I smell aftershave. Anything's possible, right?

"Your visits must remain limited. We are only allowed so many," the man states.

My father stands, and his face is red with fury. "Enough. We don't need to worry her with this."

"Father, I have to know!" I say as I stand and now put my hand on his shoulder.

He looks at me with tears in his eyes. “I wish you didn’t have to go back. I’ve missed you so much.” He hugs me, and I feel like my heart will break all over again. “But you must live your life,. You must take me out of the equation when pondering your number of visits. Okay?”

“I love you.” Looking into his eyes, I could stay in this world forever. I have to blink several times to keep tears from seeping out of my eyes. I do have to get back to Earth because this is bigger than us. We’ll be with each other in the end when we walk the stairs. “Please, I have to know.”

“You can only come back and be able to return four times. The fifth visit for the true Altered Helixes is the final one. With your fifth visit, you won’t be able to return to your world as your body will have fully acclimated to this one. That’s also why you’re beginning to lose your ability to perceive things on Earth. You’re beginning to acclimate to this world already. I didn’t know that when I came here the fifth time. I wouldn’t have come. I’m sorry I missed your teenage years, baby.”

The air’s gone from my lungs. I suddenly feel dizzy, as though I could fall. I only get a few more visits with him. He had been taken away from me after all. He didn’t want to leave me ever. He loves me. The thought of limited visits triggers a memory from earlier in the conversation. Tension releases from my shoulders.

“Earlier you said the mutant Altered Helixes only get three visits. How many times have Matt and Ed visited?” I say as I try to keep a mischievous smile from my face.

“They’ve been here twice, but rid that from your head, Austria. You would waste a trip bringing them here for good,” my father answers.

“Would they cause the sides to become unbalanced here?” I ask.

"You'd be amazed what you can talk people into when you're able to read their thoughts and they're unable to read yours," the man who had been talking to me earlier states.

My father jabs him in the side playfully, but the look he gives the man clearly says to shut up.

MEMORIES

My father calls a wrap to the meeting. He and my grandmother have set up a dinner for just the three of us. Apparently they've been doing this for some time in hopes that I might one day visit. They've prepared the chicken, asparagus, and brown rice stir-fry that was one of my favorites growing up. Grandmother even has the cloth napkins in the Mickey Mouse rings I used to love. I can't help but feel like a child. If only I could rid myself of the adult worries pressing in on me.

"Remember going to Wonderscope? All three of us went one day when your mother had to work," my father asks, a smile tugging at his mouth.

"I do remember that. They had that room. It was dark, and you'd pose in front of the wall. A light would snap on and then the walls would glow except for where you had been. We played there forever, making puppet shapes with our hands and letter shapes with our bodies," I answer, surprised at how the preschool memories flood back to me.

"I remember you being in awe of the mock spaceship. You lit up at the mention of space. You asked about a hundred questions about how things worked." My father's leaning back in his chair, totally relaxed as he says this.

"You've always been a smart kid. Older children followed your moves in that dark room." The look of endearment my grandmother gives me makes me miss her more than I ever have. A thought strikes me. Grandmother actually did die, or at least I'd thought she had died shortly after Father.

"Grandmother, what happened to you?" I ask, hoping they won't try to hide more from me like they did during the group talk.

"I'd visited this world a few times before. Some of my visits had been with your father. He was in a hurry to try to find answers. He wanted to secure a safer world for you. It had not been so dangerous in my early days. The danger is greater, but we are armed with more intelligence now. Word hadn't gotten around about us then. Your father blames himself because part of what brought us attention was his success in the Olympics. I've told him over and over again that his success had nothing to do with it. Anyhow, I'm showing my age gabbing on like this. When your father made his final visit neither one of us knew that it would be his last. So many of us have tried to stay in your world. It has only been recently as we've witnessed the Stranded Coil becoming overpopulated with Mutated Altered Helixes that we realized our visits were limited. When your father didn't return, I knew something was amiss and travelled back here to see what it was. I quickly learned that I wouldn't be returning to your world either. Can't complain. There's nowhere I would rather be than here with my son."

"Oh. It's been a rough few years for Mother and me."

"Sorry honey," my father says. "We tried and tried to get back, but once you've reached your limit, there's no returning. Although I did figure out how to talk to you when you came of age by conversing with others here."

"So how do you travel back? I don't really want to go. I'm enjoying this time with you more than anything, but we do have to stop the others from overpopulating this world. I want to keep you safe and Mother and my haunted house family safe."

Now my father sits forward in his chair, the relaxation gone. I can see this is the conversation he dreaded, but I'll be back a few more times, and I'll be sure at least one is quality time. It almost feels like I'm not really going to be leaving him since we can still communicate in my world. Is there really more to life than the conversations we have together whether they be spoken, written, or in body language? It has always been what's set us apart from other species on Earth. It's why the technological age has grown so quickly. Instant conversation via texts to close contacts or to the masses via social media, we cling to it because it's part of our essential being.

"Are you sure you're ready? We could spend some more time here, honey. You could hang with Grams and I."

"Father, I have to stop the medical research and human trafficking. Plus how quickly does time pass in my world compared to this one?"

"Well, more time passes here than on Earth. So when you return it will seem to those in your world as if you've only been gone minutes. The Stranded Coil cause this world to somewhat pause in time like a black hole. Some of those here with scientific backgrounds say the time's speeding up with the population of the mutated helixes."

"Well, I guess I could wait a little bit."

They get up and gesture for me to follow. We walk out the back door and, to my amazement, the tire swing from my childhood still hangs from the oak tree just as on Earth. I run to it in glee. I climb in and smile at my father and grandmother. Their faces light up. My father pushes me until I reach a decent height. I lean back and begin pumping my legs. The warm breeze that washes over me makes me forget my worries. I could stay here in the shelter of my father and leave all my frets behind. Josh and half my haunted house family don't care about me anyway. Tiff would understand. She's had to hold me too many times as I sobbed over my father not being able to see me grow up. I could get a note to my mother so she would know what happened to me.

As I slow down, their faces wash through my thoughts. Little Jack and Lea. They'd be torn apart if Jack were seized by the human traffickers. Emmitt, Brittany, and Landon would lose their apartment and be heartbroken if Camille were taken. Tiff, my best friend, is like a sister. If I don't return, she'll crumble like I did when I lost my father. My mother would do everything within her power to get to me, including putting herself in danger. Luke, Ceresa, Ethan, and Patrice have become family to me. They might be mad at me, but I have to believe they'll forgive me. Just the thought of Josh makes my heart skip a beat, and I drop from the tire swing. Could he forgive me? I have to give it a shot.

Thankfully, my grandmother and father both seem to comprehend the thoughts going through my head. They give me a hug and then each take one of my hands. Then they take each other's hands, forming a circle.

"You have to relax and slow your breathing," my grandmother says. Her voice soothes me into a serene state. Then memories flood back of how I'd done this on my own when I first saw the shadows at the haunted house, calming myself down with breathing and other techniques. Had I been escaping travelling to this world by calming my reactions down before? When had I stopped doing that? Once my father began visiting me? When I realized he was one of the shadows? Is that why I'd been able to see Matt and Ed, or had they visited me the way my father had? Is that why I'd finally been able to allow adrenaline to take over and travel here? There are so many questions.

I must calm down in order to travel back. "Remember how Mother always makes home-made chicken noodle soup whenever one of us is sick?" I ask my father and grandmother.

They both look at me and smile. They squeeze my hands. Mother always has a way of making me feel safe. Then I remember Josh offering to make me tea. I begin to swirl or at least that's what it feels like. It reminds me of Dorothy's flight to Oz, except this one is full of happy memories. Maybe this is like her flight back to Kansas. "There's no place like home," I whisper and open my eyes.

##

"Whoa. Now that there is just trippy." It sounds like Ceresa's voice.

"Where, where am I?" I ask as I blink my eyes against the bright lights.

"You're in the inventory room. We closed the haunted house early, kid. Jack needed to rest, and you'd disappeared. We couldn't go on without you two," Bill informs me.

"What happened?" Tiff's sitting at my hips as I lie on the floor of the inventory room.

"I, well, do I have to explain here?"

"Yes." I hadn't noticed Josh sitting on my left side. He looks deeply disturbed. I wonder what he thinks.

"I'm so sorry, Josh. I really didn't mean to not claim you as my boyfriend at the restaurant. Things were just so awkward. I didn't handle myself the way I wanted to. Please forgive me." His face looks stunned as if he hadn't seen this coming.

"Oh, who cares about that? Even new street kids themselves get tongue-tied trying to explain their fresh bonds to old ones. Plus, Josh was trying to find a way to protect you. His acting upset was a hoax in order to achieve separation from you so he could get a plan together behind your back," Ceresa pats my shoulder in reassurance. "What in the hell were you doing? First you saved Jack from being hung. I'm still uncertain as to how that happened. Then you were yelling at nothing. When you tried to tackle that same nothing, you vanished in thin air. I've seen a lot of creepy things in my time, but that beats them all."

"I travelled to the Other World," I whisper as I look around to ascertain my audience. Josh is to the left, near my face, with Ethan and Patrice behind him. Ceresa's to my right with Landon and Brittany behind her. Luke and Tiff are by my hips on either side. Jack and Lea are at my left foot. Jack looks tired, but he also has a look of awe. Camille and Emmitt are at my right foot, and Camille's jaw has dropped. I take another look at Josh and smile. So he wasn't upset with me; it had all been a setup so he could protect me.

"So you figured out how to travel there on your own?" Camille asks.

That's when Bill interrupts. I'd forgotten about him standing behind my head. "What on Earth are you kids talking about?"

ADAPTION

I begin explaining the Other World. Bill knows about the different DNA and that Camille disappeared. When I tell them about my visit with my father and grandmother, everyone's face is focused on mine.

"You were right about the blinding light, Camille. I wasn't even able to adjust my eyes when my father first appeared. Did you visit any places from your past?"

"I was too freaked out. Maybe since I don't have relatives there, I don't have any old places there either. Plus, I could only concentrate on your father's explanation of how to return."

"It does help having people you care about there, but I believe that world feeds off of your memories and emotions and produces what you want a little too."

The faces around me help me recollect what I want. I need them to be safe. Jack, my pseudo little brother, cannot live his life in fear. Camille, the one who's spoken to my father, can't run forever. I have to get a plan into action.

"My grandmother and father shared some vital information." Everyone had brought chairs and boxes over to sit around me while I talk. Josh brings me a chair and helps me into it. I grab his hand and hold it firmly. I need him now more than ever. I see Bill has taken out a notebook and pen.

"The ones after the different DNA are primarily two groups. They have people in the human trafficking industry that we're well aware of. They also have people in medical research. When an organ from a body with different

DNA is implanted into a regular (normal DNA) host, the host's DNA is changed too, but not completely. For example, Ed and Matt were not born with different DNA; they only have Mutated Altered Helixes. They're only able to travel to the Other World three times. On their third visit, they're stuck there and cannot return to our world."

"Wait, what? So how many times can we travel and why is it limited?" a worried Camille asks.

"We can travel five times, but our fifth is our last as our bodies fully acclimate to that world."

"Whoa," Jack comments.

"And how many times have Matt and Ed travelled?" Ceresa asks with a smirk upon her face.

"They've travelled to the Other World twice. Their next travel will be their last."

"Nice," Ceresa says.

"Do your grandmother and father have a plan for how to deal with the human trafficking and medical research?" Bill wisely asks. I'm grateful as he helps me stay on track. The enthusiasm in Ceresa's questions about Matt and Ed had diverted my attention.

"Yes, Bill, with the help of their group in the Other World, there's a plan. We need to corrupt the medical research. We can prohibit the medical research and human trafficking by having legislation put into place. Bill, I'm going to need your help with that. Corrupting the research will keep it from growing after it's been stopped. We want it to appear that the findings of different DNA were a mistake, so no other scientists are drawn to research it. We also need to bring charges against the human trafficking. We have the charges from our abductions and restraining orders, but it would be good to get more of their group behind bars. I'd like to have more damaging evidence when we do."

"What do you mean you need Bill's help with legislation? Don't we have enough to worry about with the homes for children bills we're trying to have passed?" Ceresa asks, letting out a sigh of disappointment.

"The bills you have in action for the homes for children will pass with ease with the help of my father and grandmother. You'd be surprised at how persuasive a spirit from another world can be to a politician. They just need you to draft the bills."

"Interesting. I'll have to see what I can do. I wish I could discuss it with your father and grandmother," Bill responds.

"How do you plan on corrupting the medical research?" Luke asks. With his medical schooling, it seems this topic has piqued his interest.

"We know the locations of the medical research involved with studies of the different DNA. One being Dr. Shipley, who informed the human traffickers of both Jack's and my different DNA. I'm still not entirely sure how they know about yours. Camille. What doctor do you go to?"

"I see Dr. Pike, but I've seen him since I was a kid. He's a sweet old man. I don't think he'd be involved in something like this," Camille says.

"You're probably right, but let's take a look just in case. We should probably have a look at the blood donation center too," I say.

"Do you mind if I take a sample of your blood to study so I can see what will be in the medical research we're looking for?" Luke's mindset is already as if he were wearing scrubs.

Uh, another vial. "Sure, no problem." Have to do what I have to do.

"Thank you. I have an idea of how to corrupt the research. You said Dr. Shipley mentioned the 95% of DNA that used to be viewed as meaningless, right?"

"Yes." Hope sparks within me. I'm so glad we have Luke on board and that he isn't as self-serving as his fraternity counterparts, Matt and Ed.

"Much of the DNA being tested now is showing marks and signs of diseases such as cancer. If I can manipulate the different DNA to mirror this, the research will be thrown into disease studies. There's so much data on that, it should be hidden within piles of other research. And, if it's found, I can also show foreign matter within the findings, rendering them for the most part useless. We can't just delete them completely because that would be easily detected."

"That sounds perfect, Luke," Tiff says as she grabs his arm and holds it.

"So it seems we have a plan for the medical research. Now, how do you plan on getting more evidence against the human traffickers?" Bill asks.

Josh's hand tightens on mine as Bill finishes.

"My father and grandmother have those locations too, but we can't really go into police headquarters claiming we know the locations because some spirits told us, now can we? I'd like to have surveillance set up at the locations. I think if we can get photographs of those involved at the sites and evidence of human trafficking activity, we can get most of these places shut down and the perpetrators behind bars. I'd like to make these reports at the same time as we corrupt the medical research, so we'll have to work quickly."

"There has to be a head. I mean all groups like this have leaders, don't they? We should find out who that is and present evidence that incriminates them," Ethan adds. I find myself smiling at his sharp thinking.

Josh stands then, letting go of my hand. "No, we're putting ourselves in way too much danger. How are we to stop a group that's been at this for years? Austria, get that smile off your face. You will most definitely not be involved. What do you intend to do? Walk up to the head-person's house and ask for a fingerprint?"

"I don't want anyone in danger, Josh. We'll find a way to collect evidence without them knowing we're doing so," I say and put my hands around his head and begin peck kissing him all over his face. "Please?" I repeat over and over with each kiss.

He grabs me and tries to push me away, but I jump up on him so that if he doesn't catch me, we'll both fall. As he holds me, I feel like everything is going to be okay. I kiss him one last time. "Everything's going to be fine, Josh."

He shakes his head and then kisses me back.

"Get a room, you two," Ceresa complains.

HEIST

Luke looks ridiculous in his costume of camouflage. He has black and green makeup all over his face. His white teeth stand out when he smiles at me. Josh looks just as ridiculous. His eyes are even more prominent now, like an owl in the dark. Tiff has dark pants, a dark long-sleeve shirt, and dark gloves on. We all look like we're getting ready to rob a bank. Brittany has her dirty blonde hair hidden beneath a dark green stocking cap. We're getting ready to go to the first location of medical research. I'm excited to finally be making an offensive move, rather than just defending.

As we park a block away from the medical building, I look out to make sure we haven't been seen. We appear to be undetected. We're close to the alley that leads up to the building. As we enter the alley, a shadow flies by me. Great, right now I don't know if the shadow is from a good or bad helix, but I'm sure it's one. If it were my father, wouldn't he talk to me? I'm going to have to be very careful as we go about this venture.

Josh picks the lock like a pro. Guess when you're stuck between living on the streets and finding a place to stay warm, you acquire a few talents. Luke enters first, shining a flashlight around to see if there are any occupants. Tiff follows him when he gives us a thumbs-up, meaning it's all clear. Josh gestures for Brittany to follow them and then grabs my hand as we bring up the rear. Luke's entering the code into the alarm system my father had seen while spying as a shadow. I'm filled with relief when it's inactivated. He then goes to the computer. We have the login information from my father too. My father had informed us the software used is from Descry, a large local global supplier of healthcare information technology. Luke has trained on this exact technology at medical school.

Ironic that the software we're using is called the Helix Flat File. As Luke begins manipulating the data to make it look like disease research, he tells us where the specimens are stored. Tiff stays with Luke as Brittany, Josh, and I go to the specified refrigerated storage. We each have multiple needles to stick through the rubber stoppers and insert the foreign data. It seems like an hour has passed by the time we're done. I'm anxious to get out of here. Josh blinks his own flashlight in Luke's direction three times to let him know our part of the mission is complete. Luke will now add the foreign data findings to the Altered Helix disease research data. He blinks his flashlight three times at us to let us know he's finished.

Luke keeps his flashlight pointed toward us as we make our way back to Tiff and him.

"Whoa, I found something interesting I think we can use," Luke exclaims as we make our way.

We're almost to them when I see the shadow dart by. I become overwhelmed with a feeling of anger. Brittany's in front of me and Josh behind me. That's when I notice Matt and Ed's features behind the metal filing cabinet. They're not hazy this time. They're here in real life. How did they know where to find us and when? I gasp a breath in. Who was the shadow then? Was someone from the Other World trying to warn us? Josh must've seen my reaction and that I'm looking directly above the cabinet. He must see Matt and Ed because he pushes me and Brittany out of harm's way just as I see Matt and Ed push the cabinet. It catches Josh on the shoulder and takes him down. His arm is caught under it. I take one look at him. Luke's already removing the cabinet. He must have started heading our direction before the push. I wonder if he saw Matt and Ed too. I'm a little surprised they didn't go after him. Why would they want to harm my body? The game's changing. They must have found more Altered Helixes than I'd thought for my body to be so useless. They know I'm coming after them. Yes, the game certainly has changed.

"Are you okay?" I ask Josh.

"Yes, but Austria…" Josh pleads.

I don't wait for him to continue. I'm attacking Matt and Ed before another word can come out. Ceresa will be pleased when she hears that I'm taking them to the Other World for good.

As the adrenaline rushes through my veins, I make sure to grab both of their arms. They try to escape my grip, but I just let my fingernails dig deeper into their skin. I focus on the image of Josh caught beneath the cabinet as I let the adrenaline take over. This time, when I land on the grassy patch near the ocean, I'm tangled with Matt and Ed. Matt punches me in the side. Ouch, I had hoped I wouldn't feel pain here. I wonder if I actually do or if it's just a psychological reaction. Ed kicks me off him.

I'm about to kick and punch back when Matt and Ed are taken away by many hands. My father, the man who spoke so much at my house in this world last time, and a couple of somewhat familiar guys have restrained Matt and Ed.

“Take them to the barn. These here are our captives. Maybe if they share some information with us, they can go free,” the man who spoke to me at the house says.

“Yeah, right, like we’re going to tell you anything,” exclaims Matt.

One of the somewhat familiar guys punches him right in the belly. “I think we should gut them like they’ve done to some of us.”

“No more talking. Just have them restrained at the barn and set up guard duty,” my father interjects.

I rub my side and stare at them as they’re carted off. Something feels wrong, like we’re now the bad guys. I guess we can get good intelligence from them, but as much as I dislike the pair, my stomach twists at the thought of them being gutted. I know they wouldn’t hesitate to do that to me, but I don’t want to stoop to their level.

Once they’re out of sight, my father approaches me. “You okay, kid?”

“Yeah, I’m fine.”

He must’ve noticed the look of reproach I had as Matt and Ed were hauled off. “You know they’re not really going to gut them. Matt and Ed just can’t tell a lie here, so we’re going to be able to get information out of them without harming them. Plus as you now see, even what seems like physical action does no harm.”

My pain seems to disappear just as he says the words. It must truly be a psychological reaction.

“Is Josh okay? I have to get back. I have no clue what’s going on down there. They pushed a cabinet on him.”

“He’s fine. Your team has done marvelously. You all successfully took down one medical research location. The other team, with what’s his name, Ethan I think, found the other human trafficking site. They’re working on getting more surveillance as we speak. Today I was able to help the homes for children legislation move forward. Bill and Ceresa are on board with helping impose laws against our enemies now. The day has been good."

"Oh, wow." I walk over to my father and give him a hug. There has been so much going on. Before I know it, he's carrying me, and he's walking. When we make it to the house, he lays me on the couch and covers me with a blanket. I fall asleep to him kissing my forehead.

Dreams in this world are different. Memories spin into premonitions and hopes spin into recollections. I see my father walking with me on his shoulders as we head to the Liberty Memorial; then he's being chased, and I'm nowhere in sight. I watch from behind a hedge. He must have hidden me to protect me, but to watch him being taken away from me is worse. I take a step to run after his pursuers when a hand touches my shoulder. I look to see who the hand belongs to and find my grandmother.

"You have to let him go, child. All he wants is for you to have a life. You'll understand one day when you have children of your own. It's harder for me to stay here, trust me, but he asked for one last favor before I go. That was to protect you, and I mean to do so."

"I don't understand." My body trembles as I respond.

"There, there. It's going to be fine."

I wake and look around. My father sits safely in the recliner next to me. That was so weird—it felt real. I know our thoughts are different in this world. Was my grandmother trying to send me a message of some sort? If so, I have to stop whatever it is that will cause my father to put himself in danger before it happens.

"You all rested up, kid?" my father asks me. His hair is all askew from sleep. He looks older, as if the stress of everything going on has aged him. I wonder if people age in this world. If it weren't for the bags below his eyes, I'd swear he had not aged a day since I last saw him alive in my world.

"Yeah I slept, but I still feel anxious. Are you guys going to be okay here while we work in my world? Will they come after you knowing you have Matt and Ed?"

"No need to worry. Matt and Ed are pretty low in their chain of command. I don't really see much action being taken."

"Are you sure? I thought their parents were involved in the human trafficking and have financial pull on Earth. It's not like you have police and hospitals you can go to here."

"We have each other, the Altered Helixes, and that's enough."

"Okay, so what's the plan now?"

"I think it's best to continue with the original plan. You have to get back, honey."

"I know, but I've been here two times now. I only have two more visits until my final one."

"I'll always be with you. I'll always look after you." A shiver causes my joints to jerk as he says this. He knows. He knows he's going to be in danger, and he wants me away from him, so I don't have to see it. He's preparing me. What can I do though? I have to keep the others safe.

"So what will you do here while we're working down there? You already have helped with the homes for children laws and now have Matt and Ed in custody."

"We're going to continue to run interference in case any of you get into trouble during your missions."

"Won't that put you in jeopardy?"

"We've been here watching them for years. We have a plan. Now you need to return before you worry everyone back home."

He's avoiding my questions. What can I do? I can't force it out of him. He's probably already aware that I'm feeling things out. I'll just have to think on it and hope to come up with something before it's too late.

"Okay, can I swing on the tire again?"

He smiles and musses my hair. When he stands, so do I. His broad shoulders seem to carry the weight of the world. He smiles as he gets the swing started. That smile makes memories rush through my head as I pump my legs.

CRASH

I wake in my own bed. Josh is lying next to me, cradling a pillow as if it can fill the emptiness. In the moonlight from the window, I see how puffy the skin around his eyes is. My eyes widen as I see what's propped on the pillow. His arm is in a blue cast. Everyone has signed it. I climb out of my bed to grab a sharpie from my desk. "To my love, I vow always to protect you from this or any world. –Austria." He begins to stir as I put the cap back on the marker. His eyes flutter as they adjust to the darkness.

"Who are you? What do you want?" His muscles are flexed, and he's searching for an object. I have to speak before he finds one and hits me over the head with it.

"Josh, it's me. You're safe." I hate that they've caused fear to invade his life again.

"How did you get here? Did you take Matt and Ed to the Other World?"

"I got back the same as last time. I'm not sure why I'm here, but I think it must have been because I had just awoken there. Yes, Matt and Ed will not be returning to this world."

His breathing slows, and I can see his muscles relax again. "That's good. I don't mind never having to see those two again."

"Are you okay? Is anything else besides your arm hurt?" I touch his cast and have to roll my shoulders to release the tension.

"Na, just the arm. I have a couple scrapes and bruises, but they're nothing."

"Were we successful with the medical research facility? It had seemed as though we were, but I remember Luke saying he'd found something interesting. What was it?"

"Let's wake up Luke and Tiff and discuss it together. Part of my memory of that trip seems to be incomplete. I think I suffered a minor concussion when the filing cabinet fell on me."

Those jerks caused him another concussion. Now part of me hopes my father's group *will* gut them. Who am I kidding, the very thought of that upsets my entire being.

"Oh, Josh, I'm so sorry. Are you going to be okay?"

"Yeah, nothing I haven't been through before. Please don't worry about it."

"Okay. What time is it?" I move in to give him a hug. It's awkward with the cast but warm at the same time.

"It's seven in the morning. They'll be up soon enough. Can we hang out here, just the two of us for a while?"

We lay down side by side with the cast propped on my hip. I've always gotten lost looking into his eyes. I find myself losing time and worry. He smiles at me with his beautiful smile and eyelashes touching his cheeks. Then his emotions seem to shift as he reads his cast.

"From this world or ANY world…really, Austria. I don't want you going back to the Other World. What if they figure out how many visits you have left and just take you without your consent, and you end up stuck there?"

"I will only go for important reasons. It's nice to see my father, but he wants me to live a normal life. Plus, now we don't have to worry about Matt and Ed."

"But aren't they able to cause physical things to happen here while they're in that world?"

"Yes, but not when they're in my father's custody."

"Whoa. Okay, but please be careful."

"Okay."

We kiss, and the seconds fly by. I wish I could just spend eternity in this electrical outburst. It feels as though my heart will explode through my chest. I grab his shirt. He runs his fingers through my hair. I hear footsteps approaching the door.

"Josh, are you okay? I thought I heard voices in there," Tiff asks from outside the door.

Shoot, the kiss has to end.

"I'm fine, Tiff. Austria's back."

She's opening the door before we can move out of our embrace. She jumps on the bed and grabs me. I see an agonizing look cross Josh's face as she lands. The arm must give him worse pain than he let on. She's hugging me from behind, and I can feel her smile through her cheek on the side of my head.

"I knew you'd come back."

"What? Did some people believe I wouldn't?"

"Well, I know how much you've missed your father. We always wonder if you won't stay there with him sometime."

"And miss out on all the fun here? Never."

I hug her back with my arm behind me.

Luke enters but seems disoriented. "I need some coffee. I don't know how you girls just pop out of bed full of energy."

Tiff gets up and wraps her arms around him. "And I don't know how you pull all-nighters studying for med school."

"I'll get the pot brewing," I say.

I get up and throw on a robe. I'm not sure how I got into my pajamas as I went into the Other World fully clothed. Josh slowly gets out of bed and holds my hand with his good arm.

"I'll help," he says, though I'm not sure how much help he can be with only one arm working. Not that I'm going to turn him down. I want to spend as much time with him as I can.

I scoop coffee as he one-handedly puts the filter in its place. The aroma as it brews awakens my memory of our strategy. I need to know everything that's happened and what our next steps should be. What methods need revising or reorganizing? If they knew we'd be at the medical research facility, how much more of our blueprint do they have? Did the others encounter interference like we did?

"So, Luke, before I disappeared I remember you saying that you'd found something interesting. What was it?"

He sits down, and I hand him a mug of coffee. He takes a sip before answering. "Yes, I did. We were successful in changing and corrupting the research, but I also stumbled upon some research I wasn't expecting to find. Apparently, they don't want their enemies to be interested in stealing their organs. Kind of ironic since they're so interested in stealing others' organs. They implanted organs from a copycat DNA individual into a test host. They probably kidnapped both of these individuals to be used in the research like lab rats. Anyway, the implanted organs altered DNA again. So, as a defense maneuver, they're developing a serum to protect themselves. Unfortunately for them, so far the serum is only effective on natural-born Altered Helixes."

"Whoa. Nice find. So does that mean Camille, Jack, and I could take this serum, and our organs would become useless to them?"

"That's precisely what it means. Pretty nice for them to do all that work for us. I need to conduct research to see how they would know you've been injected with the serum. Not really useful to us if they still take your organs and they fail on the implanted subject. I need to see if tests have to be run for them to see, or if there's another indicator. They had to have set something up to deter their enemies."

"Or maybe they just want to keep their enemies out of the Other World so they can rule. Whatever you do, be sure to take precautions," I say.

This new development is key. We may not have to target human trafficking through legislation and surveillance if they no longer have reason to steal our organs. A thought comes to mind. They do all of their research via the Helix Flat File. If we could update the data to show we've been vaccinated by the serum, maybe that would stop them from targeting us. I see the problem with this course of action immediately. Once we update the file with this data, they will know. They will surely know that we're tampering with their work. They'll know we are administering the serum to natural born Altered Helixes. This could work, but we'll have to wait to update the file until our mission's complete. We still need the legislation, medical research corruption, and surveillance until we've administered all the serum we can.

"There's one thing I would like to do before we continue on our missions," Josh says and then calmly sips his coffee while sitting at the table. He looks at Luke and Tiff, and I instantly feel the tension. What now?

"Yes, Josh, what is it?" I ask.

"I want you and Jack to learn some self-defense like Camille. She was able to elbow that man who tried to chloroform her. If there are forms of defense to be learned in the Other World, I would like you all to learn those too. Even though I'd rather you never go back there."

"I can do that. Cheer up, Josh. We're working to bring this all to an end."

He takes another sip and looks at Luke and Tiff. He then stares at the table like there's a whole book written on it. What's going on?

ELABORATION

At the haunted house, Ethan informs us of their success at the human trafficking location.

So far, we've been quite successful. We're sure to be triumphant if everything else goes this smoothly, but I have a foreboding feeling that a bad experience is lurking around the corner.

"The surveillance was boring at first. Just sitting in a car waiting for action to happen. They actually brought in an Altered Helix while we were there. This couldn't be a coincidence. They must be bringing in people daily. Anyway, we called the cops anonymously from the untraceable TracFone and then removed the battery and SIM card. We were down the street when the cops arrived and saw them remove multiple people in handcuffs. Unfortunately, we also saw a gurney roll out with a black bag on top. There had to be a body inside."

Well, at least more of them are detained. The thought of the body inside the black bag makes my blood thicken, and my hands and feet begin to tingle. I have to figure out why my Altered Helix also causes these side effects. Self-defense training will be no good if I die of a heart attack in the heat of the moment. I wonder if it's part of the acclimation process. I'm glad Ethan was smart enough to remove the battery from the phone. Since the cops have been receiving payoffs from our enemies, they could track us through e-911 searches. I'm upset that Ethan was unable to find the leader of that location. Did he even try?

"So who was the leader?" I ask, not particularly hiding my irritation but also not wanting to cause a confrontation.

"We didn't get that. We were hoping to save the person they had, but I guess we were too late for that."

"They're going to know we're tailing them with the call in," I say.

"Oh, lay off, Austria. We have more of them detained," Patrice says as she coddles Ethan.

I'm furious, but I can't turn them against me now. I'm tired of having to prove myself to people. Having to make them be on my side. Do they not understand how vital this is?

Camille answers as if she can read my thoughts. "We did get bugs on those detained. We've been recording their conversations."

"You what? How in the world? Do I even want to know?"

"It just so happens a buddy of ours is a prison employee. He's responsible for checking in inmates," Camille speaks again.

"And how does that help us?" I ask.

"He hid microscopic bugs I preemptively provided him on their clothes."

"You what? How does that work?"

"Well, these will only work until the clothes are washed, but they'll pick up all of the phone calls made within the first twenty-four hours. I think we have the leader you're looking for."

She pulls out her smartphone and opens an app I'm unfamiliar with. When the audio begins, I'm taken aback by the blatant name usage and detail given. I would think they'd be more cautious when making a phone call from jail. Wouldn't the police be scanning those? Oh wait, the payoffs. There must be payoffs to prison guards and employees as well. So this must not be the first time they've been caught in action. Maybe I had been wrong to assume they would think it was us.

"That's great, guys. I'm sorry I was upset earlier. You guys deserve props for doing what you did."

"Did you hear who they named as the lead person?" Patrice asks with a look of astonishment.

I'm really surprised that anything I do can astonish her at this point. She must have taken my questioning more personally than I realized.

"Yes, Patrice, I heard. It just doesn't come as too much of a shock for me is all. I really should have seen it before. I'm pretty upset with myself for that," I say as I wonder why my strong Perceptions didn't give me more of a clue.

"So you're saying that you believe Adam, the Edge of Hell owner and the one revitalizing abandoned buildings, is the leader?" Bill asks from the other side of the room. I can see by his expression that he's taken aback. Of course, he didn't want to work alongside Adam because of the drug usage, but I don't think he'd ever considered his one-time friend to be going down the road of leading a ring involved with the organ theft in this area.

"Don't take it personally, Bill. The group doing this is trying to get complete control of the Other World. They're more influential and threatening than we give them credit for," I say, trying to soothe his hurt ego. I mean, this guy has been his friend for years.

"Thanks, Austria." I see his recoiling even though no one else does. He's going to distance himself from us. We've pushed him to his limit. He's not going to be able to believe all of this if it means accepting that someone who was once almost a brother to him is the worst villain alive. I have to get him off this train of thought. We still need him to get the legislation against human trafficking rolling.

"Bill, you've housed those without homes for years. They're your family. I believe the Altered Helixes among them are the ones in greatest danger. I mean, most of them don't have contacts that will readily notice them missing, so this group runs less risk kidnapping them and taking their organs than they do with individuals who have a residence and steady way of living."

"Really, you still gotta throw your biases up in the air," Ceresa claims.

"These are not biases. It's a fact that a person without a home can go missing and be much more likely to never be searched for than an individual living with a family of five or a businesswoman with meetings filling her day."

"Whatever. The street family is a close-knit group. We all know each other and everyone's habits. I think some of you people with homes become more solitary than us."

"Okay. Well, either way, we can't just start administering the serum. When we do administer the serum, we're going to be broadcasting that it has been done so our enemies will lose the desire to kidnap Altered Helixes. We won't be able to administer it to every Altered Helix at the same time. We need to continue with the legislation, medical research corruption, and surveillance until we've administered as much serum as we can."

"We'll work on the legislation. It's all I can do to make up for the fact that Adam is involved. I should've stayed in better touch with him. Ceresa, I know you're upset about this taking away attention from helping the street kids, but Austria's father really got our legislation for the homes for children going. You owe them too. And, biases aside, without shelter, those without homes are vulnerable. This has to be stopped."

"Thanks, Bill," I exclaim.

"Yeah, yeah. Fine, I'm in." Ceresa pouts.

"Camille, where did you learn self-defense?" Josh asks.

"Just down the street. Some of my college buddies started a gym solely focused on it. Emmitt and Landon have helped me and Brittany train. You don't want to be sleeping on the streets defenseless."

"I think we all could use some training before going out again," Josh says as he tilts his head sideways and looks at me.

"Can I train with Josh first? I want to learn how hard to jab my elbow into his side if he grabs me." I put my arms around his neck and smile.

"This is serious. We all need this training. We're diving deeper into danger. All of us need to be prepared and take precautions." Josh puts his forehead against mine and holds my forearm.

TRAINING

It is not fun being punched in the face. I feel as though this feud is being way overdone, but in order to best prepare to defend ourselves when necessary, Emmitt claims this is imperative. I don't care if it's by a glove padded fist. It is painful. I thought self-defense training was going to be different than this. Emmitt hits me again. I guess I was paired with him because of my height, but he's more built than I'll ever be. This is unfair. Wait, I see an opening. Every time he punches me, he leans to the left first. This time when he leans, I move in the same direction he does. He thinks he's going to knock me out this time, but I quickly lean the other way and jab him in the ribs.

"Ouch." He holds his side. "Good job, Austria, you're now seeing weak spots in your opponent rather than focusing on just protecting yourself. We do need to work on that, though."

"Can we work on it without you punching me in the face?"

"Yeah, everybody head over to the red mats," Emmitt announces to us all.

Jack's face looks swollen. Landon isn't much bigger than him, but he's had much more fighting experience. I don't even want to see what my face looks like. Jack looks frustrated and furious. I feel the same. On the red mats are wood planks balanced on cinderblocks.

"What are these for? Don't we have enough injuries for one day?" I ask.

"You'll be amazed at what we can do with these," Camille says. "Have either of you tested your strength since you found out you had different DNA? I used to think I could break these because I'd practiced, but now I'm not so sure. Let's see how you do."

Jack and I look at each other and nod our heads side to side. They can't be serious. We're going to break our hands.

"Once you witness your own strength, I bet your fighting will change too," Landon inputs.

Jack and I each stand in front of a set of wooden planks. I take a deep breath in and try to focus. Landon stands on the other side of my planks in front of me. He shows me the stance I need to take and the way I should strike. I try to mimic him with a practice swing.

"Are you in pain?" Landon asks me.

"What do you think?" I say with a snarl.

"Use that anger to break the planks. Imagine the wood is Emmitt's face."

"Man, I heard that," Emmitt exclaims.

"Go back to training, Jack," Landon replies.

I think about the shock of Emmitt's first punch. I think about the scar on my abdomen. I think about my father being forced to be away from me too early. Dots begin to circle my vision of the wood. I breathe in again. I can see the grain of the wood very clearly. I can smell the pine. I squeeze my eyes shut in fear of splinters and use all the force I can to send my fist into the wood. I hope I don't break a bone. A flash of light seems to gleam from the wood as I hit it. As I stand from the squat I went into while hitting the wood, I see in the mirror behind Landon what I did. I can't believe it. Waves of emotion rush through me. I can do this. I am strong. I just broke three wood planks with my fist. I look down at my knuckles to see if there's blood. Landon puts his hand on my shoulder. I look up at him, and I can tell he's talking, but I don't hear a thing. I smile, walk to the bench, and sit down.

That's when I look at Jack. He has just broken three planks too. His eyes are huge. He looks up at me, and I pat the bench next to me. Emmitt, Landon, Camille, and Josh are all staring at the wooden splinters on the floor in amazement.

"Guess, I'm not the only Hercules around here now, huh," Camille says as she nudges Emmitt and smiles. My hearing has returned.

Jack still hasn't said a word. He keeps inspecting his hands as if he's going to find something different.

"What was that?" he asks me.

"I don't know. I've never done anything like that before, but there has been all this talk about how this DNA is supposed to make us stronger and able to heal faster. My father was an Olympian. I guess I just never really believed it would happen to me."

"I know what you mean," he replies.

"Well, let's go see what else we can do."

We both stand and return to the group. They all look at us like we're different people than we were five minutes ago.

"Quit looking at me like that, Josh, or I'll begin self-defense lessons on you." I playfully pinch his side.

"Uh, just surprised is all. I've never been against a woman who topped me." He puts his arm around me.

"Ha, ha." I nudge him away and begin bouncing from one foot to the other with my fists up like a boxer.

"Austria, put 'em down," he says.

"Make me," I reply.

"Seriously, I want you to practice defense moves some more."

"All right, all right."

I stand still. He grabs me from behind. I mock elbow him in the ribs like Camille taught me. I'm afraid that I could do some damage with a real hit. He's already in a cast. Then I mock step on his foot as I turn away and flee.

"Good. Now, Jack, try the handhold move Austria taught you."

Josh grabs Jack's wrist with his good hand. Jack twists his wrist so that his thumb points between where Josh's thumb and forefinger meet. Jack then pulls his wrist out of the hold.

"Nice, Jack," I say.

"Last, I want to see you three make 100 more hits on the most vulnerable parts of the body on the dummies, and then we'll be done. Bring it on and don't hold back. We should practice this every other day for a while so it's ingrained in your thought processes," Emmitt says.

"Really?" I don't continue because the look Josh gives me renders me speechless. We have so much to do as it is. To stop the bad guys and keep each other safe. Do we really have time to be punching dummies? I can see Josh isn't going to back down on this. My voice returns but sounds squeaky like a mouse. "Never mind."

"Austria, you three have to do this in order for us to be able to operate and not worry about you all the time. You also need to train Jack and Camille how to get to the Other World and back. You're not going to be able to make all the trips yourself."

"But, I've already been there two times, Josh. If I take them there to learn, I'll only have one more free trip there."

"This will be your last trip there. I can't risk losing you."

"What? But, Josh?"

"No, this is the last time."

"Fine," I say as I begin my hundred punches. When I'm done, I stalk off to the showers.

My father and I can talk while he's in the Other World and I'm here, but I have yet to learn how to summon him. I would like to know that before I'm unable to return to his world. I like how Josh cares for me enough to want to protect me, but I also can't help feeling a little suffocated when he tells me my next visit is going to be my last. There's got to be a way to figure things out. I have to make sure to spend some quality time with Father and Grandmother this next trip. Maybe we could make the training a weeklong event. It wouldn't be that much time here. I also need to remind Josh that I don't like people trying to control me. I thought I'd made that clear by making the first move.

NAVIGATION

"Okay, so now I need you to rush after it full of anger."

"What? We already exerted ourselves physically with self-defense training," Camille huffs.

"Yeah, I can't get angry at a photo," Jack says.

He's right. While I've travelled on my own to the Other World, I have never planned it out. It just happened while I was enraged with Matt and Ed. They'd also hurt people I cared about, causing my adrenaline to spike. I never had to make it do that on my own. So how can we cause our adrenaline to jump without someone we care about being in danger? Looking at Matt's and Ed's pictures just makes me want to tack them up to the wall and get some dart practice. As I dig through memories trying to formulate something that will get us all to the Other World, pictures flood my head. Football players slapping each other's helmets, psyching up for the game, and female kickboxers smiling through mouth guards while pounding gloves together. Maybe this will work.

"Hey, Jack. So, what're you going to do if they capture Lea and want to use her body as a test to see if a new serum causes mutated Altered Helix organs to not take?" I walk up to Jack and shove him.

"What the?" He looks at me like he's meeting me for the first time. Which I guess is half true as no one here has met this side of me. Shoot, this is the first time I've met this side of me.

"That's it. You're going to protect her with some words. A question." I shove him again. "Come on, Jack.

You have more than that. Act like I'm one of them, and I have her tied up behind me. How hard are you going to charge?"

He takes a few deep breaths. He clenches his hands into fists and bounces on the balls of his feet. "If they had her, I'd save her no matter what it took."

Then he charges me. As I brace for the oncoming tackle, he disappears into thin air. It worked. It actually flipping worked.

"He's gone. Did that really happen?" Camille asks.

"Yes, now it's your turn. Emmitt, come here."

Emmitt comes over and stands beside me.

"Camille, what're you going to do if they ever have Emmitt strapped to a gurney?" I grab his wrists with one hand and put my other hand on his throat. I squeeze enough to make his face darken. Camille doesn't say a word as she makes her move toward me. After two running steps, she's gone.

Now I'm up. I can't get myself worked up on my own. Emmitt reads my thoughts and steps toward Josh. He grabs Josh's good arm and puts it behind his back. He puts Josh in a headlock. My heart stops. I don't like how this looks one bit. I run toward them, and nothing happens. I'm about to punch Emmitt in the face when he talks.

"Why didn't you disappear? You too gentle for that sort of thing?"

"I don't know. Probably good, as I wouldn't want to disappear if I were really trying to save Josh. I wonder what the others did differently?"

"Were you thinking about the Other World at all?" Josh asks.

"No, I wasn't. I was only thinking about protecting you. I can change that."

I take a few steps away. Jack and Camille are waiting for me. I close my eyes and breathe in. I imagine the interrogation room Matt and Ed are being held in. Now I imagine Emmitt is Matt when I run toward him. I think of the Other World.

The grassy pad is the same one as the last two visits. I look around and begin feeling the emotions and spinning of this world. I see Camille trying to pet a bird, and Jack has an earthworm in his hand, and he's talking to it.

"Hey, guys. Looks like we made it. Were you two thinking of this world when you charged?"

"Yeah, I was trying to remember what it looked and felt like," Camille says.

"I was just trying to imagine what it was like," Jack says.

"That's key. You have to think about this world and have an adrenaline rush to make it here of your own accord. Oh, and Jack, you don't want to go up those stairs."

He stops where he is and turns around. "Thanks, but why don't I want to climb the stairs?"

"That's how you get to Heaven, and I don't believe you're ready for that."

"Uh, yeah. So what do we do now?"

"Yeah, where's your father?" Camille adds.

"I'm not sure. I was expecting him. Maybe since there was no real danger, he wasn't expecting our visit."

We all begin searching the gorgeous beach, the luscious green grass, and the never-ending staircase into the sky. There isn't another soul to be seen. I begin to feel the spinning sensation again, but, as usual, it doesn't cause nausea. It feels completely natural, as if this has always been where I was meant to be.

Jack looks at me like a lost puppy. "Do you feel that? What is it? Off balance, but not. It's insane."

"We're on a Stranded Coil of a Nebula. So we're spinning at a faster rate than we're accustomed to. Our bodies adapt easily to it because of the Altered Helixes," I explain to him.

"Whoa. That's intense." He reaches down and touches a blade of grass, but doesn't pick it. He must feel their emotions too.

"So what do we do now?" Camille brings us back to the point.

"Well, when I've been here I've been with my father. I concentrated on one of the happiest places and then we appeared there. I'm afraid if we all concentrate on our own favorite places, we'll end up separated. I'm not exactly comfortable with that. Are you guys okay thinking about the house I grew up in?" I ask them, hoping there's no argument.

"What does it look like?" Camille asks. "I've already met your father so I can think about him too."

"Yeah, did you grow up in a mansion or a shack?" Jack asks with a snicker.

I let myself relax a little. Looks like these two won't be arguing with me. Now how to explain my first house? Wait a minute. My mother emailed pictures during the renovation. Can we get an internet connection on a Stranded Coil? I pull out my phone and begin pulling up my email. It states that I've been disconnected from my home Wi-Fi. Kind of figured that would happen. I go to the settings to see what internet's available, if any. One is available called Runner1990. I almost burst into laughter. Thanks, Father. I type in USOLYMPICGOLD and hit enter. The phone sits with a circle spinning on the screen for quite a while. Then

I'm connected. Wow! I stare at the screen in shock for a second before talking.

"Uh guys, I'm connected to the internet. I'm going to pull up some photos of my house so you can envision it," I finally speak out loud.

"What? Really. The internet? So could I email Lea right now?" Jack asks as he leans in toward my phone.

"Let's give it a try," Camille says as both she and Jack pull out their phones and begin to connect.

I share the password with them. As they're attempting to send their emails, a light bulb comes on. Duh! I've been looking for a way to connect with my father while we're worlds apart. I'd never thought to try to use email. Of all the things.

"Here are the pictures, guys. Did your emails go through?"

"Yes. Emmitt just emailed back," Camille says, jumping up and down in excitement.

So my father and I can easily "call" one another. This is wonderful. I begin telling a hide and seek story to Jack and Camille. They looked at the pictures long enough. We're holding hands to be sure we don't lose one another. I close my eyes for a moment and, when I open them, we're in front of the house.

I still can't get over the euphoric feeling of being here. I look at Jack and Camille and smile. They squeeze my hands and smile at me, then release my hands and walk toward the front door. Something's off. Why hasn't anyone sensed us? Why are we still alone? Why are goosebumps prickling up my neck?

A shadow moves behind a corner of the house. I thought I was only going to be haunted by shadows in our world. I grab Camille's and Jack's sleeves to hold them back from approaching the house. I hold my finger up to my mouth in order to hush them. I point to the right corner of the house where I saw the shadow.

"Something isn't right here. I just saw a shadow go behind that corner. Are you guys ready to put some of our self-defense lessons to the test?" I whisper to them.

"What? We haven't been here very long. Are you sure?" Jack asks. I can see the look of disappointment in his eyes. I wish there were another way, but I don't get the feeling that this is going to be a nice visit.

"Did you get any more details than just a shadow?" Camille asks.

"No, I'm sorry, but I really do get the feeling that something is off. My father would be running out the front door to greet us otherwise."

Camille motions for us to quietly follow her. She begins walking to the corner. She stops short and looks back to be sure we're there. She peeks her head around.

The look she gives when she turns back to us is awful. "It's that stupid Adam person and, believe it or not, Matt and Ed are with him. They must have escaped the interrogation your father had set up."

Shoot. This is not good. Do we even risk fighting them? What good would it do?

"Do they have anyone in their possession?" I ask apprehensively.

"No, it's just them."

My muscles relax with her response.

"We should listen and find out what they're up to," Jack says. He's thinking the same thing I am.

"Sounds good. Be ready to fight if they or anyone on their team finds us," I say.

We hide behind the bushes at the front of the house as quietly as we can and begin to listen.

"Told you they were plotting against us," Matt's voice says.

"Don't you think I've made a plan against that? What they are is weak like a bubble floating in the air. All we have to do is poke it and watch it burst," Adam responds.

"They got so much information out of us. Let's face it, they know way too much. What're we going to do?" This comes from Ed.

"Don't worry. Trust me. You must continue to follow my instructions if you don't want your families' fortunes to disappear. I have a backup plan that will blow our competitors right out of the water. While they're jumping over hurdles, I'm going to remove the track on which they plan to land," Adam replies.

With that we hear footsteps approaching. We all sit motionless, attempting to not make a sound. Luckily for us, the footsteps pass. I peer through an opening in the bush to see where they go but, once they're ten steps beyond us, they disappear.

"Are they gone?" Jack asks.

"Yes they are," a voice from beyond the bushes replies.

We all gasp and look to our right. It's the man who spoke so much.

"You all have to get out of here. We're being watched by them, and only the experienced can truly hide."

"I always swing on the tire swing in order to relax and return to our world," I say.

"Perfect. We have three swings out back now just for that."

Jack and Camille look at me.

"We can trust him. Come on, before it's too late."

“But you didn’t get to see your father. This is your last trip here.” Camille gives me a worried look.

“Hey, no biggie. I can email him now.” I give her a friendly shoulder bump and smile, but I really don’t feel comforted. She’s right. I’m missing some quality time with someone I’ve missed for years. We should be spending a week of Other World time with him. I’m pissed, but right now we all have to relax in order to return safely. I won’t let my desires put them in danger.

We walk to the back yard, take a swing, and begin pumping our legs. It’s easy here to get lost in the peaceful emotions of the trees and the clouds. Before we know it, we’re back in the gym.

“Well, that was fast. Did you get enough training in?” Emmitt asks as he walks up to Camille and gives her a bear hug.

“Not exactly, but I feel pretty confident of being able to travel if I needed to now,” Jack replies.

“What do you mean, not exactly?” Josh asks with his jaw set.

“We weren’t able to speak with my father. Matt and Ed had escaped and were talking to Adam,” I reply with the most morose look I can muster.

“Yeah, but we learned how to email back and forth from worlds. Did Emmitt show you his email from Camille?” Jack asks.

“Yeah, that was like a minute before you returned,” Josh says.

“We need to act fast. Adam said that he has some magnificently horrible plan,” Camille interjects.

I take a deep breath. This has all happened so fast and seems to just spiral faster the deeper we get.

SOJOURN

We meet up with everyone at the haunted house, my home away from home. Lea can't sit still as we tell our story to everyone. She also seems to have caught the attachment bug. When an unaltered helix mate fears losing their partner, they seem to be glued to them. She has her hands on Jack nonstop, as if they're fused to him. Sometimes she's holding his hand and sometimes she has a hand on his shoulder while he needs both hands to articulate what he's explaining. Everyone gasps when we tell them we're able to email from the Other World. I normally would be completely exhilarated by all this, but I can't get it out of my head that I didn't get to see my father during my "last" visit.

"Seriously, it's so weird in that world. You feel emotions from everything, even the bees and the birds," Jack exclaims.

Everyone has questions for him about the Other World but Josh. He's getting more rigid as we talk about it. We haven't been effectively communicating since my return. We're on different wavelengths. He has come to terms with the loss of his parents. I haven't come to terms with losing the father I just got back.

"What Adam, Matt, and Ed were talking about scares me. What can their secret plan be? We have to find out, and we have to act fast to complete what we've set out to do. I don't think they're playing easily figured out games. I don't think they ever were. This is serious," Camille exclaims.

Everyone begins chattering. I can't make sense of all the noise. I'm glad to see them all fired up about taking action, but something is stirring within. I know what it is. I have to claim it. My father has the answers, but do I risk communication via email? With the cell-phone companies' disregard of privacy and the government's complete infringement of it, I don't think we can take that risk. I need to communicate with my father face to face. I need to travel back to the Other World.

After the talking dies down, we set plans and dates to complete the surveillance, medical research corruption, and serum administration. It feels nice to know that if all goes as planned, the Altered Helixes of this world and the Other World should be safe. This can only happen if the Altered Helixes in the Other World are able to complete their plans too, but I have a feeling that, if we do our part, they'll be successful.

As the meeting comes to an end, I can't help but wish for just a moment alone, but Josh is having none of that. We all go home, and he's right next to me the entire way. We get ready for bed, but as soon as his breathing slows, and I know he's asleep, I sneak out. I boot up my phone and begin writing an email to an address I never thought would be there. Who knows, it will probably just go to spam and Josh will be happy that I wasn't able to get hold of my father.

"*Father,*

It's me, Austria. Are you okay? Why were Adam, Matt, and Ed right outside the house? What's going on? Adam mentioned some big plan.

I'm so upset that I didn't get to spend time with you. Josh doesn't want me to ever go back. I hope this email thing works, but Father, I really want to see you again.

I know you want me to have a normal life, but I can visit one more time and still do that. Please respond. I hope this is your email, and you get internet connection too.

Love,

Austria"

I bite my nails as I wait for the response. Ten minutes later, when I'm notified of a message from USOLYMPIC-GOLD I know it's him and smile as I hide on our porch.

"*Austria,*

It is not safe now to communicate via email. You can make one last trip here. Wait until Sunday at noon. Grandmother and I will make sure you travel safely, and that we're able to spend some good time together.

I love you too (to the moon and back, and farther)

Father"

We *can* communicate via email. I can set this up on my contacts list and call my father whenever I need him. I've yearned to be able to do that for a very long time.

The days seem to trickle by like sand through an hourglass. I can tell Josh thinks something's up, but I don't care. What he's asking of me is unfair. If our roles were reversed, I'm sure he'd feel the same way. As Sunday nears, it's hard to contain my excitement. Sunday morning, Tiff makes breakfast for Luke, Josh, and I. I begin to feel a little guilty, but not enough.

When we finish, I announce that I'm going to the neighborhood nursery to get some evergreen bushes for the front of our condo. I'm tired of seeing all the plants disappear come winter, so it's plausible for me to take this action. Josh automatically volunteers to go with me, but I claim to have a mutual understanding with an employee for a discount; an understanding that would be forfeited if he were there. I don't know how, but a miracle happens and everyone believes me. As I round the corner where I cannot be seen, I instinctively imagine Matt handcuffing Josh, and I also think of seeing my father for the last time. I only have to take one lunge, and I'm there.

The same gosh darn grassy pad. A second later, I'm blinded by light.

"Father?"

"Yes, I'm here."

My eyes adjust, and I see my father. I reach for his hand with mine in the same second. He holds my hand, and I feel as though I'm a child again. All worries of the present day fade into a distant memory.

"Can we play hide and seek in the house again?"

He hesitates. I wonder if this has something to do with Adam, Matt, and Ed being so close to the house last time I was here.

"Sure, honey," he says.

"Are you positive? You hesitated."

"Yes, I'm sure. What else would I want to do during your last visit here?"

He hooks his arm in mine around the elbow as he leads the way. Now I feel like this is as simple as taking a stroll down my own street. I barely even think of the house and then we're there.

"Head on in and hide, if you think you can find a good enough place," my father says as he brushes his fingers across my cheek and smiles at me.

"You're never going to find me," I respond as I take his hand in mine and gaze into his eyes. How did I live so many years without this man there to believe in me unfailingly?

I take a step toward the house. A weight falls on my heart. I con myself into believing it's because this is my last visit, but my subconscious won't let me fully let it go at that.

"Are you sure everything is okay?" I ask.

"Of course, honey, go ahead."

I do, but it feels as though the bones in my legs are made of lead.

I know where I'm going to hide before I even spot the hexagon table. This world has contorted it to fit my current shape and size. Brilliant. I hide inside and wait. And wait. My father has still not come to find me, but then I hear voices.

"Did we really have to meet now?"

"Yes, do you need an event notification and RSVP to discuss saving the Earth?" That's my father's voice.

"Whatever. What do you have that's so urgent it couldn't wait?"

"It's something that could wipe out the entire population of Earth," my father says.

"Are you sure you haven't been hanging around your paranoid group of conspirators too much?"

"I wish. Adam has atomic bomb capabilities. He hasn't only administered serum to the Mutated Altered Helixes to protect their organs, but he's also administered serum that will enable a person to withstand all forms of radiation," my father informs the man.

As the man begins to depart, all I can think is that this is nuts. Atomic weapons, really? Then I remember seeing the articles about a nearby nuclear plant in the newspaper. I can see the picture that went with the article when I close my eyes. Yes, Adam was in the photo. So this is the real deal, as intense as it sounds. What kind of deranged lunatic is this guy? The kind that steals organs and kills people without a moment's hesitation.

“So you’re saying that Adam is going to drop an atomic bomb along specific sectors of Earth in order to wipe out all non-Mutated Altered Helixes and ordinary individuals?”

“Yeah, pretty much,” my father says grimly.

“Okay, I guess I have to do what I have to do then. Thank you for all of your research. You will be remembered among us even after you’re gone. If we survive, we’ll be very thankful for your work.”

I can’t slow my breaths as I hear my father enter the house. He’s going to sacrifice himself in order to save us. This just cannot be. I just found how I could communicate with him even when I’m unable to travel here, but if he sacrifices himself, that won’t even be a possibility. Does it really have to be this way?

“Ready or not, here I come.”

“I’m here.” I open the doors of the hexagon table and tumble out. I run up to my father and wrap my arms around him.

“That’s not how the game works.”

“I don’t care. I don’t want you to sacrifice yourself.”

“Oh, honey, that’s just a last-ditch effort. There’s only like a .5% chance of it becoming necessary. Don’t worry.”

“Promise?”

“Promise.”

I hug him so tightly I feel as though one of my muscles will snap.

“How about we have one last dinner before you have to go back? We can always discuss more via email. It’s more than we’ve had in so long.”

“I know. I just wish you could travel back with me.”

"And leave me all alone?" I hadn't noticed my grandmother entering the living room. She has a bag full of groceries.

Father and I help Grandmother cook dinner. We work as a team, as if we've been doing this for years. I wonder if it's because of our DNA similarities. The conversation is fairly pleasant, but I'm still bothered by the previous revelation.

"Grandmother? What do you think of this Adam guy? What do you think of his plan?"

"I think we have it under control is what I think, sugar bear."

"Are you sure? I mean, he's messing with nuclear stuff."

"Sugar bear, it's fine. We can handle more than you give us credit for."

I slump my shoulders and begin scrubbing some of the pots in the sink. It seems as though I'm not going to get through to either one of them. I should really just enjoy this visit. I take a deep breath and grab the dishes to set the table. My father pats me on the back as I pass. Dinner smells good. I feel starved, even though I know it's only my psyche. I keep looking at them both, trying to memorize their features.

"Do you remember when your father tried cooking the Thanksgiving turkey? I think you were about eight."

"I'm not sure. I do remember there being a lot of smoke in the kitchen once. Was that because of his cooking?"

"Hey, that was my first time cooking a turkey. Would you cut me a break?" My father begs.

"He burnt that turkey to a crisp."

"What did we end up doing?"

“Luckily, Walmart was open, and we were able to swing by and purchase a couple of rotisserie chickens.”

“We still had the loveliest time.” Now it’s my grandmother’s turn to pat my father on the back.

“That was the year you taught me hopscotch.” I remember my father hopping on the squares like a little girl would. I thought it was so silly but was thrilled that I would be able to join the girls at school.

“That’s right, honey. You picked it up pretty fast. I was so proud of you. I am proud of you. You have become a beautiful, intelligent, and caring young woman.” My father has tears in his eyes.

“Thank you, Father. I’ve always loved you, and I always will.” Now I have tears in my eyes.

“There, there, you two. I’m proud of both of you and love you to pieces.” My grandmother brings us in for a group hug. I smile at her, and she smiles at me. Then I peek at my father, and he smiles at me too.

“Well, well, looks like it’s about time for you to get back on the swing.” My grandmother smooths her apron and clears her throat. She gives my father a look.

He just grabs me in a bear hug. Then we all head to the swing. I have to breathe slowly to keep from bursting into tears. I sit on the tire and let them get me going. Then I pump my legs and force myself to relax by thinking of the smiles they gave me in the group hug.

FINALE

I awake in bed with Josh. Oh, he's going to be furious. I don't want to wake him, but I'd like to brush my teeth and put on my pajamas. I get out of bed softly and tiptoe to the lamp on the other side of the room. I get my pajamas out of the dresser quietly and put them on. As I look at Josh, I see tear streaks running down his cheeks. He cried himself to sleep. Shoot, I didn't mean to worry him that much. I turn off the light and head to the bathroom. I brush my teeth as quickly as I can and tiptoe back to bed. I gently get back under the covers without waking Josh. I put my arm around him and hold him close. He doesn't say a word but grabs my hand and squeezes. He rubs circles on the back of my hand with his thumb. After a couple minutes, he stops, and his breathing slows. He's asleep. Now, will I be able to fall as easily as he did?

That's when I notice the light on my phone blinking. I must have an email. I left it by the lamp and have to get up to retrieve it. I grab my phone and unlock it. When I pull up my email, I find a message from my father, already. Time does travel at different rates between his world and mine. I wonder if the email time stamp will reflect that. The subject line is "I love you." I click on the message. The time is the same as here. Interesting. This is what the message says:

"Austria,

It was so good to see you, honey. I have enjoyed the past few visits you've had here. I will always be rooting you on. I'm so happy you get to live the life I wasn't able to. We can win this fight against our enemies. Promise you'll enjoy your life. I will be honest. If this feels like a goodbye it's because it is. Adam is taking initiative on the nuclear plan. If I strike now, I can stop him. Please watch over Mother for me and tell her I love her.

Love,

Father"

I instantly hit the reply button and begin typing. "You can tell her yourself because I will not let you do this." Before I hit another key, I stop. If I send him that message, he'll know what I'm going to do. I can't risk it. I can't believe he's actually going to do this to me again. He doesn't want to, but he's leaving me. Recurring feelings of abandonment wash over me. Then I remember my dream conversation with Grandmother: *You have to let him go, child. All he wants is for you to have a life. You'll understand one day when you have children of your own.* Did he and Grandmother know all along? I can't let him do this. I need him in my life. There has to be another way. Can I find Adam and stop him myself? Will that save my father? It would take too much time. I've already lost quite a bit since the time passes differently there than here. I have to go to the Other World. That's the only way I can stop him. But this will now be my fifth and last trip. Did he let me make the previous visit on purpose, believing I would be incapable of interfering with this suicide plan of his?

I look at Josh and drop to my knees. I didn't mind leaving for a visit with Father, but this time I'll be leaving him for good. Pain sears through my chest. What will this do to him? The tears that had welled up in my eyes on the swing burst past my eyelids now. Why does it have to be like this? The only way to save my father is to travel to the Other World and stop him. By doing that, I will leave Josh, my mother, and my whole haunted house family behind. Or I can stay here with Josh, my first true love, and lose my father, who I just got back, forever. It's not fair. I get the feeling that, as you grow up, you find out that more and more is unfair. I stand as I weigh the options in my head. Allow my father to sacrifice himself or make Josh heartbroken? You can heal from heartbreak. You can't heal from suicide. I know what I must do.

I write Josh a note. Not really my ideal way of saying goodbye, but if I wake him, he'll try to stop me.

"Josh,

I'm so sorry for upsetting you and visiting my father. I hope you can forgive me for that and for what I'm about to do. It was a miracle finding you. I love you so much. Please live a happy life. This is the only way to honor our love. I have to go back to the Other World to save my father. Tell everyone I'm an email away and will help continue the fight against our enemies. You can email me too, but I understand if you don't want to. You're the best man on Earth I know.

Love,

Austria"

Ugh, that's awful. I can't come up with better right now, and I'm short on time. Maybe I can send an email after I save my father. Josh is going to hate this no matter what I say. I hope he understands. I hope he sees that, if things were reversed, I would understand. My hands shake as I fold the note and put it on my pillow. I want to gather him in my arms and hold him one last time, but I can't find the strength. I feel like I could faint. I have to take a deep breath. I turn around and think about Adam. Why do evil, power-hungry people like him have to exist? I think of the Other World. I angrily think of what I would do to Adam if he were here now. Then I run two steps as if Adam were in front of me, and I could tackle him. This is it. "Good-bye!" I begin to feel the spinning and unexplainable emotions of the Other World I'm drifting to. Funny how it seems like I had just struggled to hang onto life recently and now here I am floating away from it voluntarily.

PARALLELED

BOND

ANAPHASE

"Please let them be okay." If I had known I would be chanting this phrase over and over again, I don't believe I would have ever set out on this mission. If I had known that my entire world would change in just a matter of months, would I have taken the job at the haunted house? If I had been given a heads up about my DNA being different, would I have lived a different life?

I don't know; those are not options for me now. We're too far in. We are inches away from saving many lives. We can do this. I know we can. I just don't know what it will cost us. I have no clue how I'm going to find the dough to pay. The odds seem stacked up against us. Is that because it is impossible to accomplish what we want to, or is it because we've gotten too close?

REJECTED

As I wait for the grassy pad, a shadow approaches me. Instead of the scent of fresh-cut grass, I smell rosewater. What's going on? I've never met a shadow while travelling from one world to the other. My vision of everything is blurry. I can't make out a single thing. Maybe it was more than a shadow, but I'm unable to make out details right now. My nerves begin to fray. It feels like someone's taking a nail and scraping it up my arm. Something's interfering with my travel. It's so quiet wherever I'm trapped. Is this some kind of portal? A space between Earth and the Stranded Coil I've never stopped before? It's difficult to concentrate as I try to see if I can feel my father's presence anywhere nearby. Am I too late? Has he already sacrificed himself? I'm trying to make my final visit to the Other World, leaving Josh and everyone behind, to save him, but I feel more lost now than I ever have. I don't understand what's going on at all. Why am I not sitting near the beach feeling the sand particles' emotions?

"Because I made a promise to your father, that's why," a voice from nowhere exclaims. I know that voice. No wonder I smelled rosewater. Slowly her image appears. The eyes are dark as charcoal, yet glow just like charcoal does after you light it. She has an infectious smile that makes me laugh even though I can see a lecture behind it.

"Grandmother, what are you doing? I have to save him." It feels strange to talk here. Whatever this place is, I hope I don't have to stay long. My grandmother's presence is comforting, but I still feel as though I'm on the brink of an anxiety attack. The feeling of having a physical form is leaving me. If it weren't the palms of my hands would be sweating. Instead, I feel static like we're in an electrical field.

"No Austria, you don't. You're his child, and he wants you to enjoy life."

How am I supposed to enjoy life when it's ripping my father away from me yet again? My chest clenches. I'm unable to take a breath.

"What's going to happen to him?" I manage to gasp out.

"He's taking Adam to Heaven with him. I'm pretty sure, once they meet the celestial gate, that Adam will be turned away. There's only one place he'll be able to go then. I'm sure you know where that is. I'm glad because I don't want to spend my eternity with a man like that."

"Are you saying that you and Father will be in Heaven?" I'm able to breathe and talk again because now I know there's a way to see him again even if he goes through with this plan. I begin to feel the spinning. Maybe if I keep Grandmother talking, I'll be forced to the Other World anyway. Then I'll be closer to him, or at least closer to the stairs.

"Yes, dear, it's where we belong."

"I just got you guys back."

"Most people aren't given such a chance. Please treasure the moments we've had together as I will and enjoy your life."

I understand what Grandmother is telling me, but I'm not happy about it. I imagine my father and grandmother in front of Heaven's gates. I can hear trumpets sounding their arrival. The perfect symphony causes goosebumps to form on my legs. I can't do anything to keep them from moving on. She's preventing me from travelling to the Other World. The spinning is beginning to cease. Maybe if I come from another angle.

"How are we going to continue the fight without you guys around?"

"We have a team up here. You've met them. Plus we're adding a new leader. One you're very familiar with."

"Who's the new leader?"

"Why it's me, Austria." I know that voice too. It's the voice that's comforted me every day of my life. What's my mother doing here? I didn't think this could be possible. What does my grandmother mean about my mother being the leader in the Other World?

"Mother, how are you communicating with us? You're not an Altered Helix."

"Well actually, Marie is. Your father realized she was before she did and hid it from her. He didn't let anyone from the Other World contact her. He wanted her to be able to live a normal life with you. He wanted to protect her from our enemies. If she didn't know she was an Altered Helix, how would they?" my grandmother answers. How can that be? Why had she not noticed the shadows at the haunted house? Then I remember she's a couple years younger than my father and the Altered Helix abilities might not have kicked in for her until after that experience.

"She's right. I didn't know. Your father just contacted me before he left to take Adam to the next world. It was so amazing to see him again. I love him just as much as I did when he was home. I wish I had more time with him but, Austria, I understand what he's trying to do. It's a noble cause, and I also want you to have a normal life."

"So you're going to be in the Other World. You're the new leader. I'm losing my whole family." The air I'm breathing thickens, and I feel my airway constricting. The spinning I feel isn't from the Other World this time. It's from lack of oxygen to my brain.

FAREWELL

"Calm down, Austria," my mother says delicately.

"What am I going to do without you? You and I have spent every holiday together. I don't want to lose that. And I want to have some family at my wedding. I want my mother to be there when I have children."

"We'll still be able to talk, darling. Most Altered Helixes are allowed multiple visits to the Other World but, as the leader, I'm going to be anchored here. My abilities acclimated during the past decade and so I only need one visit. Hey, everything is going to be okay. I feel complete with my responsibilities here and one day, many years from now, you will be too. You'll see."

"Plus, your children will more than likely have different DNA too since both your parents do, Austria. They'll be able to meet your mother." This comes from my grandmother.

She's right. They're both right, but I don't want them to be. My hands are furiously shaking. Why is it that my mother only gets one visit? My grandmother had multiple at her age. It's because she's the leader. I wonder if Altered Helixes can manipulate that? Again I'm fraught with an apprehension that causes jitters. Then it dawns on me. If my children have Altered Helixes too, they'll be in danger if we don't stop these people. I'm about to say something when I'm interrupted.

"It's time. I have him." That's my father's voice.

"Father, I don't want you to go. I love you."

"I have to, honey. I love you too."

"What the hell do you people think you're up to?" Adam's here too.

"Adam, you're deranged. and the group and plans you've put together need to be stopped," my father says.

"You're just upset that you didn't come up with them first."

"No. I do not want a dictatorship in the Other World, just as I had not wanted one on Earth."

"There's no way you can stop what I have in place. I never lose."

"You'd be surprised what we have in place ourselves."

My father turns to us and gives us all hugs. When he hugs me, I don't want to let go. I breathe in the smell of his aftershave one last time. He pulls away and kisses my forehead.

"I'll always be watching over you. One day, many years from now, we'll be together again. I promise."

He turns to Adam. "Come on. I'll show you everything we've been up to."

My father takes Adam's arm. As Adam tries to free himself, everything changes. Instead of being in the void I'd been, I'm on my knees on the floor in my room. Now I'm watching them just through a vision, similar to how I first saw my father at the haunted house before any of this outlandishness began. Before I found out I was different. Before I found out we were in danger.

They're on the grassy pad by the beach, and Adam looks disoriented. Altered Helixes can read thoughts in the Other World, but Mutated Altered Helixes cannot. My father points up the stairs. The stairs that lead to Heaven that he stopped me from ascending too early.

"Matt and Ed are up there," my father tells Adam.

"Why do I care if they're up there? I have a bit more on my hands to deal with," Adam says.

"Because they've switched sides, and they're stopping all of your work. I told you they would. In fact, they're almost done. I told you we'd win."

Adam's face is twisted in anger. "We'll see about that," he says and then takes the first step. Once his foot touches the stair, it's as if a magnetic pull takes him the rest of the way. His facial muscles have relaxed, and he looks as if he just received a massage and doesn't have a care in the world.

My father and grandmother take each other's hands. They look back at my mother and me and blow us kisses. We both simultaneously blow kisses back. Then they take a step too. The light that surrounds them brightens. The things they have done all these years when I didn't even know they were around simply amaze me. How they've been trying to protect me all along. I had felt empty and lonely at times but maybe, deep down, I had always known they were there. They've always been supporting me and cheering me on. When I looked in the stands to see if anyone was watching my school events, I should have known they were there in spirit. No world could hold back their love.

The brilliant light isn't the only thing clouding my vision. Tears are streaming down my cheeks. I cannot swallow. This isn't the way it was supposed to be. My mother, so pretty, withstood an enormous amount of pressure raising me and keeping a secret in order to protect me. Now she's making a completely selfless move. She'll be in a world that's totally new to her. I see enormous strength in her that I never noticed before.

"Everything's going to be okay, Austria. I'm just an email away if you ever need anything," my mother says.

It all fades away—the stairs, the grassy pad, and my mother's face. I'm back in my room. Everything looks the same. The lamp's still off with the shade askew. My note on my pillow is still right where I put it. My dirty laundry spread throughout the room hasn't moved an inch. My *The Catcher in the Rye* book is still on my nightstand with a gum wrapper for a bookmark. But everything has changed. Nothing's the same. Not without my father back in my life and my mother gone. I'm alone, and now it's my responsibility to make this a safe place for my future children and all Altered Helixes. It feels as though I've aged a decade in weeks. It feels as though everything's spiraling out of control.

HEARTBREAK

I crumple to the floor sobbing. I'm not just crying now. It's one of those intense, wretched sobs that shake your entire body. I pull my knees into my chest trying to comfort myself. I try to see some way out or some way to make things right, but I know there's nothing. Nothing will ever make this pain go away. My body begins convulsing, and I can't make it stop. I see Josh's face in front of me but cannot hear what he's saying. I'm not surprised that my wailing woke him. I feel him wrap his arms around me and lift me to a sitting position. Even with a cast, he does this with ease. His lips move, and he looks in my eyes. I can't move a muscle. It feels as though I can't even blink. I'm frozen. I'm like a statue of misery.

He turns his head away from me and opens his mouth wide. He's screaming something. The vein on the side of his forehead's bulging out. Then Tiff's shaking me. She's also saying something, but I don't hear her. Luke grabs a flashlight and shines it in my eyes. He's checking my vitals. I feel him touch my wrist with his thumb and forefinger. Then he and Josh pick me up and put me on the bed. That's when Josh sees the note. I see him open it and read it. His eyes move back and forth across the page. His facial expressions change over and over again as he reads. I wish I could wrap my arms around him. I wish I could talk and explain. None of those things are available to me. He squeezes the note in his hand and says something to Tiff and Luke.

Tiff grabs my phone and unlocks it. She says something to me, but I still don't hear her. Am I going to remain in this deaf and mute state of paralysis forever? Was it the portal that did this to me, or is this how everyone is when they lose their entire family? Tiff shows me the screen. She has my father's email up. She points it at me and looks like she's asking me something, but I still can't hear. Then she turns it back to herself. She's touching the screen, but I have no idea what she's doing. What if she's deleting his message, the last message from my father? I try to will my body to move so I can grab the phone. I swear I'm flexing my muscles in my arm hard enough to lift fifty pounds, but my arm doesn't even budge. Then she turns the phone back to me. There's a message from my mother. Before I can read it, she turns it back to herself.

A tear rolls down her cheek, and she hugs me. Luke holds my hand. Josh is looking at the phone now. He's pacing back and forth. I wonder what was in my mother's message. Did she talk about everything? Then Josh stops and drops to his knees. He looks at me, and I can see understanding in his eyes. We're both without family in this world now. We're all each other have. He walks over to the bed and says something to Luke and Tiff. They get up and leave the room. Josh sits down next to me. He smells like the woods. I wish I could be hidden away somewhere in the woods. Lost in a cabin with him away from society and away from where everyone else has a family.

He picks me up and walks to the bathroom. He sets me down on the floor mat. It's one of those mats with extra padding. It feels like I'm sitting on a cloud. More feeling is coming back. Then I remember my father and grandmother walking up the stairs towards the clouds. A tear springs through my eyelashes. Josh wipes it away with his fingertip. Then he turns the water on. I can hear it hitting the tub. My hearing's returning too. I'm not sure I'm ready to be back. My father will never be back. Why should I?

Josh begins to brush my hair. I look in his eyes. They've always made me think of clear blue water. It reminds me of the grassy pad next to the beach I was supposed to land on instead of going to a portal and watching my loved ones being taken from me. Multiple tears flow down my cheeks now. I begin to shake and writhe in agony again. Josh strips my pajamas off of me, picks me up, and puts me in the water. It's warm. It calms me. His arms soothe me despite the cast and awkward moves it requires in order for him to keep it dry.

"Everything's going to be fine, Austria. Stay with me."

I focus on my muscles again. I'm able to move my hand. Hallelujah. I put my hand on his forearm as he scoops water with a cup and pours it on me. I see a very small movement in his facial muscles. He's hiding a smile. I actually want to smile back. I can feel the bubbles he must have added to the bath without me noticing pop as I move. Josh lathers soap and rubs it on my skin. Every place he scrubs takes a little bit of the pain away. He helps me lower myself to wet my hair. I can feel him lathering shampoo in my hair. For a second, I feel whole again. It quickly fades as I think about how the bath water reminds me of the beach near the grassy pad. The tears return. I try to pull myself down. I want to submerge my whole head below the water.

"Oh no you don't," Josh says.

He gets into the water fully clothed and holds me.

"You're the only family I have, Austria. We're going to be each other's family now. You have to stay with me."

MESSAGE

"When does it stop hurting?" I manage to make myself speak for the first time since I returned from the void.

The look of shock in Josh's eyes as he hears me brings a stab of guilt. I'm hurting him again when that's the last thing I want to do.

"I'm not going to lie. It never fully goes away, but as you live each day and find new joy, it slowly fades."

"It's not fair."

"Nothing is."

We hold each other for a long time without saying a word. Finally, as all of the rest of my physical feelings return to me, my stomach growls.

"Hungry?" Josh says and raises his eyebrows.

"Josh, your pajamas are soaked," I say. I'd forgotten he was fully clothed when he got in the tub. It just felt so comfortable in his arms.

"Yes, they are!" He stands and shakes like a wet dog.

I laugh. I didn't think that could be possible. He smiles in return and leans down, grabs the back of my neck, and kisses me. I grab his dripping clothes and pull him closer. Every feeling comes back to me. Maybe I can find new joy. I don't know how long we kiss. I don't care. I could stay here forever. Who cares if I turn into a prune? Eventually, he pulls away.

"You need some food."

"I'm okay. We can stay a little longer."

"Austria."

"Okay, okay."

He gets out, takes off his clothes, and hangs them on the shower rod. His muscles ripple with every move. He wraps a towel around his waist. What am I supposed to be doing again? He extends his hand to me. Oh yeah, I grab his hand. He helps me out of the tub and wraps me in a soft blanket. He kisses me again.

"Even utterly depressed you're beautiful, Austria."

"So are you."

Wait, that didn't come out right. Oh, who cares, he understands what I'm saying. He smiles at me and walks out. He returns with dry clothes for us both.

As we walk downstairs, I smell one of Tiff's special recipes to combat depression; blueberry, avocado, and tomato salsa with chips, fudge brownies, and strawberry banana protein shakes.

"Really, Tiff, are you pregnant or something? Do you normally mix foods like these together?" I hear Luke asking her.

"What if I *am* pregnant?" I hear her tease him. I wish we were already in the kitchen so I could see the look on his face.

"Well, uh, that, uh…" He's stumbling, and I'm smiling again.

"I'm not pregnant, silly. This is just a little soul food we enjoy when we're not feeling 100%. Is that okay with you, cowboy?" I can't believe I ever truly felt alone. Tiff is the best pseudo-sister a girl could have.

When we walk into the kitchen, they both stare at us.

"It's alive," Luke banters. "How are you doing, Austria?"

"I'm better."

He's beside me in a flash checking my vitals again. "Yes, you are." He smiles and hugs me.

"What did you do with her in that bathtub, Josh?" Tiff is now hugging me too. "Maybe you could give Luke a few pointers."

"Top secret. I could tell him, but then I'd have to kill him," Josh replies.

Luke fake-punches Josh in the arm. We all sit at the table and dig in. Even though Luke had mocked the food mix, he's enjoying it now. I notice my phone on the table. It's blinking, indicating another message. I look at everyone, and they all look at me. Josh begins to move his arm but, before he can grab the phone, I get it. I unlock it and check the message. It's a message from my father being sent through my mother. And I'm no longer hungry. I get up, still staring at the screen, and begin to walk to my room. I hear one set of footsteps behind me. I know it's Josh, but I don't stop him. We're family. He can hear this. I have a feeling I'm going to need someone there to support me after the wave of emotion this is sure to bring.

"Austria,

Hi, darling. How are you doing? I hope you're all right. I wish I could be there to comfort you right now. I haven't figured everything out here, like how to communicate with you via a dream or vision. I've learned how to email from here. Your father had one more message to give you, but he ran out of time.

Love,

Mother"

"Austria,

I know you're upset, honey, but remember, I'll always love you. There's a reason why I have gone to such lengths to allow you to live a normal life and see the values in the world in which you live. There's also a reason why I have gotten you so involved with stopping our enemies. I didn't realize your mother was an Altered Helix until after you were conceived. You see, the committee in the Other World has been waiting for someone like you for years.

I wish Grandmother could tell you about it. Altered Helixes come from many countries around the world. A democratic vote determined that the royal leaders would be descendants of the first true-born Altered Helix. Austria, you are the first true-born. You're the first to be born from both Altered Helix parents. You're going to be the leader, but they want you to live a complete life prior to your final trip to the Other World. Once you arrive to the Other World, you'll stop aging for long enough to rule.

I know this is a lot to take in right after going through such a loss, but it has to be said. Please don't worry. I know Josh is your family now and that your family may grow one day. I also know the last thing in the world you'll want to do is leave them. So I leave you with one blessing. The committee has worked to make a normal human become an Altered Helix without having to steal organs. This must remain a secret as we do not want our enemies to discover it. In all honesty, we would like to be rid of them when the Earth comes to an end, but that'll be something you and the committee can discuss. I tell you this so when it's your time to go you can bring your family with you if you wish. I'm giving you what I had wanted all along, honey, to have you. I love you. Take care.

Love,

Father"

My head is spinning. I don't know what to think of all this. Josh is holding me. By the lost look on his face, I can tell he read the message too.

MISSION

"You're what? Should we like call you princess now?" Ceresa's giving me a hard time after all I've lost.

"No, 'your highness' is more like it," Patrice adds as she flicks Ceresa on the arm with her hand.

I may be in pain, but these two still make me smile. I see where they're coming from now. They've been through this kind of pain. This is how they say they care. They do it by giving me a hard time instead of making me feel awkward and asking questions like, "Are you hanging in there?" I definitely like my pseudo-family right now.

"You can call me Princess Austria or your highness, whichever suits you," I answer with a sideways smile. "Just be sure to bow or curtsy when you do."

"Come on, your highness, let's go scare some people," Ethan says with a bow.

"I never thought I'd see you bow, man. Got to say, I don't mind it." Josh laughs.

"Whatever, Josh, You're not true royalty. You married in," Ethan counters.

"What's all this about married in?" Tiff's eyes bulge as she looks at Ethan.

Josh's face turns bright red. What in the world? We were just joking around. Tiff turns to Patrice and Ceresa, who are both nodding "yes" to her. "Yes" what? Everyone has become bizarre in my absence. What am I going to do with these fools? Don't they know how much we have on our plate? Tiff turns to me, and she has the biggest smile planted on her face.

"What? Why are you all looking at me like that? We have things to do."

"I think they can wait," Ethan says and then nudges Josh with his elbow.

Josh walks up to me with his hands in his pockets. Then he pulls one out. He's holding a small box. Oh. He gets down on one knee.

"Look who's bowing now." Ethan can't resist.

Josh just shakes his head. "Austria, I love you. You are my family. I want to be with you forever. Will you marry me?"

My eyes well up with tears. I hear the girls squeal. I'm happy and overwhelmed at the same time. I drop to my knees in front of him nodding my head yes, but I just can't get words out. Josh grabs me in a bear hug. I'm shaking with emotion. Even though I'm crying, he lifts my chin, smiles at me, and kisses me. He puts the ring on my finger. I look down and see it's a white gold Claddagh ring like I've always wanted, with hands holding a crowned heart; ironic that now I am "crowned." I hug him again. I want to stay in this embrace forever. Tiff grabs my hand and is inspecting the ring. Ethan jabs Josh in the side. We really are going to be a family.

Bill walks into the room and makes an announcement. "Customers will be here in an hour. We need to have everything set up and everyone in their places. What's all the commotion over here? Please tell me it isn't another disappearance."

He walks over to us, and Tiff holds out my hand. I watch Bill's eyes lighten when he sees what's going on. He smiles and hugs us both, Josh and I, together. Apparently, he approves of this union.

"Congratulations. Let me see if I have any treats in the storage room over here."

"Isn't it wonderful? I can't wait to tell my …." Then I remember, I don't have anyone else alive to tell. Josh holds me tightly.

"Uh, Tiff, can you come over here and take a picture of Austria's ring and email it to her mother?" Josh asks the question that I'm too weak to ask.

Tiff comes over and takes the photo. She puts her hand on my cheek. She can see that tears of sadness have replaced the tears of joy. "Are you going to wear the ring with your costume?"

She's changing the subject. "Yeah, the ring fits perfectly. It won't fall off. Josh, how did you know my ring size?"

"Oh, a little birdie told me, and that little birdie's name is Tiff."

Now she's smiling, and my smile has returned too. I am a lucky girl. I have one hot fiancé and a dynamic best friend.

"Let's go scare some people," I almost scream.

##

After the haunted house closes, we head to Broadway Café. I had a blast scaring people, but now it's time for us to plan for our real jobs, saving Altered Helixes. We need more incriminating evidence, so we're going to set up another surveillance operation. We also need to get the legislation passed to change national human trafficking laws from not only protecting against sexual abuse and slavery, but also organ theft. We're going to travel all over to administer the serum that'll protect Altered Helix organs from being a viable option for our enemies. Then we'll need to corrupt the medical files. We have a lot to accomplish. Oh, and apparently I need to be planning a wedding too.

As we walk into the café, I imagine what our lives would be like if none of this existed. I would have my mother, father, and probably grandmother. People wouldn't be in danger apart from Earth fading. Would we be as close as we are, though? All of the trials we've been through have made us as tight knit as family in a very short time. I realize that I wouldn't change one thing as we stroll through the café, and more than a couple of pairs of eyes stare at us. I used to wonder what people thought of our different groups hanging out together, but now I truly do not care.

SURVEILLANCE

We located most of the Altered Helixes, and it just so happens that many of them reside in Memphis of all places. Josh and I arrive in Memphis on time. We sneak up the target building's emergency stairs and find the window for 3C. A team member from the Other World came to the apartment as a spirit, ahead of time when it was empty, and forced the window to unlock. Josh tests it. The window opens but with a pretty strong creak. Hopefully, Jason's a sound sleeper. We climb into his apartment. My heart's beating about twice as fast as it should. Thankfully, Jason's snoring. I can't get my hands to stop shaking when I open the box containing the syringe. Josh puts a hand on my arm and looks me in the eyes. He breathes in deeply and then out. I follow him but am still shaking. He'll have to administer the serum this time. I put the numbing agent on a cotton ball and hold it on Jason's elbow pit as lightly as I can. When enough time has passed, I test it. I flick the inside of Jason's arm and tense, expecting him to jump. He doesn't even flinch. Josh pokes him with the needle. We make it back outside safely and down the stairs undetected. Josh hugs me. We successfully administered serum to four Altered Helixes tonight. The sun will rise in an hour, so we head back to the hotel. We're not finished, but I feel better already.

"Hola! Quiet down." I can hear Patrice over the walkie-talkie. I completely missed the whole surveillance thing as I was with the medical corruption team last time. I'm still not able to participate directly in the surveillance, but I do get to hear them in action. Since Josh and I are in Memphis, we couldn't join them. We're travelling under the guise of a street kids' project, the government actually footing the hotel bill. We're able to listen into the surveillance via a walkie-talkie app on our phones. We sit in our hotel room and listen on edge. Even though I'm not there, I can completely imagine what their faces look like. Ethan must have a serious face; which is hard to picture on him. Patrice's face is full of concern. Camille and Emmitt are probably trying to decrease the tension with sarcasm, but it won't work.

"We've set up the microphones from the van so we'll pick up conversations inside the house. This bionic ear and booster sound amplifier is sweet," Emmitt says.

"You look ridiculous in those headphones, Emmitt." Camille's laughing.

"OUCH. Watch your volume," Emmitt complains.

"You better watch where you point that," Patrice instructs.

"Okay, Camille, are you set up for the emergency phone call if they bring in someone?" Ethan adds.

"Oh, they're talking, quiet down," Emmitt interrupts.

"I'm going to try to send what they're saying over Voxer so you can record it too," Patrice says to Josh and me.

"I can't believe it's happening next week," a man's voice says. It sounds a little different than Ethan's had. The sounds from the amplifier are a little fuzzy, but clear enough to make out the words. It also sounds eerily familiar, like it could belong to one of the guys who kidnapped me at the beginning of all this. How could he be out of jail already? He sounds pretty excited about whatever's going down. My father successfully stopped Adam, so what're they all pumped up about?

"I know. Can you believe we could have over a hundred?" another man says.

Over a hundred what?

"The commissioner opened up the old racetrack just for us. They think they're coming into the city from their small towns for a concert they won tickets to," the first man says. I scoot to the edge of my seat as he continues talking. "I'm glad we've had all this transplant practice. It's going to be hard to handle that many at a time."

"This is really going to shake things up a bit. I can't wait to rule the Other World. Ever think you'd be part of the group that leads an entire world?"

"I see Jerry's headlights. It looks like we get to practice one more time."

Well, this has been an insightful surveillance.

"Camille, make the emergency call. Maybe it's not too late to stop them," Ethan says.

"We got everything on record," says Emmitt.

"So did we," says Josh.

It's silent for a few minutes as the team waits to see what else the men have to say, but they're not talking.

I can hear sirens in the background. Aren't they supposed to silence those when there's a hostage? I hear commotion in the van.

"They're bailing. Why do the cops have their sirens on?" Camille takes the words right out of my mouth.

"Look, they're already rolling a gurney out. No black bag this time," Ethan says. In my head, I can see him pointing.

"They must have had it closer to the front door this time." Emmitt points out.

“Or maybe they moved it there to give them more time to get away?” Patrice adds.

Just then, there’s a loud knock.

“What in the world?” Camille whispers.

“We know you’re in there. We know you called the cops. What else have you been up to?” It’s the man’s voice from inside the house. Shoot, how did they find the van? I hear the sound of everyone rummaging around. Then someone yells, “Get going.” Tires squeal. Camille yells a horror movie type of scream. Then I hear the shot.

"You have to keep driving. Get us out of here," Patrice says.

"It went clean through. I don't think it hit a major organ. I'm pretty sure he'd be bleeding more. Where's the closest hospital?" Camille asks.

"Seriously, it went all the way through. That's going to leave a mark," Emmitt says, and I can hear a mixture of panic and laughter in his voice.

"Guys, I'm having trouble losing them. Is there any way you can help get them off our tail?" Ethan sounds exasperated.

"I'll open the side window and throw things we don't need," Patrice answers.

Static breaks up our signal. Josh and I can't hear anything over it. Josh tries to make contact, but there's no answer. We wait a few minutes and then I try making contact.

"Patrice, are you guys okay?"

There's silence for a bit. I hear some shuffling around again.

"Whoever this is, we have your friends. If you want them back, you're going to have to turn in all the evidence you have on us. I know you must have some. Look at all the equipment in this van. Meet us tonight at 8:00 p.m. at Katarina's." It's the man's voice from the house. Crap, this isn't good.

"Okay, we'll do that, but one of our friends there is injured and can't wait that long. If he dies in your hands, we'll turn everything in to the police," I proclaim.

"Fine, lady, but then we'll have to kill your other three friends," he returns.

Shoot, I wasn't expecting that response. Josh grabs the phone.

"We'll see you at 8:00 p.m. at Katarina's." He hangs up.

I look at him furiously. If this were a cartoon, steam would be rolling out of my ears right now.

"Why did you hang up? Emmitt will die if he doesn't receive medical care soon."

"Austria, we're not waiting for the meeting at Katarina's. The bionic ear and booster sound amplifier that Emmitt's wearing is also tracking their location."

He pulls up a GPS-looking App on the phone, and I see a red dot blinking in Kansas City and a steady blue dot in Memphis.

"We're too far away to help him in the time he needs. How are we going to launch a rescue with half of our group away from headquarters?" Since we're on a mission to save lives now, we've named the haunted house headquarters.

"Bill and Ceresa are with Senator Justus right now. The senator has identified trustworthy police staff. We need to contact them and give them access to this tracker. Once they've saved our friends, we need to give them this evidence."

"You're right." I give him a hug full of the most hope I can muster. He makes the call.

Bill understands the urgency right away, and we have the police in pursuit of the van immediately. Then Bill puts us on speakerphone so we can join the meeting with Senator Justus. Ceresa is there too.

"I completely support you on this. Ceresa, you did a great job drafting this. I just wish there was a way I could get my fellow senators on board. But this will cost some money, you see, and right now everyone's trying to decrease expenses. It's what the voters want." This comes from who I assume is Senator Justus. She is amazing. I wish I were in the room with them.

"I thought we would just be modifying provisions relating to criminal law, and there wouldn't be that much cost involved," I say, hoping I'm not making a fool of myself in front of a senator.

"Well, it appears that a good number of the senators receive donations from this trafficking ring. So even though the costs are reasonable, the support isn't there because they'll lose those donations if they pass the bill. Looks like this group has coerced more than some of our police officers. There's really no telling how many pockets they've lined."

"Is there any way we could fluff the bill to look like it's for a different cause and just include this in a small section?" I ask, but then recall some politicians not passing a bill because of something small included within the text.

"We're pretty used to that, Austria. We have paid staff, and they're responsible for combing through every detail."

"Good. It took me a long time to draft this. I need to be spending my time preparing the new shelter instead of fluffing a bill," Ceresa complains.

"Well, we've been able to sway the vote before. Maybe we can do that again," Bill inserts.

"Yes, we did. Senator Justus, can you please help us by introducing this bill? We'll work on the committee it will be referred to," Josh says as he gives me a wink. He's right.

We had help from the Other World for the homes for children bill. I'm sure they'll help us with this one too.

"I can do that. Thanks for dropping by. Good to talk with you. I'll have to be going now."

I hear Bill and Ceresa leave the room. Background noise continues for a couple minutes and then I hear car doors shut.

"Are you still there?" Bill asks.

"Yes," Josh and I say in unison. My face warms as I smile at him.

"A text message came through during our meeting with the senator. The police have the van. They've arrested the men who took it," Bill says.

I jump up and down and give Josh a hug.

"That's great, Bill."

Bill hesitates before responding, "You might want to head back as soon as you can. It's Emmitt. They're not sure he's going to make it."

Now I drop to my knees. Not someone else. I can't bear to lose anything more. Emmitt's too young. He can't die for our cause.

Josh holds me as he answers Bill. "We'll be there by this afternoon." Josh hangs up and grabs my face. I can see that he's holding back tears. His kiss is deep, communicating urgency and his determination to try to protect me.

DOMESTICATE

Walking into the hospital waiting room feels like being a prisoner on death row heading to the execution chamber. Josh holds my hand the entire way. Brittany and Landon are there in overalls and boots. They've been a lot of help to Ceresa building the new shelter. Now their eyes are swollen. We walk up to them and exchange hugs. Brittany's embrace is weak, like she doesn't have the strength to lift her arms. I see a woman I assume to be Emmitt's ma holding Camille. We head over to them and exchange hugs again. Camille's embrace is so strong that I feel as though she's using me to help her stand.

Luke and Tiff come up to us and lead us to some open chairs. "They aren't letting anyone visit Emmitt right now. He's in an operating room. The bullet hit a blood vessel. The blood seeped into his stomach, which is why Camille didn't see major bleeding. It took a while for the cops to locate the van and get Emmitt into the hospital. His heart was still beating upon arrival, so the original prognosis had been optimistic. That changed when they went to clean and suture the wound. They located the ruptured blood vessel and have been repairing, cleaning, and replenishing blood since," Luke informs us. We sit and wait patiently with everyone for the doctor.

As I look at Camille, I imagine what it would be like in her shoes. We're both Altered Helixes with partners that have normal DNA. They're putting themselves at risk for us. I see the pain, fear, and guilt in her eyes. They mirror my own emotions. Should we be handling this all by ourselves? I mean, we're the ones that heal faster. We're also the targeted ones, or at least we were. Now I'm beginning to wonder if we have broadened the target to our entire group since we've been fighting against the human trafficking ring. I can't believe I allowed the ones I care about to be dragged into this mess. Maybe they dragged themselves in when they came to save me. Here I am alive, and Emmitt's possibly going to die in my place. I can't take it. I stand. I can't just sit here and wait.

"Would any of you like something to eat or drink?" I ask the group.

"Here, grab some waters and crackers. Everyone is in need of both," Bill hands me a five. Maybe I can get some cups from the coffee area. Josh and Ceresa stand to join me.

"We can help you carry everything," Ceresa says.

It feels a little better doing something. We're silent as we walk to the refreshments room.

"Ceresa, how's the shelter coming along?"

"Oh, it's tremendous. We have six of the apartments renovated. Thank you so much for hooking us up with that home improvement gal—she's innovative and decorates each one so that it looks like a home. So many shelters feel like boxes, or as if we're animals being kept in a cage. They don't have enough money to put more than the basic necessities in. With her fundraising, she's able to do much more. With the bill passing, we're going to be able to take over another rundown building and set it up as a training facility. I want to get as many street kids back into stable living as I can. It's slow going, but we're making considerable changes, Austria"

"That sounds remarkable. Can I stop by and see one of the apartments sometime?"

"Of course you can. What's your schedule like?"

"Well, we left Memphis early to come and see Emmitt. We need to get back. I'm not sure how we're going to administer all the serum we need to in time," Josh tells Ceresa.

"Jack and Lea are looking for things to do," she tells him.

I grit my teeth. I know we need the help, but I don't want to get anyone else involved in this fiasco. I especially don't want to get our youngest involved. I feel protective as a mama bear of Jack.

"Hey, let's get back. I don't want to miss what the doctor has to say," I interrupt.

We head back to the waiting room. Ceresa and Josh both carry six cups of water each. I was only able to get five packets of crackers, but I'm not sure many of us are going to be eating so it should be enough. I give Bill his change and he nods at me.

I remember when I first met Emmitt. He was the one who faked a heart attack when Ceresa surprised his group. I remember thinking how bright his smile was. His dimples definitely help it stand out. I remember Brittany's, Landon's, Camille's, and Emmitt's story of spending an evening as street kids. Emmitt was the one who snuck into a bar to get them water. This group of college graduates struggled economically but grew spiritually. They're people I admire. They're like my siblings, and now my brother is in the hospital. "Please let him be okay," I chant over and over in my head.

Finally, a doctor enters the waiting room. He has a serious look on his face, but I can't tell if this means the news is good or bad. He just looks deep in concentration. He walks over to Emmitt's ma and begins talking. I can't hear him, so we try to get closer. After two steps, Emmitt's ma leaps out of her chair and hugs the doctor. I smile as this must mean good news.

"My baby is okay. Emmitt's going to live."

We all run in to give her a hug. She raises her hands and waves them at the doctor. "Can I see my boy?"

"Of course. He's still in recovery, so he'll be very groggy. He needs rest so keep it short."

VOYAGE

"I know the rules. I spy with my little eye something blue," Lea says.

"Is it the water tower at the top of that hill?" Jack asks pointing to said water tower.

"Yes, good job."

They've been playing this game for the last hour. I know we're saving money by driving, but I don't know how much more I can take. There was no way we could talk the government into allowing four people on this paid trip. Lea called a cousin who lives in Memphis, and we're crashing with him. Guess I'm paying for a free place to stay by putting up with the childish road games.

"So, has the numbing agent worked on everyone so far? What's the plan if it doesn't work or if they wake up?" Jack asks.

"Kid, if the numbing agent doesn't work, they're more than likely going to wake up. If they wake up, you had better run," Josh answers.

"What if they catch us? I don't want Jack taken again," a concerned Lea says.

"A spirit from the Other World will be watching each time and will intervene if that ever happens. You'll need to be mindful of where your exit is at all times, pay attention and be prepared," I answer. Now I wish Lea had been part of our self-defense training.

"Could you two be quiet for a little while? I'm going to call back home and see how things are going," Josh announces.

He puts it on speakerphone so we can all hear.

Bill answers. "Hi, kids, how's the drive?"

"Long," I say. "How's Emmitt?"

"He's recovering quickly. He'll be out of the hospital in a couple days. He still needs bed rest for a couple weeks while everything heals. Then he'll be a hundred percent."

"That's great news. Any luck on shutting down the racetrack?"

"We were able to change the commissioner's mind on that one. We've also acquired the list of invitees to the event. And the list of event employees. That list was turned into the police along with the recording. We've made great headway."

"Wow, that's much better than expected. Thank you." I can't believe how lucky we are. First, Emmitt's going to be completely fine and then we completely botch those idiots' plans and land them on the path to jail.

"Tell Emmitt we miss him and hope he has a quick recovery," Jack and Lea say in unison. Even though they can be a little annoying, they're still cute.

"Will do. You kids be safe now." Is that a hint of anxiety I hear in Bill's voice?

"Thanks, Bill. We will." Josh hangs up the phone. Now it's time for us to train Jack and Lea. Then we'll separate. We have seven more Altered Helixes in Memphis. This is going to be a long weekend.

##

Jack and Lea climb the apartment emergency stairs with ease. Jack's able to open the window; that doesn't squeak. We all enter quietly. We have blueprints of every place and review them prior to entry. Not a sound is made as we tiptoe to the bedroom. Then I hear a hiss. I jump. Elizabeth's cat doesn't seem to like us. We're within view of her now. She hasn't stirred. I can hear Jack breathing hard and fast. We walk into the room. Elizabeth's face glows red in the light of her alarm clock. Jack fumbles trying to open the syringe case. Lea takes it from him and opens it. Jack takes the cotton ball with numbing agent and holds it on Elizabeth's insertion point. We watch the red digits. After a minute has passed, Jack removes the cotton ball. Lea inserts the needle and serum. Josh and I watch Elizabeth's face. She twitches, as if someone tickled her nose with a feather. Lea's done and quickly pulls the syringe away. Just in time because Elizabeth sneezes. Her hands automatically fly up toward her face. We all freeze. Elizabeth rolls over, away from us, and I hear her breathing return to its original pace. That was close. We turn around and exit as silently as we entered. The cat must've hid from us because I don't see it again.

"That was great. We got to watch you both apply numbing agent and administer serum last time, but that's nothing compared to actually doing it ourselves," Jack exclaims in the car.

We drop them off at Lea's cousin's car. They're going to administer the serum to two more Altered Helixes, and we'll roll through another three. We are to call each other if we run into any trouble, otherwise we'll meet at Lea's cousin's place at 5:00 a.m.

##

During Josh and my last Altered Helix inoculation, I feel my body dragging. I can't remember when we had a full night of sleep. I can't wait for this to be over. Hopefully, we can get some rest before we head out again. We've done this so many times now that our movements feel mechanical. We enter the building and head to the room. Josh almost trips on the Altered Helix's boots on the way to the bed. We freeze and the adrenaline wakes us up. The man remains asleep on his bed, so we continue. As I hold the cotton ball to the man's arm, he flinches.

The next move he makes takes us both by surprise. Before we know it, he has a gun held to Josh's temple. Josh doesn't move. His eyes are wide. The man sits up and assesses us.

"Please, don't shoot. We're just trying to protect you from a human trafficking ring," I plead desperately with the man.

"What in the world are you two kids doing? What's in that syringe?"

"It's a long story, but keep the syringe and have it tested. What she says is true; we're only here to save you." Josh has regained his usual composure.

"Don't tell me what to do, boy." That's when I notice a star tattoo on the guy's shoulder.

"You have a tattoo just like my father's," I breathe out, amazed.

"Who's your dad, kid?"

"Brennan Andrews." I look into the man's eyes, hoping for understanding.

"No kidding! Brennan and I were in the Olympics together. Never did find out what happened to him." Josh hands him the syringe, and the man lowers his gun. I'm able to relax a little.

He walks us over to his kitchen and invites us to have a seat at his small but neat table. He offers us a drink, but we both just ask for a glass of water. As he pours some liquor for himself, I begin to unravel the story about my father and why we're there. My emotions do a complete one-eighty as he spills details about my father I never knew, like his record-beating sprint time. By the end of our conversation, he's administered the serum to himself. I find out his name is Daniel Browning. He even comes around so far as to offer a hand in our movement. When Josh tells him we must leave for our rendezvous, I'm relieved, as I'm almost delirious with lack of sleep. Daniel gives us his number, and we give him ours.

The realization of what could've happened doesn't hit until we're back in the car. As Josh drives I begin shaking so hard I can't stop. Josh has to pull over to reassure me that everything's okay and that he's not going anywhere. We just can't be doing this all on our own. I need to consult with my mother, but I think with the identities of Altered Helixes known and with the help of the Other World's shadows, we should be able to recruit many more. It's time to set our secrets aside. Time to initiate new plans.

##

At 5:15 a.m. Jack and Lea have still not returned to her cousin's. Josh and I are pacing back and forth in the kitchen.

"Have you tried calling them again?" I ask anxiously.

"Yes, Austria, I'll send a text to Jack and Lea now."

The phone rings, and Josh puts it on speaker.

"Hi, Josh and Austria, sorry we're running late. We should be there in ten minutes." It's Jack, and I can breathe again.

"What happened?" Josh asks.

"Nothing happened. The serum applications went as planned without a hiccup," Jack answers.

Josh lets out a frustrated sigh.

"What he means is that everything went according to plan until we got lost on the way to my cousin's," Lea fills in the gaps.

"Why aren't you using GPS?" I ask.

“That’s exactly what I told him.” I can hear Jack and Lea whisper, bickering in the background. “He claimed he had the whole layout memorized. Which he did, I was really impressed, until it came time to head back.”

“Not exactly a good time to be showing off for the lady. See you soon and turn on the damn GPS,” Josh says and hangs up. I believe if he heard a rebuttal from Jack, he would find a way to reach his hand through the phone and give Jack a good slap upside the head.

“Hey, at least all the serum was administered.” I try to point out the positive. Josh grabs my hand, sighs, and sits next to me. The kiss he plants on me after that makes me forget about everything.

CORRUPTION

Jack and Lea walk in just as we get Tiff and Luke on Walkie-Talkie, and my blood's able to take in oxygen. The sunrise shining behind them blinds me for a second when they open the door. The scene of them in the doorway with the sun at their backs reminds me of an old western. Jack sticks his chin up and walks with his shoulders back like he just made a game-winning touchdown. Lea slaps his arm and rolls her eyes. It's as if they're an old married couple. Maybe some people are made and molded for one another since the beginning of time.

"Hi. How's Memphis?" It's Luke.

"We're kicking butt and taking names," Jack exclaims proudly, and Josh shakes his head side to side.

"All right, we're getting ready to exit the car and enter the medical research site so we'll have you muted, but you'll be able to hear us." I can tell Tiff is in game mode.

I can hear their footprints as they approach the building. The alarm rings for just a second before the code is punched in. Instead of the clicking of keys, I hear the tapping of fingers. This alarm must have a touch screen. This is the last medical research facility that we showed as pinpointing our kind of DNA. Once Tiff and Luke are done here, they can update the Helix Flat File, and our current mission will be complete. We're going to be administering serum and updating the file for years, but at least now all of the information our enemies have will be wiped.

I hear the clicking of keys as Luke begins finding the Altered Helix files. He's going to change them to depict disease indications and possible cures so they'll be hidden with other files. I even hear the sliding glass door to the refrigerated room the cultures are stored in. Tiff must be using the syringe to add foreign matter to the Altered Helix samples. I picture her as methodic as when she's memorizing orders made at a restaurant table.

Noises continue as they go about their work. It seems to take forever; the second hand of a watch moving painfully slow. After the last Walkie-Talkie experience and what Josh and I just went through, I'm very anxious. I begin biting my nails, which I normally don't do. Finally, I hear Tiff.

"All targeted tubes now have foreign matter in them."

"Babe, you're definitely not meant for the medical world." Oh Luke, you shouldn't have said that.

I hear footsteps and then laughing. Tiff has gotten to Luke. I haven't actually heard him laugh that much. It even sounds like giggling.

"Stop it," he manages. Tiff must be tickling him. How does she always find peoples' weak spots?

"Fine, but don't knock my slang medical terms."

"We're accessing the Helix Flat File now," Luke tells us.

I hear more clicking of keys. Then I hear a mouse click. With every click, I see an enemy in handcuffs. With every click, I see a target removed from a friend. With every click, my blood is able to flow a little easier.

"We're almost finished." I take a breath of relief with Luke's words.

That's when I hear a commotion like something was just knocked over. My memory reels back to when Josh broke his arm. I'm still amazed he's been able to help with so much one-handed. I wait for someone to say they accidentally ran into something, but it's silent for a bit. Then I hear clanging and footsteps. I can hear heavy breathing like someone running. I hear car doors slam and tires peel out. The oxygen is slowly removing itself from my bloodstream.

"Shoot, they're chasing us. How many are there, Tiff?"

"Crap, there are at least three cars tailing us. Can't you make this thing go any faster?"

I hear the acceleration of the engine. Tiff, my best friend and pseudo-sister, is being chased by three freaking cars. How in the world did it come to this? Neither Tiff nor Luke are Altered Helixes. Why are they getting the most heat? Is it because their actions are essential to this mission? I don't know. How would our enemies know? I imagine Luke and Tiff holding hands, running from a pursuit like Thelma and Louise. Well, of course, instead of being chased by the cops, they're being pursued by criminals.

"Were you able to update the data on the Helix Flat File to show the serum has been administered?" Josh asks the question I want an answer to, but I cannot focus through my worry for Tiff.

"Yeah, we got it. It's saved globally so they can't change it," Luke answers.

"That's awesome. You're a real genius," Jack says.

"Yeah, now if I can just figure out how to lose this tail."

I can hear the workings of the car. It sounds like the four-wheel drive has been turned on, and they're off-road; mud flying from the wheels. Again I am repeating to myself, "Please let them be okay."

"Tiff, I know I'm awful at expressing my feelings, but I love you." I hear Luke kiss Tiff. I'm not sure if he's kissing her hand or her cheek. I remember his ruffled hair the first morning after they spent a night together. They were adorable standing side by side in the kitchen.

"I love you too, Luke. Austria, if you can still hear us, I love you." I hear a crash of twisted metal and exploding plastic. Then we lose connection. If there is any oxygen in my blood, I do not feel it now.

COMPLETION

I fall into the state of shock instantaneously. This time, a black sheet is pulled over my face. I don't remember leaving the kitchen or rising from my chair. I don't remember any "I spy" games during the road trip back. I can't even recall if I went to the bathroom or ate any food. All I can remember is thinking, "It's my fault." The only reason Tiff had been involved was because of me. The void I feel is not like losing a parent but losing a sibling. The feeling that I could have avoided this overwhelms me. I wake in the haunted house inventory room. My friends are walking all around me in a hurry. They all seem to have something to do. There are dresses, makeup, and hair products everywhere. The door to the room opens.

Tiff walks in. "Wait, what?" Is this Heaven? Will my father and grandmother come through that door next? She walks up to me and gives me a hug. I tremble, not wanting to wake from this dream.

"Austria, hon, are you going to wake up for your big day? No one wants a zombie for a bride, even if the wedding is in a haunted house. We all worked really hard putting this together while you were in Memphis. You've already told me everything you want, and I've followed it to a T."

"Tiff." I touch her face to see if it's real. "You're really here." Tears unlike any I've experienced before sting my eyes. I didn't know tears could burn so. Tiff gets out a handkerchief and dabs around my eyes.

"Yes, I'm here. Luke and I escaped the chase. We communicated that to you right away, but you'd gone into a state of shock. You've been in a state of shock for two days now, Austria"

"I thought you were dead. I don't know what happened. The thought of losing you just made me break."

"Well, you didn't lose me, and I don't plan on you losing me for a long time, so snap out of it."

She walks to the closet and grabs a large sack covering something on a hanger. She moves over to me and lifts the sack revealing a dress. It's my mother's wedding dress. Yes, it is vintage style. This style is currently in. It's a princess style with Irish lace on the chest, but not touching the neck and just barely folding over the shoulders. Instead of the flowery lace of many vintage dresses, this one has curlicues, which are all the rage, and they've dyed the lace black as I requested. Some people would be petrified to wear their mother's dress, but I'm stoked. Not only is the dress gorgeous, but it means that I get to have a piece of her with me on my big day. Everyone says weddings bring tears of joy to many people, and I used to never get it, but now I do. Picturing my mother in that dress holding my father's hand causes a small flood to emerge right below my eyelids.

Lea comes over and gives me a hug. "Glad you're among the living again. Let me just touch up your makeup a little."

She's dabbing so many things on my face that I can't even keep up. Tiff and Patrice help me get into the dress. Ceresa and Camille roll over a full-length mirror. Oh my, who is that woman in the mirror? She looks mature, like she's experienced the world. She has a strength behind her eyes that mine never have had. It reminds me of someone.

It reminds me of my mother raising me half all on her own, applying Band-Aids on every wound, and running every project I forgot at home up to school.

"You guys really planned the entire thing, so I don't have to?" I ask all of my dear friends.

"We did. I hope you're not mad at us," Tiff exclaims.

"No, this is fabulous. Thank you."

We all come in for a group hug. As we walk to the main entrance, I become dizzy with emotion. I feel like I've reached bottomless lows and unreachable highs throughout this journey. I can't wait to see Josh. I remember when I gave him a peck kiss to show dominance in the beginning. A smile washes over me. The electric buzz I felt as our fingertips met at the rollaway rack of costumes has never vanished. I tingle every time we touch. He has gone to great lengths to be there for me. We're going to become legal family today.

Before we emerge from the hallway, I see white folding chairs adorned with satin and black ties. They're all lined up on both sides of the aisle. The light emerging from the stained-glass windows overhead and at the sides gives a moonlike glow. Each row of chairs has a round white floral decoration hanging from black iron posts. In front of all of the chairs is the beautiful organ. I see all of my friends and pseudo-family walk in front of me. Some take a seat and some head up the curved staircase on the side that leads to the front to stand next to us. Josh is next to the organ, kicking his feet at the ground just as he was when we first met. He looks at me and smiles nervously. I smile back. The look of relief that washes over him makes my heart skip a beat. I must have scared him yet again with my comatose state.

Bill waits for me behind the chairs. He extends his arm for me to take so I can be escorted down the aisle. I smile at him, then look above. *Father, I miss you. You understand, right?* I take Bill's arm and begin the march forward. That's when I hear the music; it's my mother playing the piano. I would recognize her playing style anywhere. I almost choke up when I the wedding march begins, but I can't stop smiling. How did they get this recording? Did she leave it before she left? The closer we get, the more complete I feel. Bill gives my hand to Josh. He takes it and peck kisses me on the cheek. He points me towards the organ bench and waves. There's a laptop on it. My mother's image is on it too, and she's waving back from behind a piano. The music was live. I let the tears flow now. I break away from Josh and run to the computer.

"Is it really you? How's this happening?"

"Hi, darling, congratulations."

"We figured out how to Video Chat from this world and the Other World, Austria," Josh says. "Your mother can see us get married. She can see our babies being born. She can view every big experience."

I hug Josh. I don't know how he did it. I don't know how he knew I needed it, but he did. This is just icing on the cake. Josh is the man I want to spend the rest of my life with.

"Love you," I say as I brush my tears away. Mom's doing the same.

"Love you too, baby," Mom says.

Josh and I scale the stairs. The bannister is encased in black ribbon. We exchange vows and kiss. As we walk to the reception, I look at our pseudo-family and smile. We've all accomplished so much. Bill and Ceresa have a home for street kids to run. Tiff will make it in acting and put her talent to full-time use. Luke and Tiff are about to get engaged. I know because he asked for my approval before we left town. He'll be a doctor and she a happy wife. Ethan and Patrice will still roam the streets but should have more safe-homes than before. Camille and Emmitt will enjoy a happy life together. One they will never take for granted after the scare of almost losing him. Brittany and Landon will be there to help them along. Jack and Lea can be kids for a little bit longer. All of us have accomplished so much while saving the Altered Helixes. Yes, while the haunted house did bring us many scary moments, without it we would have none of these miracles and joys to celebrate. And if you ever wake up because you feel the poke of a needle in your arm, don't be afraid, because it's me or one of my friends administering a serum, and you are an Altered Helix.

ACKNOWLEDGMENTS

The transformation this novella has been through would not have been possible without many people. There's no way I can name them all, but I'd like to give it a try. They know how hard I've worked and how many years I've dedicated to books. First, I would like to thank the readers. You breathe life into books and for that I will be ever thankful. Next, I would like to thank the professionals that helped me trudge through this thing called publishing: everyone at Hypothesis Productions, Ben Furnish, Carol Cartaino, Dr. Luthi, Michael Neff, Brendan Deneen, Randi Hacker, the Lawrence SCBWI Critique Group, Amy Brewer, Patty Carothers, and Rick Miles. Next, I would like to thank my friends who saw me through dark times and helped me celebrate the good times too: Shana Bartlett, James Young, Miranda Nichols, Amy Garton, Stacked Book Club, Sarah Smith, and Cathy Wissing. Finally, I would like to thank my family for putting up with me: Nate, Ethan, Jenna, Vic Hurlbert, Debra Scarborough, Cassandra Hurlbert, Victor Hurlbert, Vondell Neill, and Peggy Hurlbert. If I inadvertently left someone off the list please let me know so I can add them to the next book.

ABOUT THE AUTHOR

Stephanie Hansen's short story, Break Time, and poetry has been featured in Mind's Eye literary magazine. The Kansas Writers Association published her short story, Existing Forces, appointing her as a noted author. She has held a deep passion for writing since early childhood, but a brush with death caused her to allow it to grow. She's part of an SCBWI critique group in Lawrence, KS and two local book clubs. She attends many writers' conferences including the New York Pitch, Penned Con, New Letters, All Write Now, Show Me Writers Master Class, BEA, and Nebraska Writers Guild conference as well as Book Fairs and Comic-Cons. She's a member of the deaf and hard of hearing community. https://www.authorstephaniehansen.com/

FIND MORE FROM STEPHANIE HANSEN

HTTPS://WWW.AUTHORSTEPHANIEHANSEN.COM/